JOAN HESS

Maggody in Manhattan

An Arly Hanks Mystery

AN ONYX BOOK

To Laurie Bernstein, my editor and friend,
for all her support

Published by the Penguin Group
Penguin Books USA Inc., 375 Hudson Street,
New York, New York 10014, U.S.A.
Penguin Books Ltd, 27 Wrights Lane,
London W8 5TZ, England
Penguin Books Australia Ltd, Ringwood,
Victoria, Australia
Penguin Books Canada Ltd, 10 Alcorn Avenue,
Toronto, Ontario, Canada M4V 3B2
Penguin Books (N.Z.) Ltd, 182–190 Wairau Road,
Auckland 10, New Zealand

Penguin Books Ltd, Registered Offices:
Harmondsworth, Middlesex, England

Published by Onyx, an imprint of New American Library, a division of Penguin
Books USA Inc. Previously published in a Dutton edition.

First Onyx Printing, October, 1993
10 9 8 7 6 5 4 3 2

REGISTERED TRADEMARK—MARCA REGISTRADA

Printed in the United States of America

PUBLISHER'S NOTE
This is a work of fiction. Names, characters, places, and incidents either are the
product of the author's imagination or are used fictitiously, and any resemblance
to actual persons, living or dead, events, or locales is entirely coincidental.

CHAPTER
ONE

Ruby Bee squeezed by Perkins and perched on the edge of the pew next to Estelle. "You ain't gonna believe this," she whispered, her face flushed with excitement clear up to her grayish-brown roots. Her eyes glittered like little sugar cookies, and her best blue dress had been buttoned so hastily that her bust looked as lumpy as an ungraded county road. "Why, you could have knocked me over with a feather duster when I opened the letter."

Estelle glanced at her out of the corner of her good eye. "It's about time you got here," she said. Her lips barely moved, and her tone made it clear that certain people's disreputable appearance and lack of promptness would be discussed later. She herself was above reproach in her aquamarine dress with matching shoes and eyeshadow. Her red beehive hairdo towered less than usual out of deference to those in the pews behind her, but there were some fanciful ringlets below her ears and framing her face, and the overall effect was appropriately festive.

"I'd say this letter's a sight more important than an ordinary wedding, Estelle Oppers, and I don't appreciate being scolded, neither. If you're so dadburned worried about—" Ruby Bee stopped as she realized half of the congregation were openly staring and the other half pretending they weren't but listening just the same.

Even Brother Verber, his fingers entwined on his belly, was regarding her disapprovingly from the pulpit. She sat back and fumed in silence.

Having squelched the behavior in the fifth pew, Brother Verber figured it was time to get the show on the road. He nodded at Lottie Estes, who was sitting at the upright piano (the Voice of the Almighty Lord Assembly Hall was not yet able to afford an organ, although another bake sale was in the planning stages).

Lottie stopped wondering what Ruby Bee was hissing about, poised her hands, and hit the keys with enthusiasm, if not accuracy. As the somewhat familiar strains of the wedding processional filled the room, throats were cleared, eyes turned misty, hands automatically fumbled for tissues, and everybody got down to the serious business of watching Dahlia O'Neill marry Kevin Buchanon. The general feeling was that both of them ought to listen real carefully to the vows before they took 'em.

"A lovely ceremony," I said for the umpteenth time as I wiggled through the crowd at the door of the Assembly Hall. I was having to bite my lip to keep from giggling, but anything that involved Kevin and Dahlia was apt to amuse me, and bless their pea-picking hearts (and pea-sized brains), they hadn't let me down. Three inches of the groom's white socks had been visible below his pants cuffs, his knees had knocked so violently we could hear them, and he'd had to be coached word-by-word through the entire ceremony, including his name. The bride, a majestic alpine figure in her voluminous white tent dress, had gone along with the love and honor stuff, but turned ornery when Brother Verber suggested she ought to obey Kevin, clamped her mouth closed, and refused to continue until a compromise was reached in which she grimly agreed to hear him out even when he was "bein' stupider than cow spit."

"Wasn't it a lovely ceremony?" said Elsie McMay.

I nodded, but it seemed more was required of me as Elsie caught my arm and dragged me out of the flow. "Lovely," I said weakly, "and Dahlia certainly made a . . . large bride. I need to run along now."

"Your mother was acting awfully peculiar, wasn't she? I don't know when I've seen her seconds shy of being late for a wedding, and then to look like she dressed in the dark. Did she hear bad news about kinfolk? Did that cousin of hers in Texarkana finally die and leave her something?"

"I don't know, but I'm sure we'll all hear the details." I squirmed free and fled to the front lawn. As far as I could tell, there had been no explosion of crime in Maggody, Arkansas, during the last hour. Then again, a goodly portion of the seven hundred fifty-five residents had been at the wedding. The rest of them were doing what they usually did, which wasn't much of anything. The hippies who owned the Emporium Hardware Store were out back unloading crates. A drunk was slumped in the doorway of the pool hall down the road, oblivious to the hound sniffing at his shoe with wicked intentions. A car was parked in front of Roy Stiver's antique store, above which I resided in grimy, isolated splendor in what was quaintly called an efficiency apartment. Catty-corner to that, the redbricked PD sat serenely in the midst of its weedy, unpaved parking lot, the yellow gingham curtains flapping in the autumn breeze.

I headed for it to check for messages from the dispatcher in the sheriff's office. After I'd assured her that it had been a lovely ceremony, she made it clear that nobody had anything to convey to the Maggody chief of police (being me) and most likely wouldn't anytime soon, since the sheriff had gone fishing and the deputy left in charge had started a poker game in the locker room.

Which was okay with me. I settled back in my cane-bottomed chair, propped my feet on the corner of the desk, and allowed myself the minor pleasure of replaying the highlights of the wedding ceremony. The demands of my position were typically no more rigorous than this, although we'd had a few upsets since I'd slunk back home to sulk after a nasty divorce. Back home from Manhattan for those unschooled in Maggodian lore, and within shouting range of my mother, the infamous Rubella Belinda Hanks. Not that she shouted all that much; she preferred oblique barbs about my appearance being dowdy enough to put off any man worth his mettle, about my disinclination to socialize with same, and particularly about my smart mouth and woeful lack of respect—especially when she and Estelle went out of their way to help me solve crimes. Lucky me.

She was shouting this time, however, as the door banged open and she whirled into the room like a dust devil. "You ain't gonna believe this! I couldn't believe my eyes, and I had to get out my glasses to make sure of what it said!" She banged down an envelope and put her hands on her hips. Everything about her was atwitter, from her suspiciously blond curls to her grandmotherly face and short, stubby body. She looked like a respectable matron of some fifty odd years (the precise number was an issue of debate), but there was something about her that kept the would-be rowdies at the bar and grill—and yours truly—leery of pushing her beyond some hazy limit.

I cautiously picked up the envelope and noted the return address. Prodding, Polk and Fleecum Marketing Associates had a Madison Avenue office, the location not too far from where my ex had toiled with clients during the day and embroiled with female friends in the evenings. Only in retrospect had I realized his office was the only one equipped with a sofa bed.

"Why're they writing you?" I asked, not yet courageous enough to take out the letter.

"Because I won a contest, that's why." Ruby Bee snatched the envelope from me, pulled out the letter, and made a major production of squinting and blinking at it, no doubt aware that she'd gotten me curious and was in a position to make me suffer.

"That's nice," I said with a yawn. "It was a lovely

ceremony, don't you think? Dahlia's dress must have taken twenty yards of fabric, but—"

"A national cookoff contest, if you must know. I read about it in one of my magazines and upped and decided to enter just as a lark. I used my chocolate chip bundt cake recipe, the one you get all slobbery over, and just threw in a cup of Krazy KoKo-Nut so it'd qualify."

"A cup of what?"

Ruby Bee shot me a look meant to discourage jocularity. "Krazy KoKo-Nut. It's this nasty stuff made from soybeans that's supposed to taste like real coconut. I wouldn't use it if you paid me, but the contest rules said your recipe had to have KoKo-Nut in it, along with your three proofs of purchase. I thought about giving the flakes to Raz to feed his sow, but I figured he'd be madder 'n a coon in a poke if she got a belly ache. You know, I'm beginning to wonder if there isn't something a mite unhealthy about that relationship . . ."

"So what did you win?"

"An all-expense-paid trip to Noow Yark City to compete in the cookoff a month from now. It's for me and a companion, and the KoKo-Nut people are paying for the airplane and the hotel where we'll be staying right smack in the middle of Manhattan." She puffed up just a bit, and she made me wait a good ten seconds before she continued. "There'll be cocktail parties and a press conference, and when the winner's announced, the president hisself of Krazy KoKo-Nut presents the ten-thousand-dollar grand prize."

My resolve cracked, and I croaked, "Tell me you're making this up, Ruby Bee. Please, tell me this is a joke."

"It's all in this letter, every blessed word of it."

I held out my hand, trying not to whimper. "May I read it?"

"Thought you wanted to talk about Dahlia's wedding dress and wasn't-it-a-lovely ceremony? You, missy, can suit yourself. I got more important things to

do, like shopping and packing and practicing my recipe." She flapped the letter at me as she left.

"You've got your maps?" Eilene Buchanon said as
she bent down to peer through the car window. "You
just be sure and stick to the route I drew, and don't go
gallivanting off on some side road that's likely to dead-
end in a swamp. And call collect every other night, and
don't talk to strangers, and be sure and keep an eye on
the gas tank, and—"

"Ma!" Kevin protested. "I am a married man now,
and you can't treat me like a kid anymore. I aim to
take care of my bride in a befittin' manner."

His bride belched softly from the passenger's side.
"That wedding cake sure was tasty, wasn't it? Come
on, Kevvie, we got to get started. Just imagine going to
Niagara Falls on our honeymoon! I can't think of anything more romantic." She belched again, dreamily and
with a look of bovine contentment that made Kevin
feel like a frontiersman in buckskin.

"Mrs. Kevin Fitzgerald Buchanon," he said as he
patted her hamlike thigh while stealing a peek at her
wondrously pendulous breasts—his to have and to hold
from this day forward.

Earl came out of the house and thrust a sack at
Kevin. "Here's some cans of oil in case you run low.
Make sure you check it every time you gas up, along
with the water in the radiator, the tire pressure, and the
fan belt. This ol' heap's on its last legs."

"I can handle it, Pa," Kevin said in his Daniel Boone
voice. After all, he and his goddess were setting forth
into the wilderness, in a manner of speaking. Neither
of them had ever been farther north than Springfield,
Missouri, and that had been in a rusty blue church bus
with the choir. This was different. This was an adven-
ture . . . a love quest.

"Do you have a sweater?" asked Eilene. "It might
be chilly at night, and you don't want to run the

risk of getting sick in some unknown place so far from—"

Kevin cut her off with a steely look. "Good-bye, Ma and Pa. My wife and I are leaving now." He glanced at the object of his adoration. "Are you ready, woman?"

"I might just visit the little girls' room one more time. That pineapple sherbert punch was so good I couldn't seem to get enough of it."

Thus the wagon master was obliged to lower his whip and listen to his ma for another ten minutes before he was finally allowed to round 'em up and ride 'em out, rawhide.

Geri Gebhearn was finding it increasingly difficult to read through the file, since the words were distorted by the tears that filled her eyes and tumbled down her cheeks to linger on her chin and then plop like gentle rain upon the page beneath.

An outsider would be perplexed to see this display of unhappiness in such a pretty young woman, dressed in discreetly expensive clothing, her short dark hair expertly styled to draw attention from her square jaw and emphasize her exceptionally large (although currently watery) brown eyes. Her body was sleek and slender, her jewelry not one carat less than twenty-four, and her keys to an Upper East Side condo and a forest green Mercedes tucked in her hand-sewn leather briefcase beside her desk.

Her desk was in a spacious office on the twenty-seventh floor of a Madison Avenue building, and although the view was not intriguing, it was hardly the interior of an airshaft. On the opposite side of the door was a gloomy yet competent secretary who took dictation, juggled meetings, winnowed calls, picked up Geri's dry cleaning, and made reservations at chic restaurants. She came in at nine and left at five, and she never cried.

"I hate you, I hate you, I hate you," Geri muttered,

not at the splattered file but at the framed photograph
of a handsome young man. Like her, he was perfect—
except for his sudden desire to date some slutty girl
he'd met in Barbados whose father owned a dumb insurance company in Providence.

She turned the photograph face down and tried to
pay attention to the work at hand. It was utterly absurd
to have this dropped in her lap like a chunk of plaster
from the ceiling; she'd been out of college for less than
four months and was only beginning to feel able to
make valuable contributions during the interminable
meetings. Now that beastly Scotty Johanson had be-
trayed her, all she wanted to do was go home to Hartford and . . . No, not home to Hartford, where Mother
would insist the best cure for a broken heart was participation in whatever charity fund-raiser most recently
had begged for her renowned expertise. To the summer
house on Cape Cod, where she could lie on the wicker
chaise lounge, paint her fingernails black, and drown
out her sorrows with Tab.

But noooo. Her boss had walked in not two hours
ago, told her she was to handle the KoKo-Nut account,
and walked right out on his way to LaGuardia and
some Caribbean island. As if she could just cancel her
hair appointment and her lunch with Giselle, as if her
late afternoon aerobics class was inconsequential, as if
she had nothing better to do than immerse herself in
the marketing of some product that, from what was
mentioned in the photocopied ads in the folder, consisted of synthetics. Geri hated synthetics (with the exception of rayon, of course). She hated her boss, she
hated her secretary, she hated her father for making her
work while everyone else was at the club playing ten-
nis, and she hated Scotty Johanson for being such a
low-down, devious, horny bastard.

Her hand trembled as she picked up the receiver and
punched for an outside line. Daring him to answer, she
dialed her ex-fiancé's number. She was disappointed
when the machine clicked on and a sultry female voice
repeated the number and invited her to leave a message
at the sound of the beep.

"I'm delighted you and your new friend have become intimate so quickly," Geri purred. "But from what I've heard of her, I'm not totally surprised. I left a tortoiseshell brush in the bathroom. Be a sweetheart and pop it in the mail, and please make every effort to have a really nice day."

She replaced the receiver, dabbed at her eyes with a tissue, and glared at the next page in the folder. Not only would she be obliged to deal with synthetics, she would have to deal with people of uncertain backgrounds. Five of them, to be precise, and all under her immediate supervision to participate in a cooking contest. For three days.

She hit the intercom button. "Meredith, cancel my hair appointment and the lunch reservations, and try to catch Giselle before she leaves the gallery. Oh, and get my mother on the line so I can let her know I won't be home this weekend. Mr. Fleecum has simply ruined the next month of my life."

"Yes, Miss Gebhearn. There's a Kyle Simmons on the line to speak to you. Shall I put him through?"

"I cannot take any calls the rest of the day. Mr. Fleecum's notes are indecipherable, and the contest is next month. I suppose I'd better run down my liaison at the KoKo-Nut office and—"

"Mr. Simmons is from that office," Meredith interrupted without inflection. "He says he's from promotion."

"Then put him through," Geri said crossly, "and don't forget to cancel everything." She drummed her fingers on the desk while various clicks and buzzes came through the line, mentally cursing Mr. Fleecum for his treachery.

"Miss Gebhearn?" said a male voice with no hint of upper-class nasality. "This is Kyle Simmons at KoKo-Nut. I suppose I'm the ... well, just yesterday I was assigned to this contest thing. I was given your name and told to ..." His shrugs and grimaces were almost audible; his gulps were.

She was not in the mood for charity. "I'm very busy, Mr. Simmons. What is your point?"

"We're supposed to coordinate the contest. I mean, your marketing firm is in charge, but I'm representing our company and sort of overseeing things." He cleared his throat unhappily. "I'll present the prize at the end."

Geri shuffled through the stack of papers. "According to what's here, the president of KoKo-Nut is going to be doing that very chore. It's so very kind of you to offer, Mr. Simmons, but we'll just pass on that. The media will respond so much better to . . ." An articulate adult, she concluded to herself.

"That would be my father, and last night he suddenly announced he had to take a business trip. I'm afraid you're sort of stuck with me."

"Then I guess I am, Mr. Simmons," Geri said, attempting to insert a note of enthusiasm and failing miserably. "My boss just gave me the account this morning, and I'm still trying to sort it out. Why don't I give you a call later in the week and we can set up a meeting to review the initial plans?"

There was a long silence, during which she could hear him breathing over the background clatter of the city. "I was . . . I was thinking we could do it sooner than that," he said.

"Fine, Mr. Simmons, we'll schedule it for"—she consulted her calendar—"the day after tomorrow, say tennish?"

"I'm in the lobby of your building."

It was a good thing the secretary could not see Geri's expression, which was not at all appropriate for a Vassar graduate from a very good family whose mother, at that precise moment, was mailing embossed invitations to a gala for Opera Relief.

"How very clever of you, Mr. Simmons. Please come right up and we'll get started immediately." She replaced the receiver and began to flip through the pages in the folder, wishing she'd done so earlier instead of obsessing over Scotty and the slut. Now her eyes were pink, and she would be facing the client with unsightly splotches on her cheeks and hair that was days overdue for a trim.

When the door opened, she finished the page before looking up with a coolly professional smile. It faltered as she took in Kyle Simmons, the scion of Krazy KoKo-Nut, Incorporated, but her years of cotillion training served her well.

"Please sit down," she murmured, gesturing at the chair across from her desk. "Would you care for coffee?"

Kyle Simmons hesitated in the doorway. He was in his late twenties, but he had less poise (and more gawkiness) than a junior high school boy who had never dared glance below a girl's collar. His face was small and angular, with a pointy chin and recessed eyes that were blinking as if he were in a sandstorm. Thin dark hair was slicked down like a glittery skullcap. His overcoat was rumpled, and his tie quite the wrong color for his shirt. On the other hand, Geri instinctively noted, his watch was outrageously expensive, his briefcase was more expensive than hers, his shoes were Italian, and his suit had never hung on a rack.

"Please sit down," she said, then waited until he'd done so and repeated her invitation for coffee. He shook his head with such alarm that she toyed, albeit briefly, with the idea of offering him a soda pop and a cookie. "Well, then," she continued, "I've only had the account a few hours, but I think I have a grasp of the immediate concern, which, of course, is the contest a month from now."

"Next week."

"I beg your pardon, Mr. Simmons, but—"

"Kyle. Call me Kyle."

"Then I beg your pardon, Kyle, but the contest is four weeks from tomorrow. Two of the finalists have sent their acceptances. As for the other three, it might be expedient to fax them some sort of formal—"

"The contest is next week, Miss Gebhearn, and I have the updated list of finalists in my briefcase." He opened it and began to dig through its contents. Slips of paper fluttered to the floor, along with gum wrappers, laundry receipts, and a very brown apple core. He at last surfaced with a page ripped from a notebook. "Good, here it is. I suppose you'd better have a copy run off so you can contact everybody about the new date."

"Next week?" Geri glared at him, her exceptionally large brown eyes narrowed to reptilian slits. "That's impossible. I only received the account—"

"The Krazy KoKo-Nut cookoff is to begin on Tuesday."

"But I can't possibly organize it in less than a week. This is ridiculous, simply ridiculous. I'd prefer at least six months, but I'm willing to do it in one." She hit the intercom button. "Meredith, see if you can catch dear Mr. Fleecum at LaGuardia. Have him paged and say it's an emergency."

"His flight left ten minutes ago, Miss Gebhearn."

"Don't sound so damn pleased!" Geri leaned back in her chair and tried to pretend it was the chaise lounge on the deck of the summer house.

Kyle held up his hands placatingly. "I'm as perturbed as you are. I've been working in the quality control division, and I know nothing about this contest. Last night my father packed a suitcase and, on his way out the door, informed me that I'm to be the liaison for the contest."

"Why was the date changed?"

"Several weeks ago an investment group called Interspace International, Inc. managed to purchase enough stock to have a controlling interest in Krazy KoKo-Nut. Their marketing people insist that the contest be next week. Furthermore, they want it held in a hotel they own in the midtown area, so they can control the cost and take full advantage of the write-off."

Geri could almost hear Scotty snickering from under the picture frame. She dropped it in a drawer, winced at the tinkle of glass, and fanned out the contents of the folder. "This is sheer and utter madness, but we'd best get started, don't you think? May I see this updated list of contestants?" She took the page and compared it to what she had before her. "Three of the names are different. Why is that?"

Kyle shrugged. "According to my father, one of them declined and two had accidents. The investment firm called him yesterday with these names, and that's what we'll have to go with."

"This doesn't make any sense. Prodding, Polk and Fleecum is conducting the contest; we're in marketing and that's what we're paid to do. Why would Interspace International be involved with bothersome details like this?"

"Favors to friends and relatives, I guess."

"So the contest is rigged?" Geri said indignantly, having been reared in an ambience of fair play and the superior sense of morality that was affordable with wealth. "Do you have a second memo that names the winner? Why bother to conduct the contest in the first place?"

"Neither you nor I appear to be in a position to ask that question," Kyle murmured.

"Well, I appear to be in a position to make sure the outcome is fair, and unless Mr. Fleecum returns in time to oversee this absurd cookoff thing, I intend to see that it is. Now then, shall we continue?"

"Next Tuesday?" Brenda Appleton said incredulously as she stumbled to a halt in the middle of the den. Her hand fluttered to her unremarkable brown hair, then fluttered away like a disoriented moth.

Jerome nodded. "That's what the lady said when she called. You're a finalist and I'm invited to accompany you. I've got plenty of work I can do at the hotel."

"But I never dreamed I'd be invited to the finals of the cooking contest! If you hadn't pestered me, I wouldn't have bothered to enter in the first place. I don't have a thing to wear, not a thing." Now the hand fluttered to her chest. "And what about my bridge party? I'm having three tables of bridge Wednesday afternoon, and the girls will be furious if I cancel."

"Screw 'em," he said as he lit a cigar and then regarded her through a bluish haze. "You're a finalist, and you're going through with the contest, even if you have to wear nothing but an apron and your mink."

"The children, Jerome! I never told them I entered, because I knew they'd tease me about it. I'd better call them immediately. What time is it in California? Three hours earlier? Will Vernie be home yet or should I wait? I cannot stand to waste money talking to that machine of hers, especially when I know she's standing right there listening and can't be bothered to pick up the receiver and talk to her own mother."

Jerome turned to the sports page to see if the Mets had done anything worthwhile, for a change.

Catherine Vervain sat at her desk, utilizing her textbook to conjugate French verbs and recording the answers in neatly rounded handwriting. When she heard her mother open the bedroom door, she finished the column and impassively looked over her shoulder.

"The date of the contest has been changed to next week, Catherine. I'll reschedule your hair appointment for tomorrow, and after you're done, we'll spend the afternoon shopping for our outfits."

"Cancel my violin lesson." Catherine turned back to the tedious lesson.

"I've already done it. I think we'll try that new shop at the mall, the one next to the movie theater. I saw an adorable pink dress with tiny pearl seed buttons that will do, and I'll have the cleaners dye white satin shoes to match."

"I was, I am, and I will be," Catherine muttered.

"Will be what, dear?"

"Whatever you want me to be," she said softly, flashing small, even teeth as she bent further over her notebook.

"Next Tuesday will be fine," Durmond Pilverman said. "I'll take the train down and be at the hotel by five o'clock. That's right, I'll be by myself. My wife died several years ago and I really don't know anyone who might wish to accompany me." He chuckled modestly. "And the good Lord knows I don't need a chaperone at my age. I'm just a lonely old widower who loves to dabble in the kitchen."

After he hung up, he made several other calls, none of them eliciting a chuckle, then went into his study and took the .38 Special out of the desk drawer. He sat down at the desk and began to clean the barrel with an oily rag, whistling softly through the slight gap in his front teeth.

"A cooking contest?" Gaylene Feather said, scratching her neck with a scarlet fingernail. "Jesus, I don't know. Like, I can barely make the can opener work, much less make fancy food." She sank down on her bed and began to pluck at the dingy sheet. "Don't you got anybody else who can do it, honey? I'm supposed to work every night next week, and Mr. Lisbon falls all over me if I'm five minutes late. What'll he say if I tell him I gotta miss three nights in a row?"

Her boyfriend drained the last of the beer, then crumpled the can in his hand and lobbed it toward the garbage sack. "I'll explain to Lisbon why he should not bother you about missing work, and I promise you he won't object. If you'll do this for me, I'll give you a present to express my eternal gratitude."

"And what might that be?"

"Some new luggage, a first-class ticket to Vegas, and a limo to pick you up at the airport."

"You're kidding!" she squealed. "A limo?"

"Nothing but the best for my girl. As long as you do a few little favors for me, I'll do some big ones for you."

"Are you sure I should be in a cooking contest?"

Gaylene persisted, having no luck imagining herself in an apron. She could play a lot of roles (sadistic Nazi mistress being a specialty), but Betty Crocker wasn't one of them.

"I must admit if I could find somebody else on this kinda notice, I'd do it, because I am personally and painfully acquainted with your lack of expertise in the kitchen department."

"But not in other departments ..." She stretched languidly so he could admire her very admirable attributes.

"All you will do is follow the directions on the recipe card," he said as he joined her on the bed. "It's just a cooking contest, not 'Wheel of Fortune.' Now that we have settled that, I would like to buy all your vowels."

"Oooooh," Gaylene whispered.

"The contest has been moved up to this Tuesday," Ruby Bee told Estelle, who banged down the receiver and dashed to her appointment book to get to work canceling everybody.

"Not even a week away," Eula Lemoy told Elsie McMay.

"Which means I'll have to wait till the cows come home for my perm," Lottie Estes told Eilene Buchanon. Eilene was curt and unsympathetic, having hoped the call would be from the newlyweds.

"I'd absolutely die if someone was to send me to New York City," Heather Riley told Nita Daggs. They lapsed into a giggly three-hour fantasy of limousines, Broadway actors, and penthouses ankle-deep in caviar and champagne.

"A good Christian would never set foot in that sinful city," Mrs. Jim Bob told Brother Verber. "I cannot begin to imagine the depravity and perversion that takes place on the very sidewalks of that place." Brother Verber could, but he kept it to himself.

"Sending those two to a big city is worse than sending lambs to the slaughterhouse," Millicent McIlhaney told Adele Wockerman, although it was a mite hard to tell if Adele had her hearing aid turned high enough to follow her.

She was a little surprised when Adele cackled and said, "Or vice versa."

CHAPTER
TWO

"There it is!" Ruby Bee shrieked, her finger jabbing the plastic barrier like a frenzied woodpecker. "Driver, do you see it? The Chadwick Hotel, on the right, just past that little vegetable stand!"

"Would you calm down?" Estelle demanded in a spitty whisper. "You are behaving worse than a fat kid in a candy shop, and it's beginning to try my patience. I swear, you must have spotted the Empire State Building ten times so far, along with the Statue of Liberty, which I seem to recall is out in the middle of water."

"I take you there?" the driver said in a guttural accent.

"The hotel," Ruby Bee said, now pounding on the barrier meant to protect the cab driver from robbery— or his fares from his sour odor. "The Chadwick Hotel's where we're staying. But don't let me stop you, Estelle, if you want to keep riding around with this man, so you can find out what it feels like to be smashed to death by a bus."

She was sounding on the shrill side, but it had been a real heart-stopper of a trip from the airport. Somehow the driver's ability to speak regular American disappeared right after the luggage was put in the trunk, and for all she could tell, they'd pretty much careened down the same streets two or three times amidst an endless stream of yellow cabs, all barreling along like they were in a race, changing lanes every ten feet, dodging buses, honking continually, missing pedestrians by inches, and begging for an accident. She'd gasped so many times her throat ached, and she was surprised she'd been able to unclench her bloodless, icy fingers from the door handle.

The driver turned around and showed them a few brown teeth. "You want stop here?"

Ruby Bee thought of a lot of scalding comments, but held them back and nodded. "Of course we want stop here, if it ain't out of your way!"

The cab pulled to the curb, and they all looked at the front of the Chadwick Hotel, or what they could see of it through the scaffolding. As they stared, two men with toolboxes came out the door and continued down the sidewalk.

The driver grinned at them. "No can stay here. We go now, yes?"

"No," Ruby Bee said. She poked Estelle, who was making a face as she tried to read a sign on the door. "Do you aim to sit there all afternoon?"

"That says it's closed for remodeling and won't open until next year. This can't be right. Where's that last letter you got?"

"It's in my handbag and it says we're staying at the Chadwick Hotel on 48th Street. I don't care what the sign says—this is the right place."

"Not right place," the driver said. "We go my cousin's restaurant, have nice couscous, meet plenty men who like soft white women?"

Ruby Bee and Estelle scrambled out of the cab like it was beginning to sink into the pavement. While the driver removed their luggage, they debated the tip and arrived at a scrupulously fair amount. The driver spat only once as he left them on the sidewalk, and his curse was too foreign to bother about. They were engulfed in stinky black smoke as he screeched away.

"Well, fancy that!" Estelle snorted. She was going to wait for a doorman to fetch their luggage, but a whiskery man in an army fatigue jacket was bearing down with a real peculiar glint in his eye, so she grabbed hers and told Ruby Bee to do the same.

They were about to go through the door when three more workmen, dressed in jumpsuits and all carrying toolboxes, came out and brushed past them just like they weren't there. Before they could recover, a van stopped behind them and all of a sudden crates were being carried in and other crates out. The wild man in the army jacket was staring at them, most likely planning how easiest to murder them, and a woman crooning to herself in some funny language and wearing a coat so filthy you could see the fleas hopping asked point-blank for a dollar. Ruby Bee was too startled to refuse her and probably would have given her every last penny (and signed over her traveler's checks, too) if Estelle hadn't intervened.

Across the street, two men staggered out of a store, pushing each other and shouting words that were downright rude. The van was blocking traffic, and now horns were blaring and drivers were poking their heads out their windows to yell things that were just as rude, if not a sight worse. The two men began swinging at each other like playground bullies and threatening to call the cops. A couple, both with spiky orange hair, tattoos on their cheeks, earrings in their noses, and matching black leather jackets, weaved down the sidewalk, sharing a bottle in a brown bag and gawking at Ruby Bee and Estelle as if they were the funny-looking ones. A helicopter droned across the sky, and steam swooshed from a grate not ten feet away as the sidewalk trembled ominously.

"This ain't Maggody," Ruby Bee opined.

"And here I am thinking it is!" Estelle snapped. "I suggest we get our things and go inside before we get killed." She took her own advice, and Ruby Bee followed, a little reluctantly since the sounds and the sights and even the smells were interesting.

There were plenty more sights and sounds and smells in the lobby. Mysterious pieces of furniture were draped with tarps, and part of the linoleum floor had been ripped up to expose patches of black glue dotted with hairs and dustballs, and in one corner, the mortal remains of a small furry animal. A tablesaw dominated the middle of the room, and as they hesitated, a man appeared from a corridor, switched on the saw, and began to mutter to himself as the sound of screaming wood overpowered the horns still blaring outside. Someone was hammering someplace; that was hard to miss and about as welcome as a bushy-tailed missionary on a bicycle.

The man cut off the saw and disappeared down the corridor. Ruby Bee dropped her luggage and pointed at a counter in front of a dark recess. "Do you reckon that's where we check in?"

"I think we ought to check out of this place and find out where it is we're supposed to be."

"I already told you that this is the place. It's in the letter, and I don't aim to go traipsing around Noow Yark City looking for what's right here under our noses." She made her way through the patches of glue to the counter, and tapped on a silver bell. "Yoohooo? Is anybody back there?"

The wood-sawing man returned. This time he noticed them and, after a minute of frowning, said, "Closed for remodeling, honey. Why doncha call the YWCA and see if they can help youse two out?"

Ruby Bee took the letter from her purse and showed it to him. "This was sent special delivery, and it says we're supposed to stay here, so this is where we're going to stay. Do you happen to know where the manager is? If you can't spit out the words, you just go ahead and point."

Before the man could answer (if he indeed intended to), the door opened behind Estelle and a man carrying a suitcase came into the lobby. His expression of disbelief was nearly identical to Estelle's; Ruby Bee thought about commenting on it, then remembered how Arly had told her not to speak to strangers like they were ordinary folks browsing in the Hardware Emporium on a Saturday morning.

The man wasn't strange-looking, however. He appeared to be in his early forties, maybe a shade older, with shaggy dark hair going gray at the temples, a kind of messy mustache with its fair share of gray, droopy brown eyes that reminded her of one of Perkins's hounds, and such poor posture that she had to restrain herself from poking him in the back and telling him to stand up straight. He was wearing a beige raincoat that had seen a lot of rain and a tweedy hat with a single, frayed feather.

He took off his hat and nodded. With a smile as sad as his eyes, he said, "Please excuse me, ma'am. I seem to have found myself in the wrong place, although I could have sworn . . ."

"You looking for the Chadwick?" Estelle butted in. "Well, so are we, and we didn't reckon on a construction site."

He nodded at her. "Yes, the Chadwick Hotel. I've been invited to participate in"—he gave them an embarrassed look—"a cooking contest, and I thought this was the place."

"So did we," Estelle said tartly, "but someone must have gotten the name wrong, because anyone with the sense God gave a goose can see that—"

"This is the right place," Ruby Bee said, a little miffed because this gentleman was a real contestant like herself, and Estelle was forgetting that she was merely along for the ride, so to speak. She came back across the room and held out her hand. "I'm Ruby Bee Hanks, and I'm in the contest, too."

"Ah," he said, his forehead wrinkling while he appraised her as if she'd presented herself as an entry rather than a contestant. "I'm Durmond Pilverman. I'm not quite sure what we ought to do at this point, Mrs. Hanks. I was under the impression that the marketing representative would be here to handle the hotel reservations and such. Unless the gentleman in the cap is he, we may have a problem."

The subject of the remark shook his head. "Naw, but lemme see if I can hunt up Rick. He's what you might call the site supervisor. Maybe he can sort this out."

Estelle stuck out her hand. "*I'm* Estelle Oppers, Mr. Pilverman. I came along with Ruby Bee so she wouldn't get herself mugged in the airport, or get hopelessly lost before she ever caught sight of the hotel. We're from Maggody, Arkansas." She gave him a moment to respond, but he was now regarding her with the same sharply quizzical look he'd given Ruby Bee—who was not pleased with the remark about getting mugged or lost. "Where're you from?"

"Connecticut," Durmond said with a vague gesture.

Estelle opened her mouth, but Ruby Bee wasn't about to listen to any more aspersions. "Why, I used to have a second cousin who lived in Connecticut," she inserted neatly. "Elsbeth Matera was her name, but of course she died way back in 1952, so I don't suppose you'd remember her, even if you knew her. She had palsy something awful during her last few years, bless her soul, and the nurse's aides had to read the little cards and letters I sent her on her birthday and at Christmas. Did you ever happen to . . . ?"

"I'm afraid not," he said. He glanced over her head as a door behind the registration counter opened. "Perhaps we have someone to help us?"

Ruby Bee wasn't real sure the man was the one she would have picked, given her druthers. For one thing, he looked meaner than a rattlesnake, with his squinty eyes, fancy hair swept back in a televangelist's pompador, and snooty sneer. He probably wasn't even thirty years old, but he was regarding them like he owned the hotel and everything else on the block, and they were nothing but those homeless people that Arly had warned her about. Mr. Pilverman's mustache was messy but friendly; this man's was nothing more than a thin black line that could have been drawn with a felt-tipped pen. His lips were thinner than Mrs. Jim Bob's.

She wasn't a bit surprised when he said in a real cold tone, "The hotel is closed for remodeling. Please be about your business elsewhere."

Durmond Pilverman stepped forward, saving both Ruby Bee and Estelle the necessity of what might have been a fine display of indignation. "These ladies and I were told that the Krazy KoKo-Nut cookoff is to be held here, and we have letters to that effect. Are you the manager?"

"In a manner of speaking. May I see this purported letter?" He extended a hand with well-manicured nails and a ring as gaudy as a carnival prize. His cuff fell back to expose a heavy silver bracelet. If that wasn't bad enough, he had several gold chains around his neck like he thought he was one of those egotistical Hollywood movie stars.

Ruby Bee was about to warn Mr. Pilverman not to hand over anything to this fellow with all the jewelry when the door again opened. This time it admitted several folks, all of them looking unhappy in varying degrees. The unhappiest of them all was a pretty young woman in a pale green skirt and jacket, carrying a briefcase in one hand and a clipboard in the other. Her eyes were flashing like the taillights on a taxi.

"Are you Richard Belaire?" she demanded as she strode across the room. She sounded as if even a hint of affirmation would result in bloodshed. "Are you?"

The snooty man behind the counter got snootier. "No, dearie, I'm president of the Junior League, but I must have left my white gloves and pearls at home today."

"You have not returned my last four calls, Mr. Belaire, and it's caused me a great deal of inconvenience. We need to talk. In the office—now." She went down the corridor, and after a pause, Mr. Snooty Pants went through the door from which he'd come earlier.

"Goodness gracious," Ruby Bee murmured.

"What on earth is going on here?" gasped a woman in the doorway. She nudged her companion, a teenaged girl, then let her luggage fall to the floor. "What kind of hotel is this? This will not do—not at all!" She spotted them and managed a tight, harried smile. "I'm Frances Vervain, but please call me Frannie. I presume you're here for the contest? Catherine is thrilled to be selected as a finalist, but we were led to believe we would be staying in a decent hotel, and this won't do. Catherine has a terrible time with allergies. At the first hint of dust, her eyes water and she cannot breathe."

Ruby Bee looked at the woman, who seemed pleasant enough despite her inclination to talk faster than a trout goin' after a mosquito. She had blond hair that was a little too brassy, but nobody ever said there was anything wrong with helping Mother Nature every now and then. Maybe a little too much makeup, and maybe dressed more like a teenager than the mother of one. The hemline was far from flattering, to put it kindly, and the bright pink of the dress called attention to her thick waist and unfortunate hips.

The daughter, Catherine-with-allergies, was slender to the point of resembling a beanpole. She had a cloud of frizzy auburn hair and no makeup to speak of, except a hint of blusher beneath dramatically pronounced cheekbones. Her posture was erect to the point of rigidity, as was pretty much everything about her. She looked awfully humorless for someone her age, what with her sulky expression, but Ruby Bee could understand how a ride from the airport could do that to a body.

"So you're a contestant, too?" she asked the girl, giving her a friendly smile.

The girl turned to her mother. "I hope you're satisfied."

"It's going to be fine," Frannie said coolly. She repeated her name to Durmond Pilverman and Estelle, and after a few minutes of conversation, all the adults were on a first-name basis and feeling better about the immediate future. Catherine stared out the glass doors.

The woman in the green suit reappeared. "I'm Geri Gebhearn, the contest coordinator from Prodding, Polk and Fleecum," she told them. "There's been a small problem concerning communication with the hotel, but let's all hope it's under control—at least for the time being. Mr. Belaire has arranged for rooms on the second floor for you, and of course we'll be using the kitchen when the big moment arrives."

"The sawdust," Frannie said, glancing at Catherine's glacial face. "It's going to make it ever so difficult for Catherine. She's had allergies since she was—"

"The saw will be removed," Miss Gebhearn said

firmly. "Mr. Belaire says the remodeling will be confined to the upper floors until the end of the week. This means we'll have to tolerate a certain amount of noise and disruption, but there are union contracts involved that cannot be breached. In any case, there are enough rooms on the second floor to house you, and the lobby and dining room will be cleared and straightened for our use." She flipped to a page on the clipboard and scanned it. "Let's see who we've got, shall we?"

Despite lingering uneasiness on several people's parts, they gathered around her.

I was in the back room of the PD, trying to decide how vile day-old coffee could be, when I heard the door open. The clickety-click of high heels gave me an idea who the visitor was, and I took malicious satisfaction in calling, "Would you like a cup of coffee?"

"Is this a café or a police department?"

"Beats me," I said under my breath, then went to the doorway to regard Mrs. Jim Bob, who was not only the mayor's wife, but also the president of the Missionary Society, the self-proclaimed Miss Manners of Maggody, and a royal pain in the neck (and other locales farther south). Physically speaking, she was not altogether unattractive, but her perpetual expression of grim, self-righteous disapproval was enough to put even the most generous of us in a fractious mood. She and I were not the best of friends, possibly because I had been known to be less than deferential on occasion. Any old occasion suited me just fine.

"I wish to file a complaint," she began ominously.

"Anything in particular, or shall I arrest everybody in town and sort it out later?"

"I'm not in the mood for what you mistakenly find so amusing, Miss Chief of Police. There is a serious problem in Maggody, and your lackadaisical attitude toward law enforcement is at least partially responsible."

"Are you trying to flatter me?" I asked as I sat down behind my desk and settled my feet on my favorite corner. "It won't work. You'll have to take a number like everybody else."

I could almost hear her grinding her teeth, but after a dark look, she said, "Last night Brother Verber discovered three teenaged boys in the Voice of the Almighty Lord Assembly Hall. They were drunk. One of them was standing at the pulpit, less than properly clothed, engaged in blasphemy and disrespect for the good Christians of the community."

"Oh, my gawd," I murmured.

"What do you intend to do about this outrage?" Mrs. Jim Bob continued with the relentlessness of a torrential rainstorm.

"Shoot 'em?"

"The point is that they obtained the liquor illegally. You may waste your time reading magazines at the edge of town while pretending to monitor the speed limit, but I cannot sit by idly while the youth of Maggody sink into a moral quagmire of indecency and disrespect for their elders."

"Then you're going to shoot 'em for me? I can loan you my gun, but I've only got three bullets so you'll have to aim real carefully."

"The liquor," she said, sounding a bit strained, "came from Raz Buchanon's still. Everyone in town, from the youngest child to poor Adele Wockerman out at the county rest home, knows that he's running his still up on Cotter's Ridge. I'm surprised that the chief of police has seen fit to allow him to do it right under her nose, and without any discouragement or suggestion that he cease."

"The chief of police knows about this?" I said incredulously. "I can't believe it, Mrs. Jim Bob."

"Now listen here, Arly Hanks, I've had quite enough sass from you! As the wife of the mayor, who does pay your salary, I demand that you arrest Raz Buchanon and destroy the still before it destroys the moral fiber of Maggody!"

I put aside my urge to continue needling her (for

fun, if not for profit). "I'm aware that Raz is back in business, but it's a tad more complicated to stop him than you're implying. I've tried four times in the last month to find the still. I can show you bruises and scratches, although the tick bites are more private. He may not be the smartest person in town, but he's cunning enough to move his operation any time he catches wind of my imminent appearance, and not just to another spot on the ridge. In case you haven't noticed, we're surrounded by wilderness, all of it crisscrossed with logging roads. If it were a matter of watching Raz until he rented a U-Haul, I might be able to track him down. As it is, he ought to work for the Pentagon."

I leaned back in my chair and watched her beady eyes dart as she considered her response. She rarely deigned to speak to me, much less to come into the PD and attempt to bully me into action. But here she was, fuming and ready to fight, dressed for battle in a navy dress, a prim hat, white gloves, and a girdle no doubt partially responsible for her pink face (I'd like to take a little credit myself). It finally came to me—she'd been ignored recently, what with the wedding of the decade *and* Ruby Bee's well-publicized culinary triumph. Mrs. Jim Bob was feeling like a neglected middle sibling, and she was here to put herself smack-dab back in the limelight. That she intended to do so at my expense was hard to overlook.

This flash of intuitive brilliance required action. Before she could attack, I said, "It is a serious problem. I hate as much as you to see the kids drinking. If we could encourage some of the leaders of the community to become involved, we might be able to prevent the problem from escalating."

This caught her off guard. She swallowed several words and forced a tight smile. "Then you agree with me that this should be taken as a serious threat to our youth?" I nodded to confuse her more. "Well, then, I suppose I could be prevailed upon to organize a committee of concerned citizens, and I shall accept the burden of leadership, no matter how trying it will prove. Brother Verber certainly will wish to be included, as will Lottie Estes and perhaps Elsie McMay. It's just as well Ruby Bee is out of town; in that she owns and operates a saloon, she might find it awkward to join the battle against demon whiskey."

"Just as well," I said mildly. "I'm sure you'll select your committee with as much regard for their upright moral standing as for their dedication to the cause of temperance. Keep in touch, and let me know if I can help down the line."

"Tomorrow at seven, I should think," Mrs. Jim Bob said as she stood up and smoothed away the wrinkles in her skirt. "Please have coffee made, and perhaps a nice platter of cookies. Store-bought will do. Don't forget the napkins."

I was still gaping as she swept out of the PD, and I have to admit I wasn't feeling as damn clever as I had minutes earlier. There have been times when I've been known to underestimate the enemy. This appeared to be one of 'em.

"Some honeymoon," Dahlia grumbled as she spread extra-chunky peanut butter on a cracker and glared at Kevin's shoes. She would have glared at Kevin proper, but all that she could see of him were the shoes and a few inches of ankle, the rest of him being under the car. "If I'd wanted to watch folks crawl under cars, I would have gone down to Ira Pickerel's body shop and watched Ira hisself do the crawlin'. I sure wouldn't have chosen to stand on this dusty old cowpath watching someone who doesn't know a tire from a hole in his head."

Some of this was lost on Kevin, partly because he was engrossed in the oil pan and partly because she had popped the cracker in her mouth in the middle of her comments. "I'm working as fast as I can, my beloved," he called back, hoping to appease her.

"What's more," she said, not at all appeased, "I was the one who said we needed to ask directions. I told you this wasn't the right road, but you were too smart to listen to me. So where are we now? Nowhere, that's where we are—and it's all your fault, Kevin Fitzgerald Buchanon. I swear, if I'd realized how bullheaded you were, I would have married Ira. At least he's got the sense to come out of the rain."

"Why don't you take a can of soda pop and go sit in the shade?" he called to her. "I seem to recollect there's a nice patch of grass under that ol' oak tree."

Dahlia was about to tell him that was the stupidest thing he'd said yet, but then she realized it was a nice patch of grass and there wasn't any reason for her to stand in the hot sunshine, sweat streaming between her breasts and gathering in the creases of flesh.

"Maybe I will," she muttered. She put the crackers and jar of peanut butter in the picnic basket, took a can of orange pop from the cooler, and managed to transport it all across the ditch without losing her balance. Once settled in the shade, she removed everything from the basket and arranged things within reach, popped the top of the soda, and leaned back against the rough bark.

Kevin was sweating as copiously as his new bride, although for reasons beyond the stupefying heat. For one thing, the car was swilling oil the way his love goddess did orange soda pop, and he was pretty sure there was a crack in the oil pan. The fact that oil was dripping rhythmically on his forehead also made him suspicious. He'd heard you could put oatmeal in a leaky radiator, but he didn't know if that worked with oil pans.

The way the car had stopped with a wheezy shudder alarmed him something fierce. And Dahlia's remarks about this being the wrong road did nothing to ease his panic. Unless they'd gone through downtown Nashville without noticing, they were on about the wrongest road in the country. Pavement had turned to gravel, and eventually petered out into rocks and dust. They hadn't seen a cow in over an hour, much less a house or another living soul.

Tears welled in Kevin's eyes, adding to his inability

to trace the source of the leak and try to figure out what to do about it. Thus far, the honeymoon had been nothing but a series of disasters. The first three days they'd been obliged to stop every few miles because of recurring gastric distress Dahlia blamed on his ma's pineapple sherbert punch. Intimate marital relations had been out of the question (he'd asked the particular question, of course, but she'd locked herself in the bathroom, sobbing and flushing all night).

The fourth night they'd ended up in a motel with an hourly rate, and the undeniable presence of insect life in the sleazy room had resulted in Dahlia sitting in the middle of the bed directing him while he stalked critters with a rolled-up newspaper. That, coupled with the roar of trucks on the freeway—and the squeals and shrieks and groans and howls from the next room—had failed to kindle a romantic ambience.

Now they were lost in Tennessee, unless they were lost in Kentucky or Idaho or Florida, for that matter. It had been a good thirty minutes since Dahlia had mentioned exactly which of them had left the well-marked maps in one of the motels behind them, but he reckoned it was near time to hear about it once more.

He bravely wiped his eyes and spotted a bead of oil beginning to swell. He flicked it away with his finger, plucked the wad of gum from his mouth, and stuck it on the exact spot. It wasn't how smarmy Ira Pickerel would have done the job, but Kevin figured it might hold until they found a town and a garage. And maybe a motel with clean sheets, an air conditioner that worked, and the chance for cool showers, a jug of fancy wine, a loaf of bread, and ...

He wiggled out from under the car, stood up and brushed the dust off his backside, and with a manly smile, gazed across the top of the car at his little wife picknicking amongst the wildflowers. She had fallen asleep, he noted with the proprietary air of a rancher regarding his prize heifer. She was flat on her back, her legs spread apart and her skirt bunched up enough for him to catch a shadowy glimpse of that driveway to heaven. Her mouth had fallen open, and her melodious snores mingled with the twittering of birds and the lazy drone of insects on the sylvan glade beneath the tree.

He hitched up his jeans and strode toward her, lost in a vision in which he knelt beside her, woke her with a gentle yet demanding kiss, and was welcomed into her arms for the consummation of their vows (which had been consummated a lot in the past, but not since they'd become betrothed one long, cold, celibate year ago).

"My dreamer of desire," he practiced to himself, rather impressed with the alliterative ring of it. "How about we find passion in the wildflowers? Shall we give way to youthful lust and make mindless love here on the silky grass dotted with gay yellow buttercups, tiny violets, and . . ."

There was no mistaking the red, waxy, three-leafed stems on which his sleeping beauty slumbered. Even Kevin Fitzgerald Buchanon, who had trouble remembering which end of the fork to use to scratch his head, could recognize poison ivy.

CHAPTER
THREE

I was daydreaming about the automat on 42nd Street, the last one in town—Manhattan, not Maggody—and the only place where I'd felt like a perpetual winner at the slot machines. There were no maitre d's, no waiters to introduce themselves and rattle off the specials, no *haute cuisine* or *haute* anything else. All it took was a pocketful of change to win the sort of food that sustained my soul, like macaroni and cheese, limp broccoli in watery sauce, and soggy egg salad sandwiches. Even after ten years of life in Manhattan, a little bit of Maggody had still flowed within me like a secondary infection in my bloodstream. Maybe there was no cure for it, and never would be. A chilling thought.

But the automat was what I was daydreaming about when the telephone rang, and I was doing so because I hadn't had a decent meal since I'd driven Ruby Bee and Estelle to the airport in Farberville the day before and watched them disappear into the great blue yonder, feeling as if I were a mechanic watching a heavily laden bomber head for enemy lines.

It was likely to be Mrs. Jim Bob making sure I'd bought proper Christian cookies, I decided as I went to the back room to get my radar gun. It was still ringing when I returned, armed to the teeth with said weapon and a magazine. I chewed on my lip, which tasted no better than the canned soup I'd been subsisting on for more than twenty-four hours. It could be the Stump County Sheriff, good ol' Harve Dorfer, wanting me to do something I'd probably prefer not to do, such as untangle bloodied drunks from a wrecked car or help scoop a bloated body out of the lake south of town. Or it could be the man of my dreams. Him, or the Pope; the odds were about equal.

I picked up the receiver. "Yes?"

"Oh, Arly, thank the Lord I got hold of you! The awfullest thing has happened, and I don't know what to do! I keep rubbing my face and trying to tell myself it's all nothing but a nasty nightmare and there ain't no cause to go bellowing like an orphaned calf in a blizzard, but—"

"Estelle?" I said sharply. The background cacophony nearly drowned her out, and I caught myself wondering if she was calling from the concrete island in the middle of Times Square.

"Well, it ain't the mayor of Noow Yark City! Didn't you hear a word of what I just—"

"Calm down. I heard very little of what you just said, mostly because you weren't making any sense." I sat down behind the desk and took a breath, hoping she was doing the same. "What's wrong?"

"Nothing's wrong, if you don't count your own mother being locked up in jail for murder."

After a pause fraught with frowns and grimaces, I said, "I suppose I do count that, Estelle. Could you please explain what you said in a little more detail? Who, and what, and when, and where, not to mention the ever-popular why?"

"It happened last night, and if you ask me, it was her own darn fault for firing the gun at the police when they broke down the hotel room door. After that, they weren't in the mood to listen to her explain why a buck-naked man was bleeding like a stuck pig right there in her bed. She kept tryin' to talk to them in a right nice fashion, but you'd have thought she was visiting some country where they ride around on camels. I've never seen a bunch of grown men get themselves so riled up over one itsy-bitsy bullet that didn't even hit any of 'em."

Don't think for an instant that I was taking notes or formulating questions designed to elicit further information. I wasn't so much as blinking, and I wouldn't have flinched if I'd been stung by a hornet, or a whole swarm of them.

"Would you repeat that?" I managed to say.

"I said the bullet didn't hit any of 'em, but all the same they put handcuffs on Ruby Bee and took her away, just like she had been holding up a liquor store or a bank. She wasn't nearly as mad as I would have been, although I must say she was acting downright crumpy about the whole thing."

"Why on earth . . . ?" I began, but words abandoned me and I shrugged as if Estelle were across the desk from me.

"You would be too, if a smart-mouthed cop tackled you and nearly made you hit your head on the dresser. They wouldn't even let me talk to her, much less go along to find out where they were taking her. Instead, they made all of us wait downstairs most of the night, then questioned us one at a time in that snooty manager's office. I don't want to say anything unkind about those policemen, but there wasn't a one of them much brighter than Kevin on one of his better days. The one I talked to had a face uglier than a mud fence stuck with tadpoles and an accent I couldn't hardly understand. He hadn't ever heard of Arkansas, if you can believe that!"

"Estelle," I said, getting a little crumpy myself, "you still haven't told me what happened to Ruby Bee. Is she all right?"

"How would I know, Miss Hard of Hearing? I already told you how the police dragged her away in handcuffs and couldn't be bothered to tell me where they were taking her." She gasped. "Oh, dear, there's that crazy whiskery man who's been following me since we got here. I got to go, Arly. He's licking his lips something fierce, and I wouldn't be surprised if he didn't have a knife in his pocket or an axe down his britches. Talk to you later."

"Wait!" I screeched. "Don't you dare hang up!"

She hung up.

I sat for a very long while, staring at the telephone and trying to pluck tidbits of factual information out of the bizarre conversation. A naked man bleeding in Ruby Bee's bed. When the police broke down the door, she'd fired a gun at them. Humorless chaps that they were, they'd tackled her to the floor, handcuffed her, and taken her away to be booked for murder. As of the moment, she'd not returned. Estelle had been questioned. She was now being knifed/hacked by a wet-lipped man who'd been following her since their arrival.

"And that's all we know," I said just to hear my voice and reassure myself I hadn't been beamed aboard any hovering alien spacecraft. The PD looked the same—dusty, hot, seedy if not squalid, in need of a sweeping that wasn't on my agenda any time soon. Outside, pickup trucks grumbled down the highway, along with an occasional car filled with tourists searching for bucolic quaintness and finding a lot of tacky poverty. Car doors slammed as folks came and went at the supermarket across the road. Neighborly greetings were exchanged. A child wailed, a dog barked.

The telephone rang, and this time I did not dally. I lunged for the receiver, slapped it against my ear, and said, "Estelle?"

"Hardly. This is Mrs. Jim Bob, Arly. We'll need seating for six tonight, and I seemed to recall there are only two or three chairs. You need to arrange to borrow some from the Sunday school room at the Voice of the Almighty Lord Assembly Hall and set them—"

"You got it," I said and hung up. That was a link with reality, I told myself. Ruby Bee might be jailed for murder nearly two thousand miles away, but it was business as usual in Maggody.

When the telephone once again rang, I was a little more cautious. "Arly Hanks here," I said.

"This is Eilene Buchanon, Arly. I'm worried sick

about Kevin and Dahlia. They were supposed to call last night, but they didn't, and we haven't heard a peep from them for three days now. I was wondering if you could . . ."

Definitely business as usual. "Could what, Eilene?" I prompted her. "Get in my car and go find them? I thought I heard somebody say they were on their way to Niagara Falls for their honeymoon. In that they have several days' head start—and are likely to have taken enough wrong turns to be in Mexico by now, I doubt I'll have much luck."

"I know," she said limply. "I'm just so worried about them. I was deadset against this idiotic idea of theirs, but Earl just laughed and said they should take their best shot at finding it." She began to snivel, and her voice grew hoarse. "They were raised right here in Maggody, where everybody knows everybody. It don't exactly teach you to watch out for people who might be dangerous or want to hit you over the head and steal your car . . . or worse. Why, they might be—"

"Tell you what," I interrupted, "I'll call the state police and ask them to check with their counterparts along Kevin and Dahlia's proposed route. They were heading east, right?" I diligently recorded their itinerary and wasted a few more breaths assuring her I'd do something about the missing couple. I then replaced the receiver and sank back in my chair, seeking comfort from its familiar contours and tendency to squeak when I shifted.

Ruby Bee had mentioned the name of the hotel in which the silly contest was to be held. I had not written it down, nor had I paid particular attention to the name of the marketing firm that was conducting the contest. I worked on the latter for a while, but all I could come up with was a vague notion that it involved physical violence. My dim memory of the hotel's name stirred a Dickensian ember. Not Twist, not Copperfield, not Scrooge or Cratchit, and at least on my part, not any Great Expectations.

I was not in the mood for literary trivia, but I kept at it until I hit upon Pickwick, gnawed on my fingernails, and shortly before they began to bleed about the cuticles, arrived at Chadwick. I called information and was told by a male of Eastern European origin that the number was not working. I told him it damn well was, and we debated this until he got bored and disconnected me.

I could, of course, call all the precincts in Manhattan. If by sheer serendipity, I found the right one, I could then attempt to track down someone with information about the status of my mother's . . . arrest for murder.

Or I could cut the crap and do what I would have to do eventually, which was hunt up the directory and start calling those few airlines that flew out of Farberville and ultimately landed in one of the vast, flat wastelands surrounding the island of Manhattan.

Marvin Madison Evinrood Calhoun, known to his intimate acquaintances (and also to the East St. Louis police and the officers in the juvenile detention center) as Marvelous Marvin, Captain Marvel, but usually just plain Marvel, grinned broadly at the elderly woman behind the counter. "I thank you kindly for the donation to such a worthy cause, ma'am. If you don't mind, I believe I'll help myself to a carton of milk and a box of cookies on my way out the door."

The woman shook her head, too terrified to speak, much less object. Later that morning, when she tried to describe the robber to the sheriff, she would estimate his height at well over six feet, although he was shy of that by four inches, his weight at two hundred pounds, although he was closer to one-forty, and his skin to be blacker than coal tar, although it was several shades lighter. Her estimate of his age as fifteen or sixteen would be more accurate, however, as would be her description of an ugly pink scar that ran across his cheek and disappeared into a dimple.

She would also attempt to characterize his antiquated snub-nosed revolver as a cannon and would burst into tears when she described how he'd almost— but not quite—sexually assaulted her in her living room at the back of the store, adding that the only reason he hadn't was that her lard-butted husband had been sitting back there watching a game show on the television set.

She would then admit she hadn't rushed to the door to try to get the license plate of his getaway car, mostly because she'd gone straight to the living room to berate her husband for failing to prevent the maniac from making her hand over every last dollar from the cash register and leering at her while doing it.

The local police officer would pass along the description to the Illinois State Police barracks, where it would be noted with a sign and added to the growing list of Marvel escapades. It was clear he was heading east, stealing vehicles now and then, holding up stores and gas stations, flashing a weapon but always speaking courteously.

The sergeant would be pleased when Marvel crossed into the adjoining state. It wasn't wise to soil your own nest too long; at some point, the shit would drop on someone below, who might get pissed.

Brother Verber stood outside the gate, mopping his forehead and gazing unhappily at the hodgepodge of tin, plywood, rotten boards, and mismatched sheets of siding that comprised Raz Buchanon's shack. The roof over the porch tilted dangerously, and the boards of the porch itself were pocketed with rot. The only indication the shack was not some relic from bygone centuries was the spidery television antenna on the roof.

He shifted the handkerchief to his other hand and worked on his neck for a while. It was his Christian duty to march through the weedy yard, cross the porch, pound on the door, and confront Raz Buchanon with the bald-faced, no-gettin'-around-it truth that moonshining was a sin that led straight to eternal damnation. He knew it was his Christian duty because Sister Barbara (aka Mrs. Jim Bob) had told him so, and she'd done so for more than an hour, stressing the necessity of confrontation with this underling of Satan who was decimating the moral fiber of Maggody.

He'd have preferred to put off this particular battle with the devil for a day or two, giving himself time to study up on the extent of the wickedness and arm himself with Bible verses and platitudes. When he'd suggested as much, and also mentioned a baseball game on television that very afternoon, Sister Barbara had lit up like a sparkler on the Fourth of July. He'd revised his schedule real quick.

There was no denyin' she was the beacon of the church, the leading ewe of the flock, and a fine figure of a woman to boot, Brother Verber thought mistily as he hesitated on the far side of the gate. Whenever she came to him for counseling, she dressed modestly, to be sure, but he was keenly aware that she was no scrawny bag of bones. No sirree, she had a righteous bosom, a fetchingly slim waist, and a well-rounded derriere above shapely calves and trim ankles. He hated fat ankles as much, if not more, than he hated Satan hisself.

It occurred to Brother Verber that he might be harboring something akin to lust, and he firmly told himself that genuine admiration for the Good Lord's handiwork was above reproach. He closed his eyes to offer a prayer of thanksgiving for the miracles of creation, but moments later found himself wondering what the handiwork might look like in a bathing suit or a silky nightgown. Or nothing at all.

"Onward, Christian soldier," he said aloud and, commencing to hum the tune, stuffed his handkerchief in his pocket and pushed open the gate. His Bible clutched in his hand, he wound through the weeds, ordered himself not to speculate on whether the porch boards would hold him, and went right up to the door.

As befitting his officer's commission in the Lord's army, he pounded on the door and yelled, "Open up,

Raz Buchanon! Open this door or prepare to spend all eternity stoking the fires of perdition beneath the devil's own moonshine still."

The door opened to a slit. "What're ye howlin' about, preacherman?" said a surly, suspicious voice.

Brother Verber sucked in his gut and stuck out his chin. "I'm here to save your filthy, perverted, moth-eaten soul. You've gone many a mile down that wicked road, but it's my Christian duty to bring you back, even if it means hanging onto your trim ankle to stop you from taking that last step."

"Say what?" said Raz, puzzled. "I ain't gonna have the likes of you or any other feller hangin' on my ankle. I hear tell there's boys like that over at the truck stop in Hasty. You kin go over there and find yerself a real pretty one."

"How dare you!" Brother Verber thundered, mostly to cover his embarrassment. "The Good Lord says that's an abomination, just as wicked as fornication, drunkenness, lust—and making field whiskey! I'm here for your own good, Raz Buchanon. This is a mission of mercy, and I'd appreciate it if you'd open the door and step aside so that I can bring salvation into your home and your heart."

"Suit yourself, preacherman, but you'll have to wait until Marjorie's show is over. It's one of those damn fool soap operas, and she's stucked on it tighter 'n a seedtick on a mule's ass."

To Brother Verber's dismay, the door opened all the way and he was ushered inside, warned again to stay real quiet, and nudged across the room to be plopped on a lumpy sofa. On a recliner lay a bristly white sow with moist pink eyes and a drooly snout, and damned if she wasn't staring attentively at a television set. He was so bewildered that he mutely accepted a jar filled with a clear liquid and went so far as to automatically raise it to his lips. The first sip nearly jolted him out of his daze, but it didn't. The second sip went down more smoothly. Before too long, the jar was in need of a refill.

Brother Verber wasn't off and running down the

road he'd described to Raz, but he was well on his way at a brisk clip.

I scrunched as far as I could against the window and stared down at the endless expanse of flat, gray clouds, trying to convince myself I was traveling in an airplane rather than a time machine. We were moving forward in space, not backward along a continuum that ended in an elegant apartment (fv rms, ter, all mod con, full sec). I was going to Manhattan to rescue my mother from whatever disaster she'd brought upon herself. I was not going home. I'd done that when I walked out of the courthouse and hailed a cab for the airport.

I strained to believe the lecture I was giving myself but my ex's face kept popping up and breaking my concentration. For the record, he wasn't bad-looking if you like lounge lizards only one generation removed from pastel polyester pantsuits, family outings to discount stores, and forced joviality around the gas grill in a New Jersey backyard. The facade had begun to erode early in the game (we're talking months, not years), but I'd persevered until I could dredge up the courage to confront myself with my lack of judgment, lack of perspicuity, and lack of anything remotely akin to common sense. Admitting it to Ruby Bee had been even more painful, although for once in her life, she didn't point out that she'd told me so. Estelle did it for her, and at length.

I took out my checkbook and glumly noted the damage I'd done with the airline ticket. The pathetic figure, coupled with the possibility I'd be unemployed when I returned to Maggody, distracted me but did not enhance my spirits. Nor did the three-hundred-pound salesman from Toledo, who in theory was sitting in the aisle seat but in truth had oozed over into the adjoining one, and was now frowning as he read the bottom line in my checkbook.

"You got a place to stay tonight, sweetie?" he asked

wheezily. "I'd hate to see a pretty little thing like you stay in a dirty hotel with a bunch of pimps and whores. I'm staying at the Hilton, myself, and I sure could stand to squeeze you in with me."

"That's real nice of you, but I'm hoping to get my mother out on bail. Either way, I can stay in her room."

"Get your mother out on bail?"

"Murder," I said levelly. "I'm not sure if I have enough money. If she just hadn't gone hog wild and tried to blast her way through all those cops, she might have gotten off cheaply. But she's a real card, my mama, especially when she's off her medication. Say, maybe you could loan me a few hundred bucks, and come along down to the jail to meet her? Then we all could go back to your room at the Hilton and get to know each other better. Mama's scrawny, but she's feisty. You can ask anybody in town, 'cause she's taken on most of 'em and left 'em for dead by daybreak."

He grabbed the plastic card from the seat pocket and began to memorize the location of all the emergency exits. I resumed my study of the blanket of clouds, wishing I were in my bed with a more substantial blanket pulled over my head.

Kevin stared resolutely through the windshield, determined not to let his eyes drift to the rearview mirror. "Would you like to stop for something to eat, my honeybuns, or stretch your legs in a rest stop?"

"No."

It wasn't so much her terseness as her tone that caused him to clutch the steering wheel more tightly and gulp several times. He considered offering to pull over and fetch her a soda from the cooler in the trunk, then decided he'd better just keep quiet as a little ol' mouse and let her say if and when she wanted anything. His bride wasn't the shy type, even in her current condition. His job was to keep on driving northward, aimed at their goal, the spanking new roadmap folded and set on the seat where he could reach it.

They were back on pavement again, and this was good. Like a cowhand who'd had to venture into some canyons to round up strayed calves, he'd taken them off the route for a while. But now they were back on track, or at least going in the right direction.

"Lotion," Dahlia growled from the backseat.

"Yes, my precious," Kevin said, scrabbling on the seat for the pink bottle. He twisted his arm around and thrust the bottle over the back of his seat. "Calamine lotion for my beloved bride. I sure am sorry about not seeing that poison ivy around the tree. Can you ever find it in your heart to forgive me?"

"I doubt it, especially since you're pouring out the lotion on the floor of the car. It ain't the picnic basket that's covered with oozy red welts that itch worse than crabs in a fiddler's privates."

She groaned, although the noise hinted as much of simmering rage as it did of discomfort, and it occurred to Kevin that he was kinda glad she was lying in the backseat, her legs spread apart and her feet poked out the window.

He jerked his arm back, splattering the dashboard and windshield with pink spots. "I'll stop at the next store," he said as he hunkered over the steering wheel on the off chance she could reach him if she tried. "You know, this road's a lot prettier than a boring old interstate. There's some real nice flowers in the ditch, and that last house had a plastic duck and little yeller babies in a row. I wish you could have seen them, my adorable bride."

"You dumped lotion on the potato chips. You'd better be darn glad I ain't sitting up there beside you, Kevin Fitzgerald Buchanon. Iff'n I was, we'd find out if you'd be any smarter with soggy pink potato chips stuffed up your nose!"

"It's gonna be just fine," he said soothingly. "This is our honeymoon, my sweetness, and we've got our whole lives in front of us. You and me, a cottage with a vegetable garden out back, maybe the pitter-patter of little feet afore too long."

"I suppose so, Kevvie." She didn't sound nearly as enchanted with his vision as he did, but he blamed it on her unfortunate condition. "Even though it's all your fault this rash is making me wish I was dead, I still love you," she added gently. "I never looked twice at Ira on account of his warts. He ain't half the man you are."

Kevin accepted the praise with a cocky chuckle, although farther down the road he started wondering if she'd made the observation based on personal research. Twice?

CHAPTER
FOUR

"Are you sure this is the right place?" I asked the cabbie as I studied the scaffolding. "There must be another Chadwick Hotel somewhere. This is closed for remodeling."

"We're at the only one I've ever heard of, and I've been driving for eighteen years. But it makes no difference to me if you want me to cruise around for a while. East side, west side, anywhere you want to go. *Suum cuique,* as I always say."

"No, this must be it," I said without conviction. I paid him and carried my bag into the lobby, where it was cool and dim, if not elegant. The furniture was shabby and arranged rather oddly, the plastic plants coated with dust, the floor missing half its linoleum. Wondering what Ruby Bee and Estelle had made of it, I went to the reception counter and tapped a silver bell.

When nothing happened, I repeated the action several times, and then dropped my bag and sat down on the arm of a sofa to decide what to do next. I might have been mistaken about the hotel. There was no sense of occupancy, and certainly no hint of a national contest in progress. Outside, there was life, albeit screaming, snarling, honking, exploding life. Inside, there was something very wrong.

"I had to report your salary," said a male voice from the corridor beyond the desk. "I couldn't help it, Rick.

Those fuckin' buzzards at the IRS will demand an audit this year, just like they did last year and the year before. So act like a good citizen and pay your income taxes like everybody else. Maybe you'll get a medal one of these days."

"Maybe I'll shove it up your ass," said a second voice.

"I'm an accountant, not a magician. I've got enough problems with the invoices and the cash flow and our arrangement with the union bosses. I don't need you whining at me. You got problems with me, you call Mr. Gabardi and tell him all about them."

A door slammed, ending what I could hear of the conversation. At least there were people within the hotel, which was marginally encouraging. If I sat long enough, perhaps I would get to see one of them, or even find out what the hell was going on with Ruby Bee.

The front door opened and an elderly man in a white jacket, a lime green shirt unbuttoned at the collar, and plaid pants entered the lobby. The top of his head was shiny and dotted with freckles, but there were tufts of white hair above his ears, and a few more shooting out of same. His skin was dark and deeply wrinkled, his nose reminiscent of a plum. He carried a small suitcase and a newspaper.

"How ya doing?" he said to me, then went to the desk, banged the bell, and shouted, "Rickie, my boy, show yourself! I am in need of a hot shower and a cold drink. Airplanes make me nervous in the stomach and sweaty in the palms, and now I want to relax." His accent was a mixture of Brooklynese and Italian, his attire strictly Floridian retiree. All he needed to complete the ensemble was a pair of golf shoes.

An exceedingly ashen young man came through a door behind the desk, doing his best to smile. Even from my perch across the lobby, I could see the tic at the corner of his mouth and the unnatural bulge of his eyes. "Why, Mr. Cambria, how nice to see you again. No one told me you—" He spotted me, and his attempted geniality dried up. "Who are you? Another coconut from Kansas?"

The man glanced back at me with an uneasy frown. "Rick, you're supposed to have this under control. Although Mr. Gabardi decided to have me stay here for the next few days, he still has faith that you know what you're doing."

The one addressed as Rick (and the one who'd been expressing his unhappiness about his taxes) took the other's arm and tried to urge him around the end of the counter. "Please, wait in my office while I deal with this. There's a bottle of very soothing scotch in the bottom right drawer of the desk. I will be honored if you will sample it, Mr. Cambria."

Cambria refused to be urged one inch. "I would rather go to my room and make a call. A long distance call."

"Of course you would." He opened a drawer and took out a key. "You must stay in the penthouse. I'll be up shortly to remove my things from your way, and I'll bring the scotch and some ice. I'm afraid we don't have maid service, but I myself will change the sheets and—"

"First, the call," the older man said as he took the key, winked at me, and went to the elevator. Rick hurried after him in time to push the button, then stepped back and maintained a pained smile until the doors slid open.

Once Cambria had been whisked upward, Rick returned to the desk and scratched his chin with a well-manicured fingertip while we assessed each other. I waited silently, and he finally sighed and said, "Are you like a judge for this screwy contest or something?"

"Something," I said, nodding.

"Is there anything I can do or say that will induce you to go away?"

"I don't think so."

He smoothed down his narrow mustache with yet another well-manicured fingertip, glanced over his shoulder at the closed door behind him, and shook his head. "This has been some coupla days. Only a week ago did anyone bother to inform me of this contest, and nobody seemed to remember that I am up to my ass in remodeling. When you're dealing with union guys, you can't tell them to take a short hike, unless you plan to make like a submarine in the bottom of the Hudson River. After last night, that has begun to appeal." He noted my wince. "You got something to do with this shooting thing, right? Are you the dame's lawyer?"

"Her daughter," I admitted. "I flew in about an hour ago, and I'd like very much to find someone who'll explain what's going on."

"So would I, but I got problems with the accountant and Mr. Cambria in the penthouse and I think I'd better make some calls myself. The pistol-packing maniac— pardon me, your mother—was in 217. The police sealed it off, so I moved that woman who was with her to 219. It's possible she is up there now, presuming she didn't get her hair caught in a ceiling fan and her head was jerked off." He twitched a third well-manicured fingertip in the direction of an elevator, gave me a smirky look, and disappeared through the door.

The elevator groaned and shuddered, but eventually I found myself walking down the corridor of the second floor. The carpet was worn and badly stained, the unappetizing beige paint curled off the walls, and the redolence was that of the restrooms in Grand Central Station—or any ol' bus station in this great land of ours.

Some of the doors had numbers; others did not. I had no difficulty locating 217, however. It was crisscrossed with yellow tape and seals, and an officious sign threatened would-be trespassers with everything short of capital punishment. A few inches above the sign was a splintery hole ... Ruby Bee's signature, so to speak.

I tapped on 219. The door opened, and before I could speak, I was yanked inside. The door slammed so quickly my heels felt a breeze.

"Oh, thank gawd you made it," Estelle said, collapsing on me in a bony hug. "I am worried sick, and all

I've been able to do all day is sit here in case Ruby Bee calls or Geri finds out what's happening or the police come back to drag me off in handcuffs or I just go plum out of my mind like ol' Particular Buchanon. Remember when he decided there were Nazis in his attic? I could hear his shotgun all the way out at my house."

I squirmed free, caught her shoulders, and pushed her down on the narrow twin bed. "Get a hold of yourself," I said as I looked around the room. It was adequate for the two narrow beds, dresser, and night table, as long as you didn't mind stepping over the furniture and suitcases every time you moved. The flowers on the wallpaper clearly were not perennials; their season had come and gone. The artistic spiderwebs dripping from the ceiling implied other life forms enjoyed more success, as did the tiny brown beads along the baseboard. All in all, it was your average New York hotel room.

"What're we gonna do?" Estelle demanded. "You don't aim to stand there gawking while your own flesh and blood's being gnawed by rats in some filthy jail, do you?"

"I still don't know what happened." I sat down across from her, patted her knee, and suggested she begin at the beginning—slowly, thoughtfully, omitting nothing that might be important.

She omitted nothing, from the exchange between Ruby Bee and the cute lil' stewardess (Mitzi) concerning the so-called food (worse than the specials at the Dairee Dee-Lishus) served on the airplane (cramped), the airport aswarm with foreigners (potential purse snatchers, every one of them), the cabdriver (as ornery as Raz and twice as dumb), the lack of a welcoming committee in the lobby (a disgrace), and the arrival of the contestants, companions, contest coordinators, and possibly enough workmen (real pushy fellows) to remodel the entirety of the city from 48th Street to the tip of the island (and it sure could use a facelift).

"Wait a minute," I said, rubbing my face, "you were spouting off names too quickly. I met the manager when I arrived. His name's Rick, right?"

"Geri called him Richard Belaire, but a carpenter called him Rick. He's a real uppity sort whose mama should have smacked some manners into him long before now. Anyway, he acted like he wasn't gonna let us stay here, but Geri marched him off and told him how the cow ate the cabbage, and pretty soon he comes back with room keys and says this floor is okay." She glanced disdainfully at the room. "Okay if you do your redecorating at garage sales or flea markets! Why, the Flamingo Motel beats this place hands down—and costs a quarter of what that little framed sign on the back of the door says. You ain't gonna believe it, but when you open the bathroom door, it hits the bed and you have to slither in sideways. And you'd better decide aforehand what you're gonna do when you get inside, 'cause there's no room to turn around."

"Who's Geri?" I asked.

"Geri Gebhearn is the gal from the marketing firm. She's in charge of the contest. A sweet thing, with big brown eyes and a heart-shaped mouth. I'm not sure she's real pleased about her job, even though she seemed to take to telling folks what to do like a hen does to a handful of corn. She's the one who gave out the room keys, told us to get settled, and then said she'd send out for some food that we could eat in the lobby. The restaurant's closed on account of the remodeling, so I don't see how the contestants can use the kitchen, but Geri goes off again to talk to Mr. Richie Rick and comes back and says—"

"Why is the contest being held here?"

Estelle gave me a huffy look. "I ain't the one running it, so how would I know? Catherine's mother liked to have a fit over the sawdust, and I told her that if I was—"

"Catherine's mother? Is she one of the contestants?"

"Didn't they teach you to pay attention when you went to that police school?" She stood up and would have paced had space allowed it. She was obliged to stand over me; her hair was such that I felt as though I were being intimidated by a six-foot fire hydrant. "Catherine Vervain is this sour pickle of a girl, and she's the contestant, although if you ask me, her mother—Frannie— sent in the recipe and stuck Catherine's name on it. The girl does nothing but sulk, and refused to eat the Chinese food on account of it having some chemical in it. I myself thought it was real tasty."

"Catherine and Frannie," I said humbly. "Who else?"

"Well, there's nice Mr. Pilverman, who was naked in Ruby Bee's bed. He's a mannersome sort, a widower, and you can tell from looking at him that he's not keeping company, not by a long shot. No woman in her right mind would let him wear that shoddy old raincoat out in public." She paused, her good eye sweeping over me like a liposuction tube. "Not that old, either. Nothing to write home about, but kind of attractive and real polite. You might take to him."

"Then he's not dead?"

"Of course he ain't," she said with a snort. "They finally got the telephones fixed a while back, and Geri called to say that he's gonna be just fine. In fact, as soon as they get him patched up, he's coming back here so we can get on with the contest."

I looked up at her. "And Ruby Bee?"

"Geri couldn't find out anything. She said she and Kyle were gonna go down to the police station to see if they could fetch Ruby Bee, but she didn't sound real optimistic."

"Kyle," I said, zooming in on the next name. If we continued at this rate, we might be ice skating at Rockefeller Center if and when Ruby Bee was released. "Who's Kyle?"

"Kyle is the son of the KoKo-Nut company president. He's a scrawny thing with oily hair and ferrety face, sorta like that cousin of Kevin's who was in prison. That sure was a lovely ceremony, wasn't it? I heard Mrs. Jim Bob was all hissy about Dahlia wearing white like she was a virgin, and there ain't nobody gonna argue she was, not after—"

"Do you mind?" I said in an admirably controlled voice. "The contest is being run by a couple of kids, and in a hotel managed by a third. The contestants are

Pilverman, who's been shot, Ruby Bee, who shot him, and a sulky kid, who can't tolerate monosodium glutamate. You and the girl's mother are along for the fun. Is that everyone?"

Estelle put her finger on her lips, tiptoed to the door, and eased it open. After a peek, she closed it and tiptoed back to the bed, although we'd been conversing in normal voices all this time (and she'd squawked more than once).

"There's one more," she whispered. "Her name's Brenda Appleton, and she's with her husband, Jerome. They're next door in 221. She's kind of a featherbrain, always blithering about her girls in California and her house on Long Island and how she volunteers at the library and plays bridge on Wednesday afternoons. It ain't hard to figure out why her daughters moved all the way across the country. She's lucky they stopped when they came to the ocean, instead of renting rowboats and heading for China."

"And her husband?"

"He doesn't say much. He's short and tubby, and his hair looks like freshly vacuumed shag carpet. He wears thick bifocals that make him look like a toad, and I wouldn't be surprised if his tongue was long enough to snag a fly. I can't quite put my finger on him, but he sort of reminds me of the oldest Nookim boy. You know, shifty-eyed and most likely thinking awful things about people. Not saying 'em, mind you—but thinking them all the same." She wiggled her eyebrows at me. "And he was sneaking peeks at Geri whenever his wife wasn't watching him. He didn't have to say what he was thinking then. No, it was smeared all over his face like cupcake icing."

"Okay," I said slowly, "I think I've got everyone sorted out for the moment. Now, what exactly happened last night? Where were you?"

"Well, we all gathered in the lobby and ate off paper plates. Not everybody, now that I think about it. Brenda's husband said he had work to do and went up to their room. Catherine said she was feeling poorly on account of the sawdust, and she left in the elevator with Jerome. Oh, and one of the contestants hasn't arrived. I disremember the name, but a female. So on one side of the lobby was Ruby Bee and me, Brenda, Geri, and Kyle. Durmond Pilverman was sitting on a sofa next to Frannie Vervain, who was so busy trying to cozy up with him that she tumped chop suey in her lap."

"And . . . ?" I said.

Estelle stepped over my bag, navigated through their impressive quantity of suitcases and canvas bags, and stopped in front of the cracked mirror over the dresser. Once she'd made sure her hair was intact, she began to apply lipstick with a heavy hand. "And Geri said that the kitchen would be cleaned so the contestants could take turns trying out the oven and making sure they had all their pots and bowls. That was supposed to happen this afternoon, but Geri didn't plan on Ruby Bee shooting anybody and that awful mess with the police all night long."

"If you don't stick to the story, I'm going to take that lipstick tube from your hand and use it as a weapon," I said sharply—and sincerely. "Most of the group were in the lobby. At some point, Geri mentioned a rehearsal scheduled for this afternoon. Presumably, everyone came upstairs for the night."

"You can presume anything you want," Estelle retorted archly, then stopped and cocked her head. "Do you reckon that's the elevator?"

"I don't care if it's a newly installed escalator to heaven. What about last night?"

She opened the door, popped her head out, and with a squeal, vanished into the hall, leaving me to ponder how much damage I could do with a tube of Strawberry Soda Gloss.

"Will the meeting come to order!" Mrs. Jim Bob said, tapping on the desk with a pencil. "Elsie, just pass the cookies along and stop picking at them. Eula,

I thought you agreed to take minutes? You'll have to find something to write with, won't you?" She turned next to Joyce Lambertino. "We'll need another pot of coffee."

Joyce obediently went to the back room of the PD. She was there only because Jim Bob had bullied her husband, Larry Joe, into promising that she—not he— would come. That meant Larry Joe was obliged to babysit the kids, so it wasn't the worst thing ever happened to her. She wasn't real comfortable, since the others looked ready for church and she was wearing jeans and a faded sweatshirt, her hair back in a pony- tail. "How many cups shall I fix?" she called.

Mrs. Jim Bob rolled her eyes for the others' amuse- ment. "The whole pot, Joyce. Arly should be showing up any minute, and Brother Verber assured me this very afternoon that wild horses couldn't stop him from coming to our meeting. He was so inspired by the op- portunity to go to war against Satan that he went by Raz's shack to size him up. I expect him any second with a report so we'll know who and what we're up against."

"Raz Buchanon is who we're up against," Elsie said, peering more closely at the plate of cookies. The lemon ones were out; the tiny candy sprinkles always caught under her dentures. But chocolate gave her heartburn, and the sugar cookies looked stale. She poked one. It was harder than a lump of salt, just as she'd suspected.

"I know that," snapped Mrs. Jim Bob. She was irri- tated with the poor turnout for the first meeting of her committee, which she intended to call Christians Against Whiskey, as soon as everybody voted for it. Jim Bob had made up a flimsy story about having to be at the supermarket, although she'd seen right through that and let him know she'd stop by to make sure he was there. Eilene Buchanon had refused flat out, say- ing she had to stay home to wait for a call. Millicent and her husband were more interested in television than the mortal souls of the youth of Maggody. She'd gone so far as to invite the mothers of the three boys who'd been so disgustingly drunk, so they'd find out what the good citizens of Maggody thought of the way the boys had been reared without regard to solid Christian values. They'd declined—every last one of them, and in outright offended voices.

While Mrs. Jim Bob waited, she began a mental list of those who'd made it clear which side of the devil's fence they were on. It never hurt to keep a tally.

In the back room, Joyce got the coffeepot to gurgling, then, in a spurt of daring, slipped out the back door. It was so quiet and calm that she felt like she was in a cathedral. She wouldn't have been surprised if a monk stepped out from behind the lilac bush and started chanting away in a low, singsong voice. For a few minutes, she was a million miles away from her never-ending housework, screaming kids, whiny husband, leaky washing machine, blaring television set, not to mention Mrs. Jim Bob and the other self-righteous committee members busily telling each other how sinful everybody else was and how nigh unto saints they were. Joyce figured she was the one who deserved a halo for putting up with them.

Way up on the slumbering blackness of Cotter's Ridge, an owl hooted. It wasn't a monk, but it was the best Maggody could do on short notice.

"Jesus!" Marvel said as he kicked the side of the station wagon. "What kinda cars are they makin' in Detroit these days? No wonder the Japanese are running us off the road. Jesus!"

He took a knapsack and a carton of milk from the car, kicked it once more, and took off down the road, asking himself why he even bothered to steal American cars. There wasn't anything patriotic about having to walk on his own two feet like an army recruit.

He drained the milk, crumpled the carton, and hurled it at a squirrel at the base of a tree. "Have yourself a feast of cardboard, my fuzzy little man."

The squirrel, having chanced into a scattering of cracker crumbs, failed to acknowledge the missile as it sailed over him and landed in a mass of poison ivy.

Marvel continued to hike along the rocky road, determined to have a fine time and not to think about what his mama would do when he got home. He still couldn't believe that Dwayne and Terence had fingered him for the holdup at the liquor store—and that not one of the lily-white, myopic librarians could back up his story. All he'd gotten in return for three hours of reading up on dead presidents was a warrant for his arrest—and a sudden desire to visit Monticello. Maybe Tommy Jefferson might have some suggestions how to go about keeping his life, liberty, and pursuit of happiness.

"Could we get back to the story?" I said, amazed that I could speak so clearly through clenched teeth. "What happened last night?"

Ruby Bee lay on the bed, fanning herself with a church bulletin from her handbag. I almost felt sorry for her. Her dress was stained and wrinkled, and her hose looked as though she'd staggered through brambles. Her face was pale, her hair chaotic, her eyes pink and vague. "It was terrible, just terrible," she said wearily. "The only thing that might help is a cold can of soda from that machine by the elevator."

Estelle sat down on the edge of the bed and patted Ruby Bee's arm. "Arly's on her way lickety-split to fetch you one. You just lie still and rest. Nobody's gonna pester you to talk when anyone with an ounce of decency can see you're smack out of spit."

As I said, almost sorry for her. I grabbed some change from the dresser and marched down the hall to buy the damn soda. Okay, so she was entitled to play the martyr, but so was I and nobody appreciated it. The airline ticket had cost me all of my savings and most of next month's salary—if I got it. I'd stuffed clothes

in a carry-on and driven like a charioteer to the airport
to catch a plane with ten seconds to spare. I'd endured
a cramped commuter flight, only to race to the opposite end of the terminal to catch a larger plane and be
smothered for nearly three hours by Toledo Ted. I was
in the middle of the one place I didn't want to be, and
there was no way to ignore its omnipresence outside
the hotel.

I jammed coins into the slot, pushed a button, and
bent down to get the damn can out of the tray. No
damn can rolled into reach. I banged the plastic facade,
which in no way resembled my ex-husband's face.
"You sorry son of a bitch," I growled, pulling back my
foot to kick it like it'd never been kicked before.

"I wouldn't do that," said a morose voice from
behind me.

I looked over my shoulder at the man in the doorway. Despite his shabby bathrobe and bare, hairy ankles above slippers, he was intriguing enough to stop
me from breaking a toe or two. The bathrobe hung
oddly, and after a moment, I realized it was draped
over a sling supporting his arm.

"Are you Durmond Pilverman?" I asked.

He nodded, smiling just a bit. "I'm sorry to say I
am. Were I an employee of this hotel, I would take it
upon myself to kick that machine for you. However, I
am merely a guest, and all I can do is suggest you try
the machine in the lounge below. The light was flashing, which may indicate it works." He sighed. "But
very little works in this city."

"I'm Arly Hanks, daughter of your . . . assailant," I
murmured, confused by his gallant little speech, and
less than pleased to be caught in the act of attacking a
mindless machine. I was even less pleased that I was
doing so in a grimy outfit that had looked much better
seven hours and two thousand miles ago. "I'm . . . uh,
glad you're okay, Mr. Pilverman. I still have no idea
what's going on, but it's encouraging to know Ruby
Bee didn't . . ."

"Please, call me Durmond. A silly name, I know, but
my mother had a brother with such a name who was

killed in a car wreck, and she was a very determined woman. I should have half her determination."

I liked his chuckle, his quirky smile, his eyes that were as placid as pond water. Hell, I even liked his hairy ankles. "I guess I'll go down to the lobby and try the machine," I said. "Can I bring you one?"

"If you were to do that, I might spend the time searching for a functional ice machine. When you returned, I might invite you in for a drink and offer some enlightenment as to what took place last night."

"I might accept," I said, reminding myself he was my mother's victim, not a potential date.

The machine in the lobby functioned nicely. Cradling four cold cans in my arm, I returned to the second floor and went down the corridor to 219. As I lifted my hand to knock, I heard Ruby Bee say, "I'm not altogether certain, but there's something downright fishy about him." She lowered her voice to a level inaudible to eavesdroppers and continued.

Estelle gasped. "Are you saying he's a—"

The final word was drowned out by a sudden spurt of hammering from the floor above me. At least I hoped it was hammering, since it very well could have been a local version of Particular Buchanon engaged in a bit of de-Nazification. I waited for a moment, but the racket did not abate and I was beginning to imagine what it might feel like if the ceiling crashed down on my head.

I knocked on the door and yelled, "It's me!"

The door opened. A hand plucked one of the soda cans from my arm. The door closed and the lock clicked sternly.

"You're goddamn welcome!" I went back to Durmond's room and knocked once again. My reception was a good deal more cordial in 202, I must say. Durmond thanked me gravely, gestured to glasses, an ice bucket, and a bottle of bourbon on the desk, and shortly thereafter we were knee-to-knee on the twin beds.

"Would you please tell me what's going on?" I said, trying not to stare at the visible sliver of the sling, nor to be overly aware of his knee brushing against mine. As distasteful as it was to admit, Estelle had been right about Durmond Pilverman, although I'd read bedtime stories to Raz's pedigreed sow before I ever told her as much. "Ruby Bee's back, but she has yet to find a moment to tell me why she shot you."

"She didn't shoot me. She did fire a shot through the door, but I doubt the police will do anything about that."

"Who shot you—and why were you in Ruby Bee's . . . room?" I couldn't quite bring myself to mention the most interesting element of the story.

He studied me as he took a drink. "After dinner last night, I took a stroll around the block. When I returned, the elevator balked and I decided to use the stairs. It was a poor decision, I fear. It was very dark, and a punk was lurking in the stairwell. He requested my wallet, I declined, and he reiterated his request while waving a gun at me. I stupidly tried to knock it out of his hand, and it discharged, striking me in the upper arm and causing me to lose my balance and fall backward. At that point I lost consciousness. That's all I remember of the incident."

"You were mugged in the stairwell?"

"That's an accurate synopsis," he said gloomily. "There's no security in the hotel, and the mugger must have slipped in while our manager was away from the desk. I should have known better than to attempt to disarm the punk."

"But that doesn't explain why you were"—I struggled not to allow anything to creep into my voice—"found in Ruby Bee's bed without any clothes."

"No, it doesn't, but for that I have no explanation. I cannot imagine why the mugger wasted the time required to drag me in there, disrobe me, and then drop his weapon on the floor before fleeing. Miss Gebhearn, who was kind enough to escort me back here from the hospital, related what Ruby Bee told the police. It seems she'd just come into the room and switched on the light when she saw me. Before she could stop gasping, footsteps thundered down the hall and fists pounded on the door. Without thinking, she picked up the weapon off the floor, and as much to her surprise as that of the officers in the hall, it went off."

"It went off," I echoed numbly.

"It was unintentional, I'm sure, and the officers finally came to accept her version earlier this afternoon, after I'd told them my story concerning the mugger. They traced the weapon to a pawnshop in Harlem. There was no way she could have obtained the weapon, should she have desired to do so, and it was of very poor quality." He shook his head, as if depressed at the idea of being shot by a cheap gun. "Plastic, and with a loose trigger. What used to be called a Saturday Night Special, when in vogue. Now the children prefer more sophisticated weapons."

"Do the police have any theories how you ended up in Ruby Bee's room? Did you get a good enough look at this mugger to assist the police artist? Did you go through the mug shots? Were there any witnesses in the lobby when he ran out the door?"

"You sound like a cop."

"Probably because I am a cop."

"Are you now?" He held out his hand, and for a fleeting second of insanity, I thought he wanted to hold mine. I then realized he was offering to make me another drink, and I awkwardly gave him my glass. "That's very interesting," he murmured as he went to the desk. "Very, very interesting."

I wished I could see his face, but I couldn't. Not any more than I could interpret his tone of voice or stop myself from admiring the broadness of his shoulders. His hair brushed the back of his neck like dark, downy feathers.

I'd suspected as much, but now it was a certainty: Manhattan was too damn dangerous for the likes of me.

CHAPTER
FIVE

There was a gentle tap on the door. "Durmond?" called a woman's voice. "Are you awake?"

He handed me the drink, then opened the door. "Come in and join us, Geri. There's someone you might like to meet." He took her hand to usher her in, closed the door, and beamed at me as if I were a student who'd produced a clever answer. "This is Arly Hanks, Ruby Bee's daughter."

Geri wrinkled her nose at him. "Kyle's with me."

"Oops," Durmond said as he reopened the door. "Sorry about that, Kyle. Come have a drink with us."

The straggler came into the room and introductions were made. Both seemed uninterested, despite my self-perceived role as assailant's daughter.

"I'm so glad that you were able to come on such short notice," Geri said with a perfunctory smile, then opened her briefcase, took out some papers, and handed them to Durmond. "These are copies of the medical forms and insurance paperwork from the hospital. The Krazy KoKo-Nut Company will absorb all the cost, naturally. I cannot believe they're forcing us to use a hotel with absolutely no security. This is Manhattan, not some idyllic little suburb." She glared at her companion. "I assume you spoke to your father about all this?"

Estelle's description of Kyle's ferrety face was accu-

rate. He wasn't sending adoring looks at Geri, however, and he sounded miffed as he said, "I tried to call
my father to tell him about the—incident last night, but
he wasn't in his room. I left a message with the desk.
This hotel isn't my idea, either. It's a directive from Interspace Investments."

"This is not the time for excuses. Poor Durmond was
shot and then subjected to ... further indignities. If
you cannot arrange for proper security, I'll do it myself!"

Kyle flushed. "Do you want me to rent a uniform
and go stand by the door?"

"At least you'd be doing something useful, for a
change." Geri sat down on the edge of the bed and began to sort through papers in her briefcase.

Durmond and I watched all this in silence. We even
exchanged significant looks, although I had no idea
what they signified. Kyle clearly had several retorts in
mind, but after a moment of twitching his lips mutely,
he leaned against the door and folded his arms.

"So the contest will continue?" I asked Geri.

"Yes. It's totally absurd, but the show will go on.
My secretary"—she glanced at Kyle—"managed to
touch base with my boss. He was displeased to hear
what happened, but he was quite firm about our contin-
uing here in the Bates Hotel."

Durmond put his hand on my shoulder, which sent
off all kinds of adolescent fireworks—invisible, I
hoped. "You'll need to find a room for Arly. I'm sure
she's thrilled at the opportunity to watch the Krazy
KoKo-Nut cookoff in all its flaky splendor."

"Flaky is right," Geri said grimly. She slammed
closed the briefcase and consulted her watch. "I'll go
downstairs in a minute and speak to Rick. I'm quite
sure Krazy KoKo-Nut will be delighted to provide the
salary for a temporary doorman, should Rick resist, as
well as a room for you, Arly. And please forgive
me—I'm not at all like this usually. But less than a
week ago the account was literally thrown onto my
desk, and then I was assigned to work with someone
who has no experience in promo, and my boss is being

as beastly as Scotty Johanson, and Mother's livid because I—" She broke off as tears began to wobble down her cheeks. Seconds later, she was sobbing and the rest of us were patting her on the back and murmuring inanities. Even the broody Buddha relented and sat beside her, cradling her hand and sounding quite as ineffectual as Durmond and I.

It fit perfectly into the lunatic scenario. I wouldn't have been surprised if Mrs. Jim Bob, Brother Verber, and Mr. and Mrs. Kevin Buchanon marched into the room and announced they were planning a ménage à quatre in the next room. Oh, to be in lazy, hazy Maggody, where nothing ever happened.

Brother Verber stumbled along the side of the road, singing "Onward, Christian Soldiers" as best he could, considering he couldn't rightly recall the words. He couldn't rightly recall why he was doing it, for that matter, but he was having a splendid time. The night was balmy, the stars glittery, the world bathed in a most lovely glow of goodwill to all men.

And to all women, he corrected himself with a hiccup. Goodwill to all women, including Sister Barbara Ann Buchanon Buchanon Buchanon, or something like that. Why, if she should pop out from behind a tree, he'd just throw his arms around her and tell her what a perfect saint she was, from her halo straight down to her trim ankles.

He lurched to a stop at the edge of the highway. After several minutes of making real sure there was no car or truck bearing down, he started across the road, then paused on the yellow stripe to think whereall he was going.

It came to him like a bolt of lightning from the Almighty Hisself. There was no doubtin' this kind of divine inspiration. No doubtin' and no disobeyin'. The Almighty thought he should go right over to Sister Barbara's house and tell her what a saint she was and

beg her to join him on her knees in a prayer of thanksgiving for the miracle of creation.

Brother Verber gazed toward the heavens above, real
grateful for the suggestion. He then took a jar from his
pocket, unscrewed the lid and took a deep swig, took
another for good measure, and set off down the yellow
line, doing his best to walk on it but having a darn
tough time of it. It didn't make much sense for it to be
weaving like a snake, but it was.

He resumed booming out his battle hymn and doing
his best to keep time. "Marching as well wore, with the
crease of Jesus, leaning on the floor!"

Marvel hitched a ride with an old guy in a delivery
truck and listened to a lengthy story about a fishing
tournament. In that he was a guest, he didn't point out
you could buy fish at the market without having to sit
in a boat all day. When they reached the highway, the
driver let him off and told him to have himself a nice
evening.

Marvel peered both ways, not especially caring
which way he went. Problem was, he was getting hungry and there wasn't so much as a house in sight. He
had a couple bucks in his pocket, but that wasn't going
to buy him anything in no-dude's land. He'd already
learned it could get damn dark without any city lights,
and spookier than the hallways of the housing project
where he lived with his mother and sister. His mother,
who was going to kill him, that is, and his sister, who
probably needed help with her arithmetic homework.

He was scratching his head and trying to guess
which way to walk when a car came over the hill. For
some reason, there were two bare feet poked out the
backseat window. Marvel was wondering about that as
the car stopped.

"Is this the road to Cleveland?" the driver asked. His
voice broke like he was a kid, but Marvel looked
harder and decided the honky was old enough to drive.

"Why you be going to Cleveland?" he countered, still uneasy about the feet resting on the sill.

"Who are you talking to?" demanded the other end of the feet. They were mystifying, but the voice was belligerence personified—and then some.

The driver turned his head to mumble something, then looked back with a smile that hinted of terror. "We're on our honeymoon."

"You're going to Cleveland for your honeymoon?" Marvel said with an incredulous snort. "Shit, nobody goes to Cleveland for a honeymoon. Why you be doin' something crazy like that, man?"

"We're sorta off the track, but we're aiming at Niagara Falls, and we can get there if we can get to Cleveland. My bride's so dadburned itchy—I mean, feeling poorly and she seems to think this ain't the road to Cleveland. I've been telling her I'm pretty sure it is, but she wants me to ask somebody."

"Somebody with more brains than a mess of collard greens," said the other end of the feet.

Marvel scooped up his backpack and went around the car. As he got in the front seat, he took a quick look at what all was in the back. It was too dark to see much, but the aura of malevolence was enough to make him shiver.

"I've got to tell you, man," he said as he closed the car door, "getting to Cleveland's real tough. You take this road, and that road, and then another road, and if you aren't careful, you splash down in Lake Michigan. I'll just ride along with you so you won't get lost. No, you don't have to thank me; I'm happy to oblige. Lemme think . . ." He paused, watching the driver to see if he was going to buy it. The sissy white boy looked more like he was about to faint. "Yes, I thought about it, and to get to Cleveland, we go straight down this road. You just do the drivin', and your main man Marvel'll tell you where to go and when to turn."

I slept poorly and woke with a headache. Having become accustomed to nothing rowdier than dogs barking and owls hooting up on the ridge, the perpetual roar of traffic had kept me awake half the night. Trying to sort through Ruby Bee's tale had taken care of the other half. I'd gone back to her room after I finished the drink in Durmond's, but the light was out and a DO NOT DISTURB sign hung from the doorknob.

Geri arranged for me to stay in 204, which adjoined 202, which I did not fail to note. Neither did I fail to note I was entertaining ideas (okay, fantasies) that were unseemly and unacceptable. Glumly reminding myself of the reason I was there, I pulled on some clothes and took the elevator to the lobby to look for coffee.

A blond woman was speaking to a teenaged girl. The woman looked earnest, the girl exceedingly bored. I pegged them as the "sour pickle" and her mother and went over to introduce myself and mumble an excuse for my presence.

"Isn't this incredible?" Frannie said. "Your poor mother treated so harshly, and Durmond with a bullet wound! I realize this is Manhattan and people are gunned down every day, but I thought that we'd be staying in a decent hotel with—"

"Mother, it's nine o'clock," Catherine said sullenly.

"Don't interrupt, dear." She gave me an apologetic look. "Catherine has an appointment to get her makeup done for the press reception this afternoon. Geri's hoping there will be some television coverage and reporters from some of the major food magazines. I'd like to think there will be an adequate showing to justify our expenses."

I nodded obediently, if not enthusiastically.

Frannie took Catherine's arm. "I do wish there were a doorman to get us a cab. I feel so vulnerable standing on a curb with my hand in the air, and I always worry that some homicidal maniac will run us over without so much as a glance in the rearview mirror. Come along, Catherine. We'll have to make the best of it."

"I don't want to have my makeup done."

"Don't whine, dear. You must look your best for the media. We're not here for our health, are we?"

She tightened her grip and propelled the girl out the door. I was amused to see a doorman on the sidewalk and waited to see if it might prove to be Kyle in his threatened rental uniform. When he turned to respond to Frannie, I realized it was the Italian retiree who'd come into the lobby the previous afternoon. Mr. Cambria, the manager had called him.

It was so curious that I sank down on the arm of the sofa and replayed the conversation. Rick had been deferential, nearly obsequious, when Cambria arrived. Had he plied him with expensive scotch, settled him in the penthouse, changed the linens—and asked him to be a hotel doorman?

A man in a blue suit came into the lobby from a hallway. We blinked at each other until I determined he was a plumber rather than a policeman. He stuffed a considerable wad of money into his pocket and continued out the door, spoke to Cambria, and then hurried up the sidewalk toward, I supposed, the next aquatic crisis.

I was still puzzling over the identity of the doorman when Geri swept into the lobby with a briefcase, a clipboard, and an unhappy expression. "Good morning," she said to me as she went to the desk and banged the bell. "This whole thing's just impossible. How can I be expected to put together a decent press conference when the food editors won't even take my calls? I'd have more luck with the tabloids; it's right up their sleazy alley. That vile KoKo-Nut is apt to cause hair to grow on your palms, and there are extraterrestrial overtones."

"At least you have a doorman," I said.

She banged on the bell three more times in rapid succession, then frowned at the indentations on her palm. "At least I have a doorman. I made it clear to Rick that I'd arrange it if he didn't. Now, if I only had a hotel manager, and a fifth contestant, and photographers and judges and time to check the kitchen and . . ." She sniffled, but withstood tears. "Where is Rick? This is so maddening!"

Horns began to caterwaul outside. As we both watched, two men hopped out of a truck and began to unload cardboard cartons. Cambria observed them from his post, his hands behind his back and his head bobbling in approval. He held open the door as the four cartons were brought in on a dolly and came in after them.

"Ah, good," Rick said from behind the desk.

Geri spun around. "Where have you—"

"Busy. Guys, take those up to 319 and stick them just inside the door. It's unlocked."

"Wait just a minute," Geri said, clearly ruffled by his interruption. "Those are the cases of KoKo-Nut for my contest, and they're not going upstairs. They're going straight to the kitchen, and right now! I have more than enough problems without losing track of the key product." She paused and shook her head. "Although why there's so much of it is beyond me. I put in a request for one, which was one too many to begin with. We have enough to contaminate the water supply for the entire city."

Rick rubbed his temples. "No, Miss Gebhearn, the kitchen isn't cleaned yet, and the cartons will be in the way of the crew. They can be safely stashed upstairs until it's time to bring them down."

"They are going to the kitchen. There's ample room along the wall." Barely stopping short of stamping her foot, she pointed imperiously at the deliverymen. "Take them down that hall and put them in the kitchen."

"They need to go upstairs," Rick insisted.

Geri slammed the clipboard down on the counter and turned on him with all the fury of a prep school princess. "I've had it with you, buster! I am in charge of this travesty, but there's damn little to keep me from taking the next train to the Cape. You can call the CEO of whatever the investment company is and tell him how you screwed up this promotion and you refused to cooperate and you failed to provide security until this morning so that you ended up with the police. While you do that, I'll be changing into sweats and pouring myself a Tab!"

Rick looked as if he might come across the desktop to throttle her, but Cambria intervened, saying, "Rickie, my boy, this is not the time to make waves. I believe you ought to allow the little lady to do as she wishes, and without interference. There's no reason why the cartons cannot be stored in the kitchen."

The deliverymen waited, as did I, for the next round. It wasn't Broadway quality, but it had potential. Geri had her fists on her hips, her jaw squared like a pugnacious boxer, and her mouth was stretched to expose glistening white teeth. Rick looked from Cambria to her, slowly uncurled his fists, and said, "Take the cartons to the kitchen, guys."

Geri was too well-bred to gloat, but I could see it took effort on her part. "Fine. I'll need the key to the kitchen door."

"Why should you need the key?" said Rick. "That's out of the question. I need to have it handy for when the cleaning crew shows up. I don't have time to call your fancy office and wait until you come back here to open up for us."

"I've decided that we don't need a cleaning crew," she said with a shrug. "It's a bit dusty in there, but I'll have Kyle wipe down the surfaces and run a mop. In the meantime, I want those cartons kept stored in a secure place, and I have no doubt that the minute I step out the door, you'll have them moved to God knows where."

The KoKo-Nut wars did not escalate, to my disappointment. Rick snarled under his breath, but went into the office and returned with a key with a cardboard tag. Geri took it, beckoned to the deliverymen, and led them down the hallway. Cambria returned outside to guard the gate.

And I remained on my perch, remembering what life in New York had been like. Daily confrontations had been the norm. No one bothered to remark on hostile exchanges with cab drivers, vendors, pedestrians, skaters, clerks. In Maggody, a single cross word was repeated, analyzed, debated as to its merit. I could easily imagine Mrs. Jim Bob saying, "Well, Eula had no call to say that Millicent's daughter looked like a tart, even though she does. Of course, Millicent did tell Lottie that Eula's meringue was sticky, and . . ."

"That's settled," Geri said as she returned to the lobby and retrieved her clipboard to make a flamboyant checkmark. She waited until the deliverymen trudged out the door. "I wish I had my mother's zeal for this sort of publicity thing, but I don't. I'd much prefer to handle nice, quiet little accounts for detergents and pet food."

"You said last night that this was dumped on you at the last minute," I said, aware that sympathy had been tacitly requested.

"A week ago. I'm the new kid in the office, so I'm given all the assignments no one else wants. Have you ever tasted this Krazy KoKo-Nut? It's so nasty I almost barfed. Now I'm obliged to chirp its praises to the media, when I'm dying to do nothing more than lie in the chaise at the summer house. It's simply not fair!"

Before she could do a rerun of the previous night's tears, I said, "I have a question about the incident the night before last, Geri. According to Durmond, he was mugged in the stairwell and lost consciousness when he fell. Someone carried him to Ruby Bee's room, although I can't see one person handling him. My question is this: Who called the police, and how did they know to go to Ruby Bee's room?"

"I have no idea," she admitted, frowning.

"Is someone trying to sabotage the contest?"

The frown disappeared and she gave me a pitying smile. "Please, Arly, this is the national Krazy KoKo-Nut cookoff. Why on earth would anyone bother to sabotage it? I'm knocking myself silly trying to get anyone at all to even notice it. I had to go through my father to speak to the food editor at the *Times,* and I've never been so embarrassed in my life when she finally stopped laughing and declined to be a judge. *Travel and Leisure* couldn't find so much as an assistant to an assistant editor who was willing to set foot in this place, much less sample food containing coconut-flavored soybean flakes. I couldn't bring myself to call an old friend at *Gourmet*. If anyone had the decency to sabotage this contest, it would be I."

I was about to agree with her when the door opened and a woman entered the lobby. Cambria staggered after her with four large, worn suitcases and a plastic cosmetics case. The woman had pale, thick hair and a kittenish face, and she wore a black leather miniskirt, a pink blouse that neared translucency, and fringed boots. Her makeup was more suitable for a stage than a street, although it wasn't challenging to imagine her conducting business on a street corner . . . near Times Square.

"Mr. Cambria, you are such a doll," she said, giggling at him. "I am so flattered that you remember me from that show at the Blue Heaven! The boss pointed you out to us girls, but there were ten or maybe more of us in the line. You are a regular sweetheart."

"I should forget legs like yours?" Cambria responded gallantly. "I have thought of nothing else since then, not even in my dreams."

Still giggling, she kissed him on the cheek and gave him a little wave as he went outside, then spotted Geri and me and waved at us. "I'm Gaylene Feather. Are you in the contest, too? Isn't this exciting?" She spoke with a heavy New York accent, forming the words in the front of her mouth and sending them up through her nose like cigarette smoke.

"I'm Arly Hanks, daughter of a contestant," I said.

"Arly?" she repeated, her finger on her cheek. "I don't guess I've ever met anyone with that name before. It's kinda exotic, if you know what I mean."

"Oh, I do." I looked down modestly, not inclined to lie and claim kinship with the sprite in *The Tempest*, nor to be truthful and admit I'd been named Ariel, albeit with a glitch in the spelling, after a photograph of Maggody taken from an airplane.

Geri introduced herself and acknowledged that she

was the coordinator from the marketing agency. "We were expecting you yesterday evening, Miss Feather, but it's just as well you waited until today."

"Please, you should call me Gaylene. My real name's plain old Gail, so I changed it a while back when I began my career. I heard about the man getting shot." She sat down across from us, her heavy eyelashes fluttering like convulsed spiders, and added, "I had to work last night, anyways, so I couldn't have come. My boss is real upset about me missing the next few nights. I have to admit I'm losing money by doing this, but maybe the publicity will help my career, and a trip to Vegas can't hurt."

Geri raised her eyebrows a polite millimeter. "And what might this career be?"

"I am a dancer. I worked at the Blue Heaven for two years, then Mr. Lisbon offered me a better deal, so I'm now appearing nightly at the Xanadu, which is named after a fancy hotel in a poem."

"No kidding," Geri said as she made a notation on the clipboard and stood up. "You'll be in 213; the manager will give you the key. I'm going to use his phone to see if I can't find at least one paper willing to report the contest. Maybe Mother knows someone who can help." She went down the hallway to the office, and as the door closed, I heard her mutter, "If she's a dancer, you can call me Prancer!"

"I'm only doing this for the publicity," Gaylene confided to me as if we were bunkmates at summer camp. "I don't really like to cook, but like my boyfriend says, surely I can follow a recipe." She offered me a piece of gum, and when I shook my head, popped several in her mouth. "I have to make Krazy KoKo-Nut Kabobs. You roll strawberries in sticky jam, then in the flakes, and put them on long wooden toothpicks. I tried it at home, and it was real good. The package says the stuff is less fattening, and we girls have to keep an eye on that, don't we?"

"We certainly do," I said. "I'll leave you to check in. I need to see if my mother and her friend are up yet."

"Is she the one who shot the guy?"

Shrugging, I went to the elevator. As I reached for
the button, the door wheezed open and Ruby Bee and
Estelle stepped out. They were dressed in their Sunday
best, and each had a massive, bulging handbag sup-
ported by a shoulder strap.

"In case some criminal tries to snatch it," Ruby Bee
said, noticing my gaze. "I put some rocks in the bottom. I can swing it hard enough to make him see stars
until springtime. We ain't gonna take any foolishness
from these folks."

"That's good," I said weakly. "Where are you going?"

Estelle took out a travel book riddled with markers.
"We're going to the Statue of Liberty first and then the
Empire State Building. We talked about going on one
of those tour boats that go around the island, but we
decided to wait until another day for that."

Ruby Bee brushed past me. "Come on, Estelle, we
can't waste our time if we want to see Macy's, Tiffany's, that Trump man's building with the waterfall, Saks
Fifth Avenue, and the Bronx Zoo. It's already nine
o'clock, and we're supposed to be back here at four. I
am, anyway. It doesn't matter if you're here or not."

"Wait a minute," I said as I trailed them across the
lobby. "How are you going to get to all those places
and be back at four?"

Estelle, still rankled by Ruby Bee's remark, said, "We
plum forgot our mules, so I suppose we'll have to find
other means of transportation, Miss Travel Agent. We
ain't got all day, Ruby Bee. Have you got the map?"

"What map?" I asked.

"The map of the subways," Ruby Bee said, flapping
it at me. "We weren't born yesterday, missy, and we
don't aim to spend a fortune on taxicabs when we can
take these trains all over the city."

"You two have fun," Gaylene called from the sofa.

Ignoring my admittedly incoherent sputters, they
sailed out of the door, consulted Cambria, and took off
down the sidewalk as if they were heading down the
road to Jim Bob's SuperSaver Buy 4 Less.

CHAPTER SIX

For those who are a mite confused by all the comings and goings of people in the oddly parallel universes of Manhattan, Maggody, and Tennessee (or maybe Kentucky by now), rest assured that everyone was pretty much in place for the duration.

The fifth and final contestant, Gaylene Feather, had arrived and was in her room unpacking while she listened to a talk show that concerned the secret lives of transvestite Episcopalian priests. Down the hall from her, Durmond was wincing as he dressed. Brenda and Jerome were in their room; he was dealing with work he'd brought and she was fretting about the time zones and her daughter's lackadaisical attitude about picking up the telephone.

Farther afield, in a charmingly swank salon, Catherine was having makeup done under hawk-eyed maternal supervision. Ruby Bee and Estelle were heading down a flight of stairs to the vast labyrinth of dark, odoriferous tunnels and graffiti-riddled trains, both so determinedly fierce that they were unnerving the regular psychotics who inhabited the station. Neither realized they were being followed, but they would before too long.

Geri was on the telephone in the hotel office, desperately pleading with a receptionist. The desk was littered with lists, most of them scratched to the point of illegibility and splattered with a saline solution of per-spiration and tears. Kyle was cleaning countertops in the kitchen. Rick was on the third floor with two men sporting the insignia of an electrical contracting business. Mr. Cambria smiled benignly at pedestrians from his post outside the door of the Chadwick Hotel.

Back in Maggody, the newly elected president of the Committee Against Whiskey was sitting at the dinette on the sun porch, drinking tea and making notes as she plotted an appropriate course of action to save the youth of Maggody (and some others who could use a righteous shove) from demon whiskey. It was a nice day, what with the sun shining and the foliage aglow with autumn colors, but the newly elected president wasn't admiring nature. She was pursing her lips and wondering where Brother Verber had been the night before—and that smart-mouthed Arly Hanks, who, from all accounts, had torn out of town without so much as a word of explanation to anyone and thus far had not returned. The newly elected president finally put down her pen and went to make some calls to see if anybody knew what was going on.

The husband of the above was out back picking up garbage scattered on the lawn. It looked as if dogs had gotten in the cans, or maybe a coon. Odd thing was, dogs and coons hardly ever left behind a Bible under a limp lettuce leaf. Jim Bob started to toss the Bible into the garbage can, then stopped and opened it on the off chance there was a name written within the inside cover. There was. Frowning, he set it aside and re-sumed his chore.

Brother Verber lay on the couch inside the silver trailer that served as the rectory for the Voice of the Almighty Lord Assembly Hall. Like the newly elected president, he was oblivious to the day unfolding out-side, since he was keenly and painfully preoccupied with his pounding head, moldy tongue, bleary red eyes, tumultuous stomach, and general feeling of being trampled by an endless herd of bison. Which, for all he could recollect of his previous evening's adventures, might well have happened. Whatever lust he might have been harboring had been replaced with righteous heartburn.

Raz Buchanon was on Cotter's Ridge, as was Marjorie. She was snuffling contentedly for acorns, but he was up to no good.

Eilene Buchanon was well on her way to losing her mind, having spent the night alternately pacing the floor and sitting by the telephone, willing it to ring. Well after midnight, her husband had gone on to bed with a few grumpy remarks, and earlier in the morning had gone on to work with a few more, even grumpier, since Eilene had not been of a mind to fix him breakfast.

Joyce Lambertino was vacuuming the front room and trying to remember if she had enough sugar in the cannister to make peach cobbler for her in-laws, who were coming for supper. Shortly afterward, she discovered there would have been enough had the kids not made Kool-Aid and left snowy white hills all over the counter and the floor. No use crying over spilt sugar, she wearily told herself as she went for the broom and dustpan.

Somewhere in Tennessee (or maybe Kentucky by now), Marvel was cruising along in the passenger's seat, his feet on the dashboard and the warm breeze buffeting his face, gazing at the bucolic panorama and humming along with the whiny country music from the radio. The road to Cleveland had turned out to be damn empty thus far, and they'd been obliged to sleep in the car. He was in the mood for food.

"When we gonna eat, man?" he asked Kevin.

"As soon as we find a place," Kevin said, glancing in the rearview mirror. "Doesn't that sound like a good idea, my sweetums? Eggs and sausage and grits? Biscuits and gravy? You'd like that, wouldn't you?"

Dahlia was still in the only position that gave her relief from the insidious itching. She grunted and said, "All I'd like is to see you being dragged behind the car in a gunny sack. I must have told you twenty times that this is the wrong road, but you just kept driving and now we're so lost that the cows probably speak a foreign language. It's all your fault."

Marvel turned around and smiled at her. "Hey, Big Mama, you got to trust me on this. We're not lost. I know exactly where we are. Why, if you were to blindfold me and spin me around three times, I'd still know where we are."

"Yeah," Kevin said, bobbing his head like a dashboard figurine. "Marvel knows where we are."

"So where are we?" she demanded.

Kevin stared pleadingly at Marvel, who was a little bit uneasy about the direction of the conversation (and of their desired destination). The latter finally cleared his throat and said, "On the road to Cleveland. Your man Marvel ain't gonna steer you wrong. I been to Cleveland so many times I could find it in the dark. You just relax and leave the navigating to me, Big Mama."

Kevin accurately interpreted the noise from the backseat as a mixture of disbelief and of displeasure with the increasingly frequent use of the phrase "Big Mama." He wanted to believe Marvel more than anything (except the consummation of the marriage), and he was aware that he didn't have a passel of options at the moment. "Look up there," he said, struggling to sound like a hearty trailblazer. "We're coming to a town, and if that's not a cozy café, then I don't know what it is. It doesn't look busy, so we can be settled in for a nice big breakfast afore you can count to ten."

He parked right as Dahlia reached eight, hurried out of the car and opened her door, and with some exertion, managed to slide her out of the car and get her steadied on her feet.

"Not much of a town," she said, squinting at the few buildings, ramshackle house, and rusted mobile homes on cinder blocks. "It's uglier than Maggody."

Marvel was equally unimpressed. "Or East St. Louis long about January, when the snow turns to slushy mud."

"This looks like a mighty fine café," Kevin said with enough enthusiasm for all three of them. With Marvel trailing behind, he herded his beloved across the rocky parking lot, through the doorway, between the tables, and to a booth where he gestured for her to tuck herself in.

"Ain't this nice?" he said hopefully.

Dahlia looked real hard at the interior and then at him. "I wouldn't let my dog eat here." Nevertheless, she managed to slide into the booth, pick up a menu, and begin to read, saliva gathering in the corners of her mouth as she savored the promise of carbohydrate heaven.

"It's cool, Big Mama," Marvel said as he slid in across from her. "We gonna have ourselves some food and drink. Sure we are." He grinned at the two elderly men sitting at the counter and at the waitress in the kitchen doorway. Something about the way she was eyeing him made him uneasy, but he figured his main man and Big Mama weren't going to drive another mile until they ate. His instincts were very good.

There were people I could call and announce my presence, if not my triumphant return through the gates of the city. There were women with whom I'd done lunch, men with whom I'd worked in the security agency. Lining the gray gullies of the city were stores and shops I'd patronized. Museums, galleries, bars, restaurants, delis—the whole gamut: the sidewalk where I'd first been mugged, the corner from which my car had last been towed, the apartment building where I'd bathed and slept and cooked and told my ex that I was unwilling to continue to feign ignorance of his philandering (I'd called it something else at the time; what we'd called each other afterward was too unimaginative to repeat).

Yeah, I could make a few calls and sally forth, serene in the notion I had neatly severed all emotional entanglements with the people and the place. Or I could hang out in the lobby, waiting to hear that Ruby

Bee and Estelle had been murdered in a subway station. Mr. Cambria would protect me from the intrusion of the ghosts (of yuppies past), as well as muggers and others less desirable.

I turned away from the window and determined that I had the place to myself. On my left were double doors that led to a dimly lit dining room, the site of future antics. The registration counter was directly in front of me, with the elevator and stairs on the right. On the left, between it and the dining room, was a hallway which led to an office and ultimately the kitchen, where the cartons of Krazy KoKo-Nut were safely stored.

For lack of much else to do, I went quietly down the hallway, pausing by a closed door long enough to overhear Geri snarl, "Mother will be terribly disappointed, Tina," then continued to a scarred metal door at the end.

The key was in the lock and I was curious, or perhaps merely bored. I eased the door open. The overhead fluorescent lights were on, and water was gushing and splattering in a double sink. As I hesitated, Kyle stood up from behind the stainless steel island, his arms laden with bowls and utensils, and dumped them into the sink. The ensuing foamy splash was accompanied by an expletive more often heard in the alley behind the pool hall in Maggody.

"Doing the dishes?" I inquired politely.

"What do you think?" he said, then bent down and began to withdraw more paraphernalia from within a cabinet. "Geri decides she doesn't need a cleaning crew—not with good ol' Kyle handy. Doesn't need someone to inventory the cabinets—not with good ol' Kyle handy." He appeared with yet another armload and disposed of them as before. "She doesn't even need someone to run out to some damn kitchenware store and buy whatever's missing—not with good ol' Kyle handy. I was on the CEO track not that long ago, not the handy-dandy gofer track."

"CEO of Krazy KoKo-Nut?" I said, trying not to

smile in a situation in which there were cleavers within reach.

"My father sold a couple of blocks of stock to an investment firm in Miami, enough to give them the majority position, but they've assured him he can remain president until he retires. I'm the logical successor. There aren't too many MBA's who are frantic to assume the helm of a company that makes soybean flakes, plain and tinted."

"Tinted?"

"We market it as Krazy KoKo-Nut Konfetti. It still tastes like the contents of Ollie North's wastebasket, but it's exceedingly low in fat and cholesterol."

I glanced at the four offending cartons stacked along the opposite wall. "Do they contain . . . tinted things?"

"I really don't care," he said as he plunged his hand into the water and dislodged the drain stopper. He waited until the water obediently gurgled away, then grabbed various items and placed them on the counter of the island. To his credit, it was sparkly clean. Once he'd transported the last measuring cup, he took a paper from his pocket and scanned it, his lips curling downward as if he were reading the hymns to be played at his funeral. "I don't suppose you might want to help me with this?" he said, glancing up with a nervous smile.

I felt a pang of pity for him. His father had thrown him to the wolves, in this case, Geri, and she'd wasted no time letting him know her opinion of him. He reminded me of Kevin Buchanon, who was forever cringing and simpering under Dahlia's beady disdain, fearfully begging for a pat on the head like a mistreated puppy. Kyle was trying not to appear that way, to maintain an edge and a slim measure of control over a situation in which he had none, but he was fooling none of us.

"Sure," I said, going into the kitchen. "It's not like I've got anything else to do."

Veritable castaways that we were, we spent an amiable hour at the island. He read out the utensils, bowls, and so on for each recipe, and I located what I could and put them in marked boxes. Skewers for Gaylene, a bundt pan for Ruby Bee, an oblong cake pan for Catherine. I felt as if I were a genial Ms. Santa stuffing stockings for the little tykes.

When we were finished, he bent down over the page and counted those items not checked off. "I'd better get on this now," he said unhappily. "We need at least two large sacks of things, and if I don't have them tucked away before the reception at four, she will have a fit."

He didn't quite manage to capitalize the "she," but he came close. "Kyle," I said, feeling like a gray-haired granny down from the hills, "she can't be any older or more experienced than you. Okay, so she majored in marketing and knows the field better, but you"—I had a small problem here—"have a head start on the product. Think of all those years of growing up in a Krazy KoKo-Nut environment. She's clearly incapable of expressing genuine enthusiasm, so it's up to you to convey it to the media and the world. This isn't her contest—it's yours! She can't make it happen without you."

He brightened at this final bit of banality. "She really can't, can she? I suppose I'd better follow through with this list. If my father were here, he'd pass it to a minion in the office. What the hell—it'd probably be me, anyway."

He switched off the lights, and we walked toward the lobby. As we passed the closed door, we both heard Geri say, "But Buffy, we were roommates for two years! If you recall, I was the one who took you to the clinic and never said a word to anyone afterward. All I'm asking for is an itty-bitty photograph and a paragraph in the 'What's Cooking?' column."

Durmond was sitting in the lobby, flipping through a guidebook. His jacket hung more normally without the sling, but he winced each time he moved his arm. "Good morning," he said as we appeared. "Have you any idea if there's coffee available on the premises?"

Kyle snorted. "I wouldn't count on it. I'd better get to work on the shopping list. See you at the press reception." He went out the door, nodded to Cambria, and disappeared down the street.

"I haven't seen any sign of coffee," I said to Durmond. "There's probably a place nearby, though." I felt myself flush as he regarded me with an expectant smile, and had it been anatomically possible, would have given myself a quick kick to the fanny. "How about the automat? I used to inhale the danishes."

"It closed a couple of years ago, I'm sorry to say."

Feeling as if I'd learned of the death of a beloved pet, I managed a small smile and said, "Well, someplace else."

"A lovely idea," he said as he put the guidebook in his pocket and stood up. "Then, if you're not busy, perhaps you might like to accompany me to the Museum of Modern Art? We could eat lunch there, or farther afield if you have any suggestions, and be back here for whatever it is Geri has in store for us."

"I don't know," I said, now suspecting that my face was beet red and liable to ignite. "Ruby Bee and Estelle took off for the subway station, planning to do the entire city, and I'm afraid that—well, maybe I ought to be here in case something happens. I mean, they really have no idea—"

"I understand perfectly," he said, sounding exactly as if he did—to my regret. "At least let's have coffee at a nearby shop. Your mother and her friend won't be able to bring the entire underground transportation system to its knees that quickly."

"Probably not, and I certainly could use a cup of coffee." We headed for the door. "Is your shoulder any better today?" I asked as he held open the door for me.

"It hurts, but not so much that I need the pain medication the hospital gave me. Certainly not so much that I can't compete in the contest."

"Good morning, good morning," Cambria said, twinkling at each of us as if we'd done something remarkable by maneuvering through the door. "And where are we off to this lovely day? The park for a carriage ride, a cozy restaurant for brunch?"

"Merely a coffee shop," Durmond said, sighing.

"The young lady professes to have other plans for the day. I shall find a park bench and sit among the old men, watching the children play and flicking popcorn to the pigeons."

Cambria gave me a stern look. "Is this true?"

Durmond was biting his lip to maintain his sorrowful expression, but his chin was trembling and his eyes patently guileless. "I fear it is."

"We're going for coffee," I said to Cambria. "Is there a place nearby?"

He pointed out a restaurant on the corner and wished us a pleasant day. As we walked down the sidewalk, I heard a slightly suspicious noise from my companion, but refused to so much as glance at him until we were seated in a booth.

Once we'd ordered coffee, along with bagels and cream cheese, I gave him a level look and said, "So why did you enter the Krazy KoKo-Nut thing? The other contestants are . . . shall we say, more suitable for this kind of lunacy?"

"And I'm not?"

"Not from what I've seen thus far," I said, then paused while the waitress from the Rambo School of Table Service banged down our order and challenged us to ask for anything else. Neither of us dared. I took a sip of coffee and resumed my oh-so-delicate inquisition. "Have you always enjoyed cooking?"

"Since my wife died, I've found it an amusing occupation." I waited, and after a moment, he said, "Inoperable cancer. Grueling, but brief. I took off for the remainder of the semester, sat in my boat and stared at the gulls, and pulled myself together in time to start the spring semester."

"What do you teach, and where?"

"Connecticut, a small liberal arts college. You wouldn't have heard of it. I teach obscure things." He slathered a piece of bagel with cream cheese and carefully took a bite, all the while feigning preoccupation with the process instead of the postulator.

"How obscure?" I persisted.

"Very, very, obscure. Now how about you? You're a

cop, you mentioned last night. In this little town your mother mentioned?"

I was searching for a way to explain Maggody when two figures dashed by the window, faces contorted, bags thudding wildly, a guidebook loosing a stream of papers, and one red beehive at a perilous tilt.

"That was . . ." I said, stunned, then put down my cup and struggled out of the booth. "I'll catch up on the bill," I said as I rushed past the waitress and out the door (in retrospect, I admitted this wasn't wise; customers are shot for much less than skipping out). I caught up with Ruby Bee and Estelle as they reached the door of the Chadwick.

"Oh my lord," Ruby Bee said, grabbing my arm and gaping over my shoulder, her eyes as round as I'd ever seen them. "There's a maniac after us! We got to call the police before he gets here and kills us on the spot!"

"Ladies, ladies, calm down." Cambria put arms around both of them. "You are safe now. I personally will see that this maniac does no harm to you."

"He's been aiming to kill us ever since we set foot in this place!" Estelle shrieked. Like Ruby Bee, she seemed to be anticipating an assault from the direction they'd come. "Get out your gun, Arly! I plan to die in my own bed, not in this dirty filthy place!"

I looked down the sidewalk. There were hordes of people, of course, but all of them appeared to be preoccupied with missions more mundane than murder. A few of them may have noticed the excitement in front of the hotel, but they maintained the introspective expressions of big-city pedestrians and continued around us.

"Who's trying to kill you?" I asked.

"That maniac," Estelle said in a slightly calmer voice. "Doncha remember? I told you about him when I called."

"How silly of me," I said as Durmond joined us. "So what happened a few minutes ago?"

Ruby Bee clutched her bosom, one of her more elegant and well-rehearsed gestures. "Well, first off, we went down the stairs and followed signs to where there was a nice lady in a booth. She sold us tokens, but she wasn't real clear on which way to go to get to the place you take the boats out to visit the Statue of Liberty."

"I had already said a number of times which train we needed," Estelle cut in with a sniff. "I studied the map this morning while others of us dallied in the bathroom for a good hour."

The accused bristled. "You said *one* time that we needed the downtown train."

The accuser bristled back. "And I suppose *one* ain't a number anymore?"

I barely restrained myself from assaulting them. Both Durmond and Cambria sagely had decided to refrain from asking questions, and they'd also shown enough sense to back away from the twosome. "One is a very good number," I said irritably, "and I would like *one* of you to tell us what happened. Did this person actually approach you and make threats?"

After an exchange of dark looks, Ruby Bee shrugged and said, "Estelle decided to consult this big dirty map on the wall, and some old geezer started trying to explain how we had to change trains somewhere down where the map was so smudgy it was a disgrace. That's when I saw him. I told Estelle to stop yammering and come through the little gate so we could get on a train. She couldn't find her token, and by the time she remembered it was in her pocket, why—the maniac was not ten feet away."

"How did you know he was a maniac?" Durmond asked.

"I did not get off the watermelon truck yesterday," Ruby Bee retorted. "Anyway, we got by the track, kinda down toward the end where he couldn't see us, and then, just as the train pulls up, there he is coming at us like a rabid skunk."

"Then," Estelle said, "the train doors open and all these people come spewing out like ants out of a flooded hill, and people from behind are shoving us and nearly knocking us down, and we finally get on, but there he is in the same car, grinning and licking his lips, so I scream at Ruby Bee to get off—"

"And we did," she interrupted smoothly (they'd perfected the routine over the last thirty years). "But so did he, and we didn't know where the exit was, so we had to climb over the little gates. The lady in the booth starts yelling at us, and Estelle has to go and spill her purse, and by the time she's gathered up everything, this policeman shows up."

Estelle tightened her grip on her purse. "The strap got caught, which was hardly my fault. The policeman was right friendly about it, but the maniac, who was no dummy, had disappeared."

"I don't think he believed us," Ruby Bee said, winding down. "But I'd like to know something—how come you can't ever find a policeman when you need one?"

We all mulled that one over for a minute. Durmond sighed and said, "I'm sure it's my fault, but I don't understand why you were so sure this ... man was following you, determined to harm you? Did he say or do anything?"

"He's been following us since we got here," said Estelle, making it clear she didn't appreciate being doubted for one teensy second. "I saw him leaning against the wall over there when we got out of the taxi, and yesterday morning when I went to call Arly from a pay phone on the corner up there, guess who turned up like a bad penny not five minutes later? This is the third time, and he probably thought it'd be the charm. He just didn't realize who he was tangling with!"

Cambria lifted his bushy white eyebrows. "Isn't it possible he simply lives in the neighborhood? That would explain his presence on the street and in the subway station. And why shouldn't he have noticed two attractive ladies like yourselves, noticed and admired?"

Patting her hair, Estelle said, "That's right kind of you to say so. He did sorta smile, so maybe he thought he was being friendly." She and Ruby Bee moved away from us to evaluate this newest theory.

I glanced down the sidewalk, then nudged Durmond in the opposite direction and in a low voice said, "I'm not comfortable with the explanation. It's possible they've attracted the attention of someone with less pure motives than Cambria assigns him. I'm not suggesting this man is a serial killer out to get them, but there are a lot of screwy people on the streets. However, if I try to warn them, especially now that they've decided the city is thick with secret admirers, I'm afraid they won't take my advice." I made a face at the hissing pair. "Not that they ever do."

"Then we have no choice," Durmond murmured. "It would be irresponsible of us to allow them to resume their day's plans on their own. While we keep an eye out for the maniac, you and I must escort them—for their own safety, naturally."

"Naturally," I echoed unenthusiastically, recalling my uneasiness about venturing outside the hotel.

Durmond squeezed my arm briefly. "Then it's settled. Come along, ladies. Let's see if they're serving breakfast at Tiffany's."

Ruby Bee and Estelle were still debating the name of the cat as we slammed shut the taxi doors and took off into the slate gray maze of Manhattan. I'd long since given up trying to convince them it didn't have one.

CHAPTER
SEVEN

It was approaching four o'clock when we returned to the Chadwick Hotel. It felt more like midnight (in the Arctic Circle, no less) to me, but I'd just spent six hours in the company of two exceptionally unimpressed tourists, who were still verbalizing disbelief that a crowded little coffee shop (and by no means spic and span) had the audacity to charge seven dollars and fifty cents for a cheeseburger—and then put the coleslaw in a paper bonbon cup. And some of those silly things at the Museum of Modern Art! Both of them had made known, loudly, that someone had sure pulled the wool over the museum folks' eyes. Why, anyone with half a brain could see that big picture was nothing but a black square. Minimal art? About as minimal as you can get with nuthin' more than a can of black paint! And look at that, Miss Art Expert—it ain't anything more than a bunch of ropes curled up, and a mite sloppily at that. If we was to gather up the junk out behind Raz Buchanon's barn and send it to these folks, they'd probably send back a generous check and a thank-you note. As for those other so-called paintings, prettier pictures were taped on Joyce Lambertino's refrigerator, and you could tell what they were supposed to be, presuming you were charitable and remembered how old the children were.

And so on and so on, until I was no longer amused,

or bemused, and was reduced to offering sullen explanations and wishing I were wearing a hood ... and a noose. Even Durmond, who'd initially made an effort, had quieted down after we'd been asked to leave Tiffany's (Ruby Bee had been determined to get Gloria Swanson's autograph, and the woman thus identified all the way across the showroom had taken the accusation rather poorly).

Geri was in the lobby, the clipboard clutched in her hand and a faint frown marring her flawless brow. "Oh, good," she said, taking attendance with a gold pen. "I can't promise which media people will show, but there were a few who didn't curse at me or flatly refuse. It's shaping up nicely. The caterers are here, and the bar is set. The flowers came at noon, and ..." The frown deepened just a teensy bit. "I haven't seen Kyle all afternoon. The grocers delivered the ingredients an hour ago, but since he'd danced off with the key, I had to have the boxes left outside the kitchen. I do hope he didn't say to hell with it and head south to join his father and dear Mr. Fleecum."

"I saw him midmorning," I volunteered. "He was going out to buy the utensils that were needed for the contest. He didn't mention suntan lotion and a beach towel." A genetic disposition to meddle in romantic endeavors made me add, "He wasn't too happy to be treated like a combination of a scullery maid and an errand boy."

Geri stiffened. "I was working on the media contacts, which is my area of expertise. There's absolutely no reason to sponsor these things if coverage isn't forthcoming, and Prodding, Polk and Fleecum does have a reputation in the field. In any case, Kyle'll be in the spotlight tomorrow when he presents the grand prize."

"Ten thousand dollars," inserted Ruby Bee, much brighter now that she could dismiss the nonsense passin' for art in Noow Yark City and focus on more important issues.

"In a manner of speaking," Geri said uneasily. She poised her pen over the clipboard and began to murmur to herself as she perused the page. She glanced up as the door opened.

Kyle carried two bulging sacks, with a third balanced atop them. "I hope I never have to go through this again," he said as he headed toward the kitchen. "There was a sale on crockery, and I barely escaped intact."

"Did you get everything?"

"Every last damn thing. As much as I'd like to stand here and chat, my arms have lost all feeling."

"How dreadful for you. I do hope they spring back to life, since you'll need to put away all the little things you picked up and then distribute the ingredients to the proper boxes. Once you've done that, lock up and be back at five. And, please, try to wear something suitable for the media."

Kyle's neck muscles tensed, but he continued down the hallway. While our group stood like children awaiting permission to go to the bathroom, Geri complacently resumed her study of her clipboard.

The elevator doors opened and a trim, middle-aged woman joined us. "Oh, Geri, dear, have you seen Jerome? I popped out earlier to shop, and I thought he was intending to work in the room all afternoon, but he's gone. I cannot face the idea of television cameras and newspaper reporters without him beside me to keep me from making an idiot of myself. My daughters say that every time I open my mouth, there's room for a discount shoe outlet to fit inside, and—"

"No, I haven't seen him, Brenda," said Geri, "but the press reception doesn't start for an hour. I'm sure he's just gone for a walk and will be back shortly."

"I suppose so," she said, sighing in much the fashion Eilene Buchanon did when informed of Kevin's latest mishaps. She acknowledged my introduction with yet another sigh and was hovering near the door as Ruby Bee, Estelle, Durmond, and I went to the elevator and rode to the second floor. The two intrepid tourists continued to their room, now engrossed in the spectre of a large sum of money.

"A quiet drink?" Durmond said as we paused in the

hall to locate our respective room keys. "I think I need something after today's ... outing. Gloria Swanson must be laughing hysterically from the great beyond, along with Picasso and Warhol, and poor old Monet, who probably intended all along for his paintings to be blurry."

"I wish I were with them. Let me wash my face, then I'll tap discreetly on the adjoining door and we can do the dirty deed without stirring up any gossip."

The elevator door slid open. Brenda and Frannie stared at us, then nervously twittered as if they'd been accused of conspiring to rig the Krazy KoKo-Nut cookoff.

"Frannie's coming to my room for a little drink," Brenda said in response to our less than inquisitive expressions. "I know we shouldn't be imbibing at such an hour, but I'm so excited about the press reception, and, as Jerome says, it must be five o'clock somewhere in the world."

"I've been out shopping," Frannie said, somehow equally compelled to explain herself—and the highly suspicious presence of shopping bags in her hands. "I sent Catherine back here earlier to take a nap and prepare herself for the press. She's been in numerous beauty pageants, talent contests, that sort of thing, and she does much better if she's well rested. The DO NOT DISTURB sign's still up, so I guess she's asleep."

"What time is it in California?" Brenda asked as the two went down the hall. "I never can keep it straight, although I do know it's much earlier or much later. Vernie's a freelance writer, as I told you, and works at home. She's sold articles to—" The door closed on Vernie's career.

"I'll be ready in a minute," I said to Durmond, then went inside my shabby little sanctuary and sank down on the bed. The ghastly foray had left me so tense that I was trembling, as if I'd confronted my past on every corner. I hadn't scrutinized every face for that of my ex, nor had I really worried that I would run into him or anyone else. In Maggody, population about 755 (depending on who was off visiting relatives), you bet. In

Manhattan, population 10,000,000 (give or take a million), not likely—but too close for comfort, nevertheless.

The red bulb on the telephone was blinking. I punched for the operator and waited, although I was more interested in the far side of the adjoining door than I was any messages.

Rick responded with a surly, "Yeah? Whaddya want?"

"My message light's blinking. This leads me to believe there's a message."

"Hang on." He banged down the receiver, cursing, and several minutes later, came back on, cursing. "Goddamn Gebhearn dame swept everything off the desk. Here it is, no thanks to her. Some broad named Ellen called, said to call her back, said it's an emergency." This time he banged down the receiver in its cradle.

I replaced mine more gently and flopped back on the limp pillow. I'd been expecting the message to be from Ruby Bee, concerned with the presence of cockroaches in their room or a desire for sodas from the machine in the lobby—both of which she would have construed as emergencies no less volatile than a neighborhood nuclear meltdown. But Ellen who?

There was a mild tap on the adjoining door. I pulled myself up, rubbed my eyes, and opened it. Durmond held two glasses, the ice cubes tinkling seductively, a bagged bottle, and a bag of potato chips. "Your place or mine?" he said.

I waved him in and, while he fixed drinks, said, "I've had a message from someone named Ellen. I have no idea who it might be. Could it have been meant for you?"

"A woman calling me?" With a self-deprecatory chuckle, he sat down on the bed and began to open the bag. "Who'd be interested in a dreary old professor who's desperate enough to mutilate a perfectly decent cake recipe with Krazy KoKo-Nut?"

"She said it was an emergency," I said, ignoring his melodramatic display designed to elicit a tender response from yours truly. "I guess I'd better ask Ruby Bee and Estelle if they have any idea who it might be. I'll be right back."

"Don't worry about me. I'll just sit here by myself."

"Do that." I went down the hall and knocked on their door. When Estelle opened it, I made a rather natural attempt to enter the room. Natural and unsuccessful. "What's the deal with the security in this room?" I asked, irritated. "Are you entertaining sailors or something? Boozing it up with traveling salesmen from Toledo?"

"Ruby Bee is gettin' herself gussied up for the press reception," Estelle said, glancing over her shoulder. "She's wedged in the bathroom at the moment, while I try to figure out what she's gonna wear. The room's too darn small to have other people traipsing in and out all the time like a bunch of gawky outlanders. Now, what's your problem, missy?"

Manhattan was unnerving me, but it was unhinging them. I told Estelle about the mysterious call from "Ellen," and was told that they were a sight too busy to worry about my anonymous callers. On that note, the door was closed.

As I retreated toward 204, a man with erect peppery hair and thick-lensed glasses came out of one room and headed for the door through which Frannie and Brenda had gone earlier. The missing Jerome, I surmised as I smiled vaguely and made a move to pass him, wrinkling my nose as I caught a whiff of perfume tainted with cigar smoke.

He stepped back to block my way. Although we were the same height, he seemed to think he could tower over me and intimidate me with his masculine authority, or at least his bad breath. "Who are you?"

"Not my mother's keeper," I replied mildly. "How about yourself?"

He moistened his lips with a normal tongue. "I'm Jerome Appleton, honey. My wife's one of the contestants, and I came along for moral support. How about yourself?"

I recognized his voice, although it was no longer

roaring about the blankety-blank buzzards at the IRS. I introduced myself and admitted I was in a similar role. "I guess this is convenient for you," I added, "since the Chadwick Hotel is one of your accounts."

"This dump? You gotta be kidding." He moved toward me, and as Estelle had sworn, it was damned easy to see the mental icing on his face, not to mention the real dribble on his chin. "I handle a coupla clubs not too far from here, though. Maybe while the contestants are busy, we might go have a drink to console ourselves for missing out on the limelight? Don't get me wrong, honey. I'm not suggesting anything more risqué than that—unless you're in the mood . . . ?"

"You really are a toad, aren't you?" I said evenly. "Do you have dead flies stuck between your teeth?"

"Jerome?" Brenda said, opening the door and frowning as she noticed his face, which was frozen in a fine imitation of a gargoyle. All we needed was a flying buttress on which to perch him. "Is something wrong?"

"Nothing." He brushed past her and closed the door.

I was not popular on the second floor of the Chadwick, I thought as I trudged on my way like an errant mail carrier. The last time I'd received the cold shoulder from Estelle and Ruby Bee, they'd been up to no damn good, not to mention enmeshed in a thoroughly idiotic kidnapping plot that had backfired and then some. It was hard not to suspect they were up to something now, but I had no idea what it could be.

There was something damned fishy about the so-called mugging in the stairwell, but everyone seemed content to dismiss it as a typical New York close encounter of the wrong kind. I was the only person who remained unsatisfied with the story. But it was hard to explain why Durmond had been dragged to Ruby Bee's room and stripped, and the police alerted to storm the same site. To myself, anyway—since no one else was asking.

I stopped in front of the stairwell door around the corner from the elevator. Almost invisible in the terminally dingy pattern of the carpet was a round brown speckle. I knelt and looked for others. There was a trail of sorts, and I determined that it began by the door and went in the direction I'd just come. Like Raz's sow on the scent of a wily truffle, I crawled down the hall, restraining myself from actually snuffling as each speckle lured me on.

"Arly?" Durmond said from behind me. "Are you okay?"

I stood up and tried to think of something clever to explain my porcine imitation. In that nothing came to mind, I was relieved when he said, "There's something on the news that ... well, did you say the name of your town is Maggody?" He pronounced it "mu-GOH-dee," but I forgave him since he'd saved me the necessity of a lie.

"Maggody," I said, stressing the first syllable. "It rhymes with 'raggedy.' But I can't believe it's on the news. Stoplight go dead? Fish kill downstream from the sewage plant? Pedigreed sow on the rampage?"

He hurried me into my room and turned up the volume on the television set in time for the tail end of the story. When the flat-faced anchorwoman moved on to footage of sump holes in Florida, I found myself numbly staring at the now dark message button on the telephone. "Not Ellen," I heard myself croak. "Eilene."

Her white gloves clutched in one hand, Mrs. Jim Bob rapped on the rectory door, determined to go on doing it until she received a response. "I know you're in there," she called sternly. "When I came out of the Assembly Hall, one of those licentious hippie women across the road said you hadn't been out all day. She also said she was thinking about bringing you some carob cookies and a pot of herbal tea, but I put a stop to that." She increased the fury of her fist. "Brother Verber, you are trying my patience. Open up this minute!"

The door opened, and Brother Verber blinked down

at her with the unfocused gaze of someone who has been knocked up the side of the head with a two-by-four. "Why, Sister Barbara," he said, swallowing several times between each word, "how nice of you to come visitin' like this."

She took in his bathrobe, pale puffy face, and eyes zigzagged with red lines. "Are you sick?"

"I've had a touch of a stomach virus," he said as he held open the door for her and tried not to wince as her high heels clattered like a machine gun across the living room floor.

"We missed you at the organizational meeting last night," she said, twisting her gloves and tapping her foot, clearly not in the mood to proffer sympathy for the invalid's woeful condition. "I was disappointed, Brother Verber. You and I must join forces to lead the community away from the wickedness. No one else has the kind of dedication to decency, the commitment to righteous and old-fashioned Christian morality." She eyed him narrowly, and her lips all but disappeared. "The meeting ended at ten, and I drove by here afterward. The lights were off, and I could only assume you'd found something more entertaining elsewhere."

Brother Verber pulled the bathrobe around him more tightly and searched his maladroit mind for an explanation that might gain him temporary parole (a full pardon was most likely out of the question). He took his handkerchief from a pocket and began to mop his forehead, doing his best not to squirm as her eyes bored into him like skewers. "You and I surely are the generals in the Almighty's army," he said, wishing his mouth wasn't drier than a wad of cotton. "That's right—the brigadier generals leading on the Christian footsoldiers, marching against the forces of evil."

"I believe we were discussing your absence from the Christians Against Whiskey meeting, Brother Verber."

"So we were." He realized the handkerchief was so wet he was gonna have to wring it out in the sink before too long. "By the way, that's a most fetching dress, Sister Barbara. It must be new, 'cause I'm sure

I would have noticed it if you'd worn it to church or Wednesday evening prayer meeting."

"You would have seen it last night—if you'd been at the police department." She sat down and made sure her skirt was pulled down to cover her knees. Her gloves placed squarely in her lap and her hands folded beside them, she once again made it plain she was waiting for an explanation and was willing to do so until she was completely satisfied.

"Would you like a glass of iced tea?" Brother Verber whimpered. She shook her head, and after a painful minute of silence, he came up with something. "I was on a mission last night," he began tentatively, watching her from the corner of his eye, "a mission assigned to me by our Commander-in-Chief. Praise the Lord!" She failed to react, so he blotted his neck and moved along. "I went to Raz's like you said to do, forced my way into his den of degradation and decay, and offered to go down on my knees with him on his area rug to beg for divine forgiveness. He resisted, so I grabbed his bony shoulders and said to him, 'Woe unto them that draws iniquity with cords of vanity, and sin as if it were with a cart rope.' "

"You did?" said Mrs. Jim Bob, mystified.

"I did, indeed. Isaiah, chapter five, verse eighteen. While he was mulling this over, I dug my fingers into those same bony shoulders, shook 'em so hard his eyes liked to pop, and said, 'Joy shall be in heaven over one sinner that repenteth, more than over ninety and nine just persons, which need no repentance.' " He smiled modestly. "From the Gospel of Luke, chapter fifteen, verse seven. Well, that stopped Raz cold in his tracks, if I say so myself. A strange look came over his face and he began to cry like a newborn baby. It was something to behold, this miserly old wreck of a man, blubbering and mewling and begging me to put my hand on his head and grant him forgiveness."

"He did?" Mrs. Jim Bob usually wasn't the terse type, but she was having a hard time grappling with the scene. "We're talking about Raz Buchanon, right?"

Wiping away the hint of a tear, Brother Verber sat

down next to her on the sofa and put his hand over hers. "It was the most intense moment of my entire ministry, Sister Barbara. I was so moved by this unexpected triumph over Satan hisself that my throat seized up and I could barely speak. Sweat blinded me. My heart pounded like a big bass drum. The only reason I didn't crumple to the floor was the angels on either side of me like celestial bookends, holding me steady so I could save the soul of the wretched sinner. Praise the Lord!"

"Praise the Lord," she echoed weakly.

His hand, guided by an equally omnipotent force, abandoned her hands and began to squeeze her knee. Unlike Raz's purportedly bony shoulders, it was soft and supple. "So that's where I was last night," he concluded with a moist smile, a little confused about where he was in the narrative. He shifted so his thigh was against hers, and he could drink in her redolence that was as pure as spring water.

He was about to suggest they fall to their knees when she said, "Then Raz repented his wicked ways and promised to destroy his still and whatever whiskey he has?"

Every story needs a happy ending. "Of course he did," Brother Verber said, emphasizing the words with a tighter grip on her knee. "Soon as he has a chance, he's going right up on Cotter's Ridge with an axe. He's gonna smash the still until it ain't nothing but a heap of rubble, and pray for the Almighty to guide his arm as he throws those jars of evil moonshine onto the rocks. The youth of Maggody can go back to their innocent ways, playing ball and doin' schoolwork and attending Sunday school."

Mrs. Jim Bob was doing her best to ignore his hand, which drifted from her knee and was massaging her thigh—and heading in a direction she found most unsettling. She'd been married nearly twenty years, and since the very night of the honeymoon, had resigned herself to her marital obligations (carried out once a month, in total darkness). But Jim Bob had grown per-

functory over the years, and disinclined to dally about
his business. But, she thought, as an unfamiliar sensa-
tion began to seep into her body, her dedication to the
preservation of Christian standards had not made her
less of a woman.

Their thoughts were running in a somewhat similar
direction. However, she yanked hers to a halt well
short of anything less than respectable, hastily stood
up, and said, "We'll have to go along with Raz when
he destroys the still, Brother Verber. Without us to help
him maintain his resolve, he might change his mind.
It's our duty, and we have to see it through."

With a gurgle, Brother Verber clasped his hands together and lowered his head as if in prayer. Actually,
he was praying, and as hard as he'd ever prayed since
he'd mailed back his final exams to the seminary in
Las Vegas, although he wasn't silently exalting in the
glories of the Almighty. "Our duty," he repeated in a
reverent tone, "and we have to see it through." Now all
he had to do was figure out how in tarnation they were
gonna do it.

"In Lebanon?" I said between Eilene's hiccupy sobs.
"They're being held hostage in Lebanon, Kentucky—
right?" I waited out another one. "But they haven't
been hurt?"

"Not yet," she wailed, "but the policemen haven't
seen them in over an hour, so they could be bleeding
to death right this minute . . ."

I grimaced at Durmond, who was listening to the
conversation from the other bed, then persevered.
"But, Eilene, they've been held hostage for more than
six hours by now. There's no reason to think this . . .
person will do something violent after all that time. Do
you know how it happened in the first place?"

"How could I? They're halfway across the country
in some town nobody's heard of . . . I knew something
terrible was gonna happen to them, Arly. It's all my

fault for letting them go off like this. Wait, Earl wants to talk."

"Arly," Earl said, clearly having lost patience with his wife's failure to communicate, "the trooper what ran down the license plate and called us said Kevin and Dahlia went in some dumpy little café with a black guy. The waitress recognized him from something she'd seen on the news, called the cops, and then skedaddled out the back door with two of her regulars. When the police parked out front and yelled at the guy to come out, he came to the door with a gun and said he had hostages. It don't take a college degree to figure out who they are."

"What about the black guy with the gun?"

Earl snorted. "The police know all about him. He's got some fancy name, but they call him Marvel. Said he's been committing armed robberies all the way across Illinois and part of Kentucky. How he got hitched up with those fool kids is a mystery, and probably to them, too. Everything else is." He snorted again. "Hold on a minute. I cain't hardly hear myself think." He covered the receiver and began a muffled conversation with Eilene, who'd wailed steadily throughout this last exchange.

"Shiite rednecks?" Durmond asked, offering me the potato chip bag.

"Not exactly." I took a chip, frowned at it, and dropped it back in the bag. "You know, this has been a helluva week."

"And it's not over yet," Durmond said with a sad smile.

CHAPTER
EIGHT

At five o'clock we drifted out of our rooms for the press conference. I was still concerned about Kevin and Dahlia, but there wasn't a blessed thing I could do beyond calling Earl and Eilene for updates. I admitted only to myself that I was as worried about the physical and emotional well-being of the hostage taker as I was about that of the hostages. He couldn't have known what he was getting himself into, but I figured he was regretting it by now. Red Chief was only a kid, after all.

Durmond joined me at the elevator. "You look nice," he murmured, "and not at all like a bumpkin cop. You should wear your hair like that more often."

Okay, so I'd let my hair down, but only in the tangible sense. And run hot water in the shower in hopes the steam would undo the wrinkles in my unspectacular dress. And put on some makeup. None of it meant anything whatsoever. After all, I wasn't wandering down to Ruby Bee's Bar & Grill for a beer; I was attending a catered affair in midtown Manhattan. I wasn't a rube at heart. I was hip enough to don the appropriate camouflage for the big city.

"Well, yeah, maybe so," I responded cleverly.

Ruby Bee and Estelle came down the hall, both gussied to the hilt. Eyebrows may have risen, but they merely exchanged told-you-so looks. We discussed the situation in Lebanon, but without any keen insights, or even dull ones.

Before the elevator arrived, other doors opened and the crowd swelled. Frannie kept tugging at Catherine's sleeve and brushing at the faint creases. Her face pale, Catherine gazed at a reality of her own making. Gaylene Feather tottered along in spike heels and yet another leather skirt that barely covered the top of her thighs.

We jammed into the elevator and creaked down to the big event. The doors to the dining room were open. Geri stood just inside, her ubiquitous clipboard in hand, and a determinedly bright smile on her face. Her simple black dress and single strand of pearls gave her an elegance I couldn't have achieved with a fat checkbook and a week in Paris. It wasn't challenging to imagine her as the sentinel of a sorority house on the first day of rush.

"Don't you all look charming!" she said to us. "Brenda and Jerome are already here, and now we're all accounted for. Let's come right in and have a drink, shall we?"

We obeyed. The dining room was of moderate size, with seating for sixty or so customers. Each round table had a linen cloth, pristine ashtrays, and a vase of flowers. At the far end of the room was a long table covered with platters and trays, overseen by a pimply young man in a white jacket. A bartender waited behind a smaller table in the corner. Pedestrians on the far side of the windows glanced incuriously at us as if we were mundane freshwater fauna (i.e., guppies) in an aquarium.

Brenda and Jerome sat at a table near the window. She had a multicolored drink in front of her, he a more lethal martini. His eyes flickered at us over the rim of the glass as he downed his drink, shoved back his chair, and wound his way through the tables toward the makeshift bar. He moved carefully, which led me to suspect it was not his first martini—or second.

"Isn't this fun?" Brenda said, fluttering her fingers. "Jerome, dear, I'd love another of these wonderfully fizzy drinks. Frannie, that color is just marvelous on you. Catherine, you look absolutely darling! When Vernie and Deb were your age, they wore nothing but sloppy T-shirts and jeans with holes in them. I can't count the number of times I told them that they looked worse than ragamuffins off the street."

Gaylene clucked sympathetically. "These darn kids today—they lack class, if you know what I mean." She took off for the bar, her skirt creeping up her rump with each step. By the time she reached it, there was no doubt as to the color of her panties.

Ruby Bee and Estelle put their handbags on the nearest table and homed in on the food like airborne missiles with heat detectors. Frannie sat down next to Brenda, and after a moment, Catherine followed Jerome's path. This left me in an awkward position, as in standing next to Durmond in the doorway. I was quite sure we resembled a pair of freshmen at the first sockhop of the year.

"Thank you so much for coming!" Geri trilled from the lobby. I looked back at the two men in business suits, who were frozen just inside the lobby door. They were not identical, but their gray suits, hats, briefcases, and dumbstruck expressions were close enough to qualify them as salt and pepper shakers. She hesitated, then extended her hand and continued. "Are you from *Travel and Leisure*? I just knew Tina would come through for me, and I'm so very, very pleased that you're here. Come right in here and we'll get you settled with drinks and let you meet our five superfinalists! They're so eager to meet you. Do you have a photographer coming?"

"I don't think so," muttered one of the men. They conferred for a moment, then allowed Geri to escort them to the bar. As Jerome and Catherine turned around, I noticed she was holding a glass not unlike his—right down to the olives. Across the room, her mother winced, but continued to chatter with Brenda.

Durmond and I drifted toward the food. It looked good, especially to someone who hadn't had a decent meal in so long she felt as emaciated as one of Perkins's dawgs. I picked up a plate and allowed myself a visual feast: meatballs, imported cheeses, seafood platters, cold cuts nicely curled around fillings, crudités, and fruit dipped in dark chocolate.

As I poised a serving fork over the shrimp, Ruby Bee sniffed and said, "It's not bad, but I'd be embarrassed if I was Geri. Lord only knows how much this cost, and there ain't a wienie in barbecue sauce to be seen, much less any potato chips or mixed nuts."

"Or onion dip," Estelle said, smirking. "How much trouble is it to whip up a batch of onion dip, for pity's sake? Now, your fried okra is a sight more trouble, but I always say it ain't much of a party without fried okra." She peered more closely at a platter. "You'd think they could afford to pay someone to peel the shrimp for 'em."

"That cheese looks like it's been bleached," added Ruby Bee, pointing at a slab of Brie. "And this one smells worse than Boone Creek in August, when the fish take to flopping in the mud. What do you reckon this stuff costs?"

Don't think for a second that they weren't piling up their plates with the objects of scorn, or that I was about to jump into that conversation. I escaped to the bar, praying that their hisses were inaudible and no one from the press would realize I even knew the two gourmands.

Said gentlemen were being served cocktails. I nodded to them, asked for a beer, and fled to the farthest table to devour meatballs and bleached cheese (in Maggody, if it's not Velveeta, it's highly suspect).

Geri herded a man into the room. "This is simply marvelous of you, and I cannot begin to tell you how grateful I am." She gave him a conspiratorial smile. "You're from *Gourmet,* aren't you? You've got that look, if you know what I mean."

"Whatever you say, doll." The man winked at Geri and headed for the bar. She managed to close her lips, although it took a moment for her smile to slip back into place, and once again, the tiny frown line appeared.

It was still there as Ruby Bee and Estelle approached my table, staggering under the weight of their plates. "But the Buchanons all look alike," Ruby Bee was saying in a low voice as they sat down. "Maybe he's kinfolk on the less successful side of the family. Not everyone can be a plumber, Estelle. Some folks got to settle for less."

Estelle chased down a meatball and popped it in her mouth. "It's more likely I'm seeing things after all this time in this crazy town. Afore long, I'll probably see Mrs. Jim Bob selling pretzels from a pushcart and Hiram flapping the reins on one of those fancy carriages in the park. Brother Verber panhandling at the subway station. Perkins's eldest driving a cab."

"But you have to agree there's a favorance that ain't easy to miss. A right strong favorance."

Before I could dredge up the courage to ask what the hell they were talking about, Durmond appeared at my elbow and said, "If I may presume to intrude on such a lovely trio . . . ?"

"Goddamn it!" Catherine exploded. We all stared as she banged her glass down on the table and grabbed her mother's arm. "For once in my life, why don't you leave me alone? I am not your Barbie doll! If you've got a problem with that, you can go straight to hell!"

It should have been an exit line, punctuated with the slam of a door. Instead, she released her mother's arm, sat back in the chair, and calmly picked up her glass. She wasn't exactly smiling, but she had a vague aura of triumph that made me uneasy.

Frannie tried to laugh. "Oh, dear, let's watch our temper and our language. We wouldn't want these representatives of the media to get the wrong idea." She waved at the three people hovering near the bar.

All three turned back and demanded refills. Frannie lowered her hand and again forced a laugh, although it reminded me of a drill sergeant on the verge of announcing a twenty-mile hike. "We'll be sure to go to bed early tonight. Lots of rest will make us feel so much better for the big contest tomorrow."

"Oh, yes," Catherine said complacently. "I can

hardly wait to go to bed. All the little piggies want to go to bed, don't they? We can't have any little piggies crying wee, wee, wee all the way home."

Geri's lips quivered, but she clearly was at a loss for a response. No one else did any better, and we were all waiting for inspiration when the lobby door opened. Geri exhaled and looked over her shoulder. "Why, if it isn't the representative of Krazy KoKo-Nut, a mere twenty minutes late for our little reception! The media will be so pleased that you've deigned to grace us with your presence."

Kyle stopped in the doorway. "I had to shower and change after spending the day doing your chores. One would think the marketing firm could handle the mindless details, since that's what they're getting paid for. What a shame no one with experience was put in charge."

Geri's chin shot up, and her shoulders rose as if she were wearing inflatable pads. "What a shame no one from Krazy KoKo-Nut has enough sense to behave properly in front of the media."

"My goodness," Ruby Bee whispered, "the good ol' boys at the bar are less fractious than these folks. When I had to throw out that one-eyed fellow from Hasty, he managed to apologize real nicely before he threw up all over the hood of his truck."

"It happened to be my station wagon," Estelle said tartly, "and I'd just washed it that very morning."

Catherine stood up and began to move around the table, touching heads as she chanted, "This little piggie went to market, and this little piggie stayed home." She dug her fingers into her mother's lacquered blond hair. "Should have stayed home, anyway." She continued past Brenda, saying, "This little piggie had roast beast, and this little piggie"—she sank down on Jerome's lap and stroked his bristly hair—"had some. Didn't you, piggie wiggie?" Before he could answer, she returned to her chair, smiling modestly, as if she'd aced the talent portion of the pageant.

Durmond leaned toward me. "I'm not sure this is what Geri had in mind."

"At least no one's been killed," I answered in a low voice, then mentally cursed myself for tempting fate. This was not a gathering of happy campers. At the table near the window, Brenda was nervously watching Frannie, who was scowling at Catherine. Jerome was staring at the olives in his glass, his lower lip thrust forward and his knuckles white. Catherine serenely awaited the scores from the judges. Geri and Kyle were glowering, Ruby Bee and Estelle were hissing, and the three men near the bar looked as if they were wishing they were history. Gaylene was grazing contentedly, however, and Durmond was sipping his drink with a faintly amused look.

"I want another drink," said Catherine, shoving her glass across the table to Jerome.

"Now, Catherine," Frannie protested, "why don't we have some ginger ale? It's not becoming for someone your age to—"

"She's old enough." Jerome took her glass and started for the bar. "Old enough for a helluva lot of things, including some you've never thought of."

Brenda glanced at Frannie. "Jerome, I really don't think you ought to—"

"Then don't think," he said over his shoulder. "It's a little late in the game for you to take up a new hobby, anyway. If little Miss Vervain wants a goddamn martini, she's going to goddamn have one."

Stricken, Brenda covered her face and began to sniffle. Frannie patted her shoulder, while the rest of us tried to pretend we hadn't heard his remarks. Gaylene was the only one of us with any success. Oblivious to the chill in the air, she marched over to one of the reporters (the salt shaker), fluttered her eyelashes, and cooed, "I'm actually a dancer at the Xanadu Club just off Broadway and 52nd. You ever been there, honey?"

"No, but I'll damn well make the effort," he said, slipping his arm around her waist. His hand dropped to her derriere. "Can you get me a table right up front?"

Geri cleared her throat. "Well, then, shall we all mingle just a bit and do some interviews? These lovely representatives of the press must have busy schedules, and we don't want to detain them any longer than necessary."

"She can detain me all night," said the pepper shaker, drooling into Gaylene's cleavage.

The last of the reporters winked at Geri and said, "So who's gonna detain me? You look like the sort who might go for something like that, hey?"

To add to the fun, Rick came to the door. A startled look crossed his face, but he rearranged his smirk, put his hand solicitously on Geri's arm, and said, "Oh, dearie, I'm so sorry to bring bad news, but some lady from a food magazine just called to say she won't make it. She has a hangnail."

Geri's eyes welled with tears. She knocked away Rick's hand and slammed the clipboard into Kyle's abdomen. "I've had it with all of you! This is more than anyone should have to bear! I don't care if every last one of you chokes on Krazy KoKo-Nut and dies! I cannot stand the sight of you! You're all worse than Scotty Johanson, and he's nothing but a turd! I hate you!"

With a howl of a coyote, she dashed across the lobby and out the front door. We couldn't hear what she said to Mr. Cambria, but he came into the lobby, scratching his head and mumbling to himself.

"I want another drink," Catherine repeated in the ensuing silence.

"I didn't mean anything when I called you a ho," Marvel said, flashing his warmest, whitest smile. He turned around to peek through the dusty venetian blinds, then cautiously looked at Dahlia, who was sitting in the booth all the way across the room. The distance didn't make him feel real safe, not with her dark eyes almost lost under her lowered brow and her lips puckering in and out every second or so.

"I ain't a whore," she growled. "If Kevin had half

the gumption of Ira Pickerel, he'd whomp you some-thing fierce for sayin' that kind of thing."

Her defender, seated across from her, gulped and said, "But, sweetums, he has a gun, and he said he'd shoot us if we so much as moved from this booth. It'd just ruin our honeymoon if we both ended up dead."

"He called me a whore."

After he'd checked once again to make sure the cops were keeping a civilized distance, Marvel sat on a stool by the counter. "I've already explained a hundred times that I didn't mean anything. It's street talk, Big Mama. You know—jive?" He rubbed his face with his free hand, wishing he were at the schoolyard shooting baskets with his friends. Even sitting at a desk in a school that should have been condemned before he was born had appeal. Shit, watching television with his mama and little sister didn't sound half bad.

"I ain't a whore," Dahlia insisted. "I am a respect-able married woman, and I've been a member of the Voice of the Almighty Lord Assembly Hall my entire life. Robin Buchanon was a whore; there's no gettin' around that. And I've heard stories about girls who hang around the bus station in Farberville, their dresses tighter than sausage casings and their hair dyed funny colors. Brother Verber says they'll be spending a good long time in Satan's bedroom, doing the same wicked and perverted things they're doing with men from the bus station."

"Like what?" asked Marvel, momentarily diverted.

Dahlia stiffened as much as she could, since she was wedged in so tightly she was barely able to breathe. "We are not gonna talk about things like that. You've got a filthy mind for even asking." She glowered at Kevin, who had slithered down as far as he could with-out ending up on the floor. "Do you aim to sit there like a napkin dispenser while he calls me a whore? What're you gonna do if he attacks me right here in this café?"

"Marvel's not gonna do that," Kevin said weakly. He reminded himself that he had vowed to defend his wife till death did them part. The possibility that it might happen sooner than he'd expected didn't help much, but he straightened up and said, "If he so much as touches one hair on your head, he'll be sorry he was ever born."

"I wasn't referring to him mussing my hair," she countered.

"Stop it!" Marvel commanded. "I promise I won't muss or mess or do anything to either of you, so just chill. Jesus, you white folks are tight. No wonder you can't dance worth shit. As soon as I figure out how to get out of this with my hide intact, I'll be on my way to some place that's not Cleveland. I'll find some place where they've never even heard of Cleveland."

"Soon as you figure it out," Dahlia simpered, making it clear she didn't think it would happen anytime soon.

"Honey bunny," whispered Kevin, "don't go riling him like that. That ain't exactly a water pistol he's holding."

Marvel considered giving them a demonstration, but the sound of gunfire would agitate the cops outside, maybe even provoke them into storming the doors. From what he'd seen and heard, they were nothing but rednecks with itchy fingers and no great fondness for black boys.

He went back to the window to see if they were up to something new. No, a few were hunkered behind their cars, keeping their weapons trained on the door, while others stood in a group on the far side of the road, gabbing and waving their hands and playing with their walkie-talkies. None of them had donned white robes and pointy hoods, but that didn't mean they weren't debating it.

"Figured it out yet?" Dahlia said in the same simpery voice.

In the sanctuary of her own bedroom, where nobody could see her, Mrs. Jim Bob was on her knees beside the bed, her elbows spread on the pink bedspread, her hands clasped, her eyes rolled toward heaven, her lips sucked in so tightly that her chin trembled. On the far side of the door, Jim Bob was snorting and har-rumphing like he always did before settling down, but there was no way she was going to get any sleep until she and the Almighty agreed upon an answer.

Her immediate problem was that she couldn't bring herself to formulate the question. The very question it-self . . . well, it was unthinkable. She wasn't about to invite it into her mind, not one lurid word of it.

"For better or worse, till death do us part," she murmured over her bent thumbs. As far as she could tell, neither one of them was planning to die anytime soon, which meant she had many a hard row to hoe down the line. Oh, Jim Bob thought he'd fooled her all these many years, claiming he had to work late or had to run into Farberville for a meeting, but she wasn't stupid, for pete's sake. Whenever he started snuffling after a new hussy, he'd turn genial and mannersome and stop whining about having to dress up for prayer meeting on Wednesday nights. He'd also lose interest in crawl-ing into her bed, which was fine with her.

Mrs. Jim Bob wiggled her elbows more firmly into place and let her forehead fall onto her entwined fin-gers. But was there something out there that she'd been missing? In the trashy novel she'd confiscated from one of the girls in her Sunday school class, there'd been all sorts of nonsense about . . . well, romance. About moonlight, supple lips, and electricity racing through one's veins, throbbing and pulsating and de-manding and forcing and . . .

Was it possible to enjoy It? It, of course being the marital obligation that her mother had so rightly warned her about just before the wedding. The thought had never before occurred to her. She'd just kept her eyes closed and reminded herself that what seemed like disgusting animal behavior was actually encour-aged by the Good Book itself. Although she hadn't been fruitful or done any multiplying, she felt obliged to do her duty . . . month after month after month.

Mrs. Jim Bob reminded herself that she wasn't all that old. If nothing else, she was young enough to be married to a self-proclaimed stud willing to indulge his carnal desires from one end of the county to the other. She'd kept her figure. There was life within her, albeit buried pretty darn deep.

Adultery was out of the question, of course. "Till death do us part," she repeated sternly to herself. She could smell a mortal sin from a long way away, and she valued her eternal soul too much to consider the very idea.

But then, despite the surge of piousness that might have allowed her dreamless peace, she recalled the feel of another man's hand on her thigh, and she was overcome with an image. Overcome and overwhelmed.

She crept into bed and yanked the blanket to her chin. Moonlight danced seductively on the ceiling, causing shadows to melt in and out of each other like amorous amoebas. For the first time in her life, Mrs. Jim Bob wished she were a Catholic. Everybody knew they did whatever they wanted all week long, including murdering and raping and robbing and fornicating and all kinds of sinful things, and then just sashayed into a funny wooden box and confessed their sins to a priest. He canceled every last one of them, just like that.

"Not fair," Mrs. Jim Bob murmured, pulling the blanket up farther so she wouldn't have to watch the shadows copulating on her ceiling.

"This is a fine mess," Ruby Bee said from within the bathroom. "I come all the way here to be in a cooking contest, then the prissy little thing goes flying off the handle and storms out the door. They may have paid for the airplane tickets, but I spent a goodly sum of money for clothes for this shindig. On account of bein' given less than a week's notice, I didn't have time to see what all was on sale. Furthermore—"

Estelle closed the door and sat back on the bed. "It's

not like she's the only one who made any sacrifices. I had to cancel all my appointments, including two perms and a frost." She paused, but before I could get in a word, said, "For the Riley girl. I think it's gonna look real sweet, what with her auburn hair. You know something, Arly? If we were to take off about six inches and—"

"No," I said curtly, although I was aware of the risk of being booted out of 219 once and for all. I'd been invited in only in order to gossip about the debacle at the press conference. If they'd been up to no good within the room, they'd tidied up nicely—no blood, no stray body parts, no lingering traces of sailors and salesmen. I glanced up as Ruby Bee edged out of the bathroom, dressed in a flannel gown and her face slathered with cream. Pink sponge rollers made bumps under her plastic shower cap.

"The contest may continue," I said to her. "There's no reason to start packing your bags. Kyle may be able to convince Geri to come back, and if not, perhaps he can get someone else from her firm to take over."

Estelle gave me a pitying look. "Kyle couldn't convince someone to come out of a blizzard, much less take over something like this. Why, I wouldn't consider it for all the tea in China, unless it meant I could turn that Catherine over my knee and paddle her, wash Jerome Appleton's mouth out with soap, put tape over Brenda's mouth—"

"Well, you can't," Ruby Bee said. She sat down on the foot of the nearest bed and sighed. "I sure can think of ways to spend ten thousand dollars. My television set's been flickering something awful, and I happened to spot a fine-lookin' one in Sears not too long ago."

She sounded so disappointed that I felt guilty for secretly enjoying the melodramatics in the dining room. I patted her slumped shoulder and said, "As I said, don't start packing yet."

"Or counting your chickens," added Estelle. "There are four other contestants, after all."

"I ain't worried about them," Ruby Bee said with

measurable smugness. "There's no doubt in my mind that I'll win, presuming the contest goes on like it's supposed to."

I frowned at her. "Why is there no doubt in your mind? For all you know, Durmond could have created the world's most insidious way to disguise the taste of soybean flakes. As could Brenda, Catherine, or even vapid Gaylene, who's extremely proud of her kabobs."

She responded with an indulgent smile, then wiggled her eyebrows at Estelle and said, "It's getting late. Doncha think we ought to get ourselves some beauty sleep? Run along now, Arly. You look a mite haggard yourself, and a good night's sleep can't hurt."

"It might help," Estelle said as she opened the door and waited for me to leave.

I left, although I was far from assured that all I needed was sleep to erase the dark smudges below my eyes and the tendency to twitch whenever a horn blared from the street. In any case, I ambled down the hall, idly wondering why Ruby Bee was so damn sure she would win. Her chocolate chip bundt cake was divine, but she was at the mercy of the judges and needed to acknowledge the possibility that one of them might have an abiding fondness for strawberries and jam. She wasn't counting her chickens before they hatched; she was anticipating the very existence of the eggs.

Unless, of course, she was up to something, which was hardly inconceivable. As I passed the door of the Appletons' room, I heard voices—one low and surly, the other high and tremulous. One of the contestants (kontestants?) might be on the shaky side in the morning, I thought as I went right on by and headed for my room.

From behind the Vervains' door, I also heard sounds indicative of an argument. I slowed down long enough to hear Frannie say, "I am so ashamed of you. I will not allow you to behave like this, Catherine."

Deciding not to hang around and discover how Catherine felt about the matter, I pulled my key from my pocket, glanced at Durmond's door, and opened my own. I did so stealthily, not because I was too much of a ninny to face him, but because I was as sick and tired of the situation as Geri. Unlike her, I couldn't stomp out the door to take refuge in some other part of the city. I needed to take refuge in some other part of the country, say two thousand miles from the door of the Chadwick Hotel.

I undressed, then sat on the edge of my bed and called Eilene to find out if she knew anything more. Amidst a great deal of sniveling and sniffling, she admitted she had heard nothing new despite numerous calls to the Lebanon police. The newlyweds were still inside the café with their captor, condition unknown. The police were content to wait outside, and it seemed this Marvel person was equally willing to wait inside.

I made a few reassuring remarks, promised to call in the morning, and lay on my bed to stare at the mottled ceiling. The lights from the street flickered in a nebulous pattern of colors and images. I supposed they continued to do so long after I drifted into sleep.

CHAPTER
NINE

The elevator awakened me several times, as did what sounded like a massive traffic jam a block from the hotel, a spirited rendition of a Bob Dylan dirge by a tone-deaf tenor, and an argument that peaked below my window. A car backfired, or so I told myself. The tenor retraced his steps, incoherent but still enthusiastic Eventually everybody quieted down, and I was able to take the pillow off my head and breathe the musty air wheezing from the air conditioner.

I lapsed into a convoluted dream involving Kevin, Dahlia, and a faceless assailant in a baggy raincoat, all cowering in the shadow of a nuclear reactor while Raz Buchanon circled them in a horse-drawn buggy. He was snapping the reins so loudly that it took me a moment to realize someone was tapping on my door.

I banished the last of the bizarre dream, went across the room, unlocked the deadbolt, and opened the door as far as the chain would permit. "Who is it?" I whispered.

"Who do you think it is?" Estelle whispered right back. "It sure ain't the mayor wanting to give you a key to the city. Open the door right this minute."

"What time is it?"

"Time to open the door, Miss Third Degree. We are disinclined to be murdered in the hallway while you ask stupid questions."

I closed the door to disengage the chain, then opened it and waited irritably as Estelle and Ruby Bee slipped inside. They were wearing robes and slippers, which at least implied they hadn't been riding the subways or prowling the sex boutiques at Times Square.

I squinted at the clock. "Okay, what's the problem? It's nearly four in the morning. Back home, you may get up with the chickens, but in this neck of the woods, the only chickens are in the moo goo gai pan."

Estelle poked me in the chest. "Here's your poor mother, who's just gone through a terrible ordeal, and you're making smart-mouthed remarks. I'd like to think you can show her some compassion, instead of spouting off like a snotty teenager." She poked me again for good measure.

I bit back a retort and glanced at Ruby Bee. Even in the murky lights from the street, I could see she was upset. She stumbled to the bed and sat down with a muffled moan. "Terrible, terrible," she said, rocking back and forth, her arms wrapped around herself. "I can't think when I've seen something that terrible."

"What?" I snapped, having become inured to her thespian skills well before the onset of my adolescence.

"A body in the kitchen," Estelle said.

I numbly switched on the light and sat down next to Ruby Bee. "Did you have a nightmare?"

She shook her head. "I wish I had, but what I saw was as real as it gets. And the blood! I ain't never seen so much blood in all my born days. There was blood on the floor, blood on the wall, blood on the counters, and blood all over him like he took a bath in it." She covered her face with her hands and slumped forward. "I get all woozy just thinking about it."

I was a little woozy myself. "And this was in the kitchen? You were in the kitchen and found a body? Whose body?"

"It was dark and I didn't stop to ask for identification," Ruby Bee said testily, apparently not as close to a swoon as she'd been two seconds ago. "Nobody would have. For all I knew, the murderer was hiding right there in the broom closet, a butcher knife in his hand. I skedaddled out of there like the hem of my robe was on fire, and I didn't look back."

Estelle sat down on the other side of her. "You did just what any one of us would have done." She gave me a dark look for hinting that Mother had not acted appropriately upon the discovery of a blood-drenched body. "So what are you gonna do about it?"

"About what?" I said more loudly than I'd intended. "I don't even know what we're talking about, for chrissake! For one thing, the kitchen is locked, so there's no way there could be a body down there—or that you could have stumbled over it and fled before you met the same fate. I realize you're anxious about the contest. You had a very vivid nightmare set in the kitchen." My theory was not well received, or so I suspected from the snorts and glares coming at me as if I were a hapless toreador. "The kitchen is locked," I repeated, enunciating slowly and carefully.

"No, it ain't," Ruby Bee said. She took an old-fashioned hairpin from her pocket and showed it to me. "I planned to use this to get the door open, but it wasn't even locked. I eased it open in case it squeaked, took a couple of steps inside, and saw the blood splattered on the wall. I didn't know right off it was blood. There was only a little bit of light from the hallway, so I thought it might have been shadows or even mildew."

I stared at her. "But why did you go to the kitchen in the first place?"

Estelle twitched disapprovingly. "Would you let her finish the story without this constant interrupting?"

"Sure," I said as I lay back on the bed. "I'll hold my breath to the very end."

"Then," the narrator said in a hushed voice, "I started to tiptoe around the island in the middle of the room, and I happened to put my hand down to steady myself. I felt something wet, and when I looked at my hand, it was smeared with brown stuff. I was pondering it as I took another step and caught sight of the feet sticking out from the far side. I liked to jump out of my skin, lemme tell you. I took a fast look at the rest of it, but there was a noise like someone was lurking in the darkness. I turned tail and ran out the door, along the hallway to the stairs, and right on up to the room without wasting one second."

"She pounded on the door," Estelle added, "and when I let her in, an icy hand seemed to grab my heart and I knew then and there that something terrible had happened. I haven't seen her shaking like this since that ornery escaped convict was on the verge of killing us up on Cotter's Ridge."

I waited for more breathless prose, but it seemed I'd heard the entire story and it was my turn to fabricate. A gentle tap on the door saved me the effort.

"It's the murderer!" Ruby Bee shrieked. "He followed me up here! You got to do something, Arly!"

Estelle shook my arm so violently my head bounced on the bed and my teeth clattered. "Do something!"

"Indeed." I stood up and pulled on my robe, went to the adjoining door, and held it open. "Come on in, Durmond. We're just sitting around the ol' campfire telling spooky stories. Don't suppose you have any marshmallows with you?"

He tightened the belt of his robe as he came through the door. "I hope I'm not interrupting, but I heard voices and I was worried that there might be a problem of some sort." He waited for a moment, then smiled uncertainly and said, "But I can see that you're all safe and sound, and I don't want to intrude."

Ruby Bee and Estelle sensed a more receptive audience. They snagged him, settled him on the bed (my bed), and related the entire story once again, from the hairpin to the pure panic down the hall in 219. I leaned against the wall and listened, somewhat amused by the varying degrees of shock and incredulousness that crossed Durmond's face. Only somewhat amused because it was well past four o'clock by now.

"I don't know what to say," Durmond said when they ran down. "I suppose we ought to take some action, but my only experience in this sort of thing is from television. Should we call the emergency number for the police?"

"No!" I said, startled out of my benign trance.

"We have to do something, missy," said Estelle. "There's some poor soul dead in the kitchen. It's up to us to call the authorities." Ruby Bee nodded, although she looked a shade less enthusiastic about doing her civic duty.

I made a face at Durmond. "Before we do something quite so definitive, why don't we go have a look at this purported corpse?"

"Purported?"

"At this point, it's purported," I said in a grim voice. I wasn't in the mood to explain to him about Ruby Bee's and Estelle's propensity for fanciful tales anymore than I was to explain it to the police. "Estelle, take Ruby Bee back to your room and give her a shot of that brandy you've got stashed in your suitcase. After such an ordeal, she must be thirsty. Durmond and I will go downstairs to the kitchen, and if there's ... what Ruby Bee says there is, we'll call the police and deal with them."

Estelle started to protest, then clamped down on her lip and nibbled on it while she studied her cohort. "I get your drift, Arly. You're thinking the police will leap to the wrong conclusion again and drag your poor mother off to jail. She's not exactly Miss Popularity of the Precinct, is she?"

"Not exactly," I murmured with heartfelt sincerity.

We went out to the hallway. Durmond and I watched the two until they were safely inside their room, then mutely rode the elevator to the lobby. He looked as if he had a lot of questions, but I knew damn well I didn't have nearly enough answers even to start a conversation, much less to sustain one.

The lobby was quiet, although the traffic beyond the glass doors had abated only slightly. I'd never been able to figure out why the streets were crowded all night long in Manhattan, who the busy bodies were and where in the hell they were so eager to be in the hours before dawn. One of life's little mysteries.

"Let's just get this over with," I said as I took off down the dimly lit hall to the kitchen.

"You're the cop," he said from behind me, his slippers softly slapping the floor.

I hesitated in front of the kitchen door for a moment, then eased it open and found the switch on the wall. The room flooded with harsh white light. Taking a deep breath, I forced myself to step inside and look at the stainless counter for signs of a bloody handprint. The surface was clean. The five boxes, each with a contestant's name scrawled on the top, were in a neat row.

I exhaled noisily and went on around the island. The wall wasn't splattered with anything I could see, and there certainly were no feet poking out from beyond the far corner. I completed my circumnavigation of the island and joined Durmond at the door.

"No body," I said with a shrug. "No blood, no nothing. It looks pretty much the way Kyle and I left it this morning." I reached for the light switch, but my hand froze in midair and I turned back around with a puzzled frown. "No, it doesn't," I said, mostly to myself, as I struggled to form a mental image of the room as it had been earlier.

Durmond put his hands on my shoulders. "There's certainly no body, as you said. Your mother had a nightmare about creeping down here, and convinced herself and Estelle that it really happened. Let's see if we can get a little more sleep." He began to massage my neck, which must have felt like a bundle of ropes. "Then again, if we can't sleep, we can find other ways to pass the time."

"There's something missing. Four somethings, to be more accurate." I pulled free of his hands and went back around the island to make sure I wasn't as addled as Ruby Bee. "This morning there were four cases of Krazy KoKo-Nut stacked against this wall. They're gone."

"Are you sure Geri didn't have them moved?"

"To tell the truth, I'm not sure about anything anymore. We'd better go tell Nancy Drew that she was seeing things, and then I'm going to lock myself in my room and go back to bed. If someone's crazy enough to steal Krazy KoKo-Nut, no telling what else he or she might do before the sun rises."

"I'd be delighted to serve as a bodyguard," he said, advancing slowly.

"Good," I said, retreating briskly. "You can sit outside my door the rest of the night. I'd loan you my gun, but I left home without it. Silly me."

"I have a gun, but I'd hate to use it on someone who's obsessed with pseudo-coconut. It'd be like shooting a hopelessly sick animal, wouldn't it?" The ends of his mustache twitched as he smiled, and there was something going on behind his gentle brown eyes that I couldn't begin to read.

"I think I'd better let Ruby Bee and Estelle know that everything's okay," I said. I held my ground until he turned and went out of the kitchen, then looked once more to make sure there was no blood, switched off the light, and closed the kitchen door.

"Kevin!" hissed Dahlia, reaching across the table to shake his shoulder. "Wake up!"

"Wha . . . ?" He lifted his face, which had been flattened like a pancake from being on the table for more hours than he could count. It was so dark that it took him a minute to think where he was, and why there were fingers biting into his shoulder like a vise. "Is that you, my beloved?"

"Shush up," she continued, still trying to squeeze some sense into him. "This is our big chance to escape. Marvel's gone off somewheres. All we got to do is creep out the back door. Come on!"

Kevin rubbed his eyes and tried to spot Marvel somewhere in the shadows of the café. He listened real hard, too, but all he could hear were birds and insects outside and the low rumble of a car or truck way far in the distance. "Where is he right now?" he whispered to his beloved bride.

"I dun told you he's off somewheres, most likely

asleep. We can sit here till dawn trying to guess, or you can get off your runty butt and follow me out the back door so we can go to Niagara Falls."

Grunting ever so softly, she began to slide out of the booth. Kevin was far from convinced this was the best thing to do, but he wasn't about to argue with her, not when she'd been through such trials and tribulations these last days, all of them his fault. He wouldn't have been surprised if she regretted ever marryin' him. Wouldn't have blamed her if she did, neither.

Once she'd popped free of the booth, she grabbed his wrist and led him ponderously yet relentlessly through the tables. "You'd think I was taking you to the dentist—instead of risking my own life to save your hide. It's a good thing one of us has the smarts to do something other than snore."

"I'm awful sorry about how this honeymoon is—"

"Will you shush up?" Clamping harder on his wrist, she navigated through the gap at the end of the counter, pulling in her elbows to make sure nothing got toppled off, and dragged him into the kitchen. There was enough light from a utility pole for her to make out the back door, and once they got closer, to make out the key in the deadbolt lock.

In that she was steering, Kevin decided he'd better guard the flank and kept his head turned accordingly. There was no Marvel silhouetted in the doorway, his gun raised and his eyes as cold as a killer's. Encouraged, Kevin tried to report as much to Dahlia, but she shushed him again and busied herself with the key.

The door obligingly opened with nary a squeak. "Once we're outside, we'll run over to those trees," she said in a low voice. "Keep your head down unless you aim to have it blown right off your shoulders and mounted on the wall alongside that buck in the front room. You ready?"

Kevin was a little dismayed at the image she'd evoked, but he swallowed several times, reminded himself of his duty to his wife, and nodded. She began to push open the screened door. The tiny ticks seemed louder than firecrackers, but there wasn't anything they could do but grit their teeth and pray Marvel was tuckered out from all his crimes.

Still hanging on to Kevin in case he lost his nerve, Dahlia lifted her foot to step onto the concrete block steps that led to a weedy path.

The gunshot was a darn sight louder than a firecracker. The flash of light from behind the tree was followed immediately by the sound of wood splintering not more than an inch from her face. Shrieking, Dahlia instinctively flung her three hundred pounds plus backward, unmindful that she was taking Kevin with her as they crashed into a table near the door, and then in dizzyingly quick succession, into a kitchen counter, a collection of mops and brooms propped in a corner, a metal bucket, and the stove, at which point a skillet brimming with grease clattered to the floor.

A second shot came from the same direction, although at this point neither newlywed was keeping a tally. The grease splashed all over the floor, and all of a sudden they were slipping and sliding like novice rollerskaters, hanging on to each other and screeching something awful.

The next shot shattered the window above the sink and showered them with glass. "Let go of me!" Dahlia howled, too frantic to realize she was the one hanging on for dear life. "You're gonna get me killed!"

Kevin obediently attempted to jerk his wrist free, and this was enough to send Dahlia's feet out and up. The rest of her went down with a boom that made the entire café tremble. Tin cans fell off the shelves, as did coffee cups and plastic tumblers. Jars of pickles and jam exploded as they hit the floor. Silverware tinkled in a drawer.

Marvel came to the doorway of the kitchen, his gun in one hand and a paperback book in the other. "I swear," he said, watching Kevin and Dahlia on the floor, "I leave you two alone for five minutes, and you take to wrestling in bacon grease. I know it's your honeymoon, but do you think you could restrain yourselves a little while longer? There're a dozen red-necked cops out there hoping to shoot me between the eyes, and I don't have time to worry about you two." He waved the gun at them. "Get off that floor and try to behave, you hear? Didn't your mamas teach you anything?"

They continued to flop on the floor, making animal noises and grabbing at each other. Disgusted, Marvel went back to the front room and watched the cops as they scurried around on the far side of the road. There was still a lot of moaning going on in the kitchen, but he decided to let them have their fun in private.

"Yes, I'm quite sure there were no bloodstains anywhere in the kitchen," I said to Ruby Bee and Estelle, neither of whom looked convinced. We were alone in the dining room, but as I paused to reiterate what I'd just iterated for the tenth time, Rick came in with a coffee urn, banged it down on a nearby table, and stomped out. Mr. Cambria, dapper in his blue uniform, appeared with a tray piled with cups, saucers, and other pertinent paraphernalia, twinkled at us, and set the tray beside the urn.

"Rickie will be back with donuts and danish," he said with a courtly little bow. "May I have the honor to serve you ladies some coffee?"

"You'd better get back to your post, Mr. Cambria," Rick said, returning with the predicted pastries. "She'll have a tantrum if we are missing a doorman, and that's the last thing we need. If everyone will cooperate, maybe we can get this contest over with and all of you can go home. These have not been my favorite few days."

Cambria put his arm around Rick and squeezed him tightly. "Rickie, Rickie—don't you listen when I tell you the importance of a good sense of humor? You young kids today, you push too hard, try to make everything happen all at once, think you can go from gardener to president in the blink of an eye. Believe me when I tell you to sit back, relax, smell the roses, or in this case, the coffee."

"How true," Ruby Bee said with a sharp look at yours truly, who hadn't intended to dispute the premise.

"There, Rick, you hear the lady?" Cambria slapped him on the cheek, then nodded at us and went into the lobby to assume his post, whistling all the while. He arrived in the nick of time to open the door for Kyle, who rushed past him without a word and came into the dining room.

"No sign of Geri?" he asked between gulps of air.

"None, but I'm sure my luck will change." Rick gave us a humorless smile as he left.

Kyle fixed himself a cup of coffee and sat down. "I talked to her an hour ago, and she agreed to come back. We've decided to skip the trial runs in the kitchen and get straight down to business this afternoon. We'll draw lots for position, and the first finalist starts at one o'clock." He took a slurp of coffee and managed to return the cup to the saucer with a lot of rattles but only a minimum of sloshes. None of us mentioned the droplets on his tie. "If we stick to the schedule, all the recipes should be ready for judging at seven tonight. I'll announce the winner, present the prize, and you people can get busy packing."

"You mean the ten-thousand-dollar prize," Ruby Bee said, softening the reproach with a grandmotherly smile.

"In a way." Kyle consulted his watch, then ran his hand over his hair, wiped his palm on his trouser leg, and busied himself with the remainder of his coffee. "Shit, I wish the other contestants would get here. I called and told them to meet here at ten. It's already a quarter till. You people are on time. How hard can it be to take the elevator down one entire floor?"

"Real hard when it doesn't work," Gaylene said as she came into the dining room. She wore skin-tight shorts and a gossamer blouse, and her ash-blond hair was pulled back in a ponytail. "It's a good thing I didn't twist an ankle coming down those slippery ol' steps. How could I play the slots on crutches?"

It must have been a rhetorical question, in that she headed for the coffee urn without waiting for our opinions. Ruby Bee and Estelle agreed to allow me to bring them coffee and donuts, and we were all settled as Frannie and Durmond came out of the stairwell door and came across the lobby.

"That makes four—no, three," Kyle muttered, oblivious to the crumbs on his chin and lapels, and also to the smudge of powdered sugar on the tip of his nose. "All we need are Brenda and the kid, and we'll be set." He rapped his cup on his saucer. "Listen everybody, Geri should be here any minute to take charge, and please don't give her any grief. Do whatever she says, okay? She'll take you on a tour of the kitchen, at which time you can check your individual boxes to make sure you've got everything you need. The boxes will then be sealed, and no one will be allowed in the kitchen until it's his or her turn to prepare an entry. Only the contestant and Geri will be in the kitchen from that point on. As each entry is finished, it will be locked in the pantry under Geri's supervision, and she'll have the only key."

"Did you look in this pantry?" Ruby Bee whispered at me, then caught Kyle's beady stare and sat back. I nodded, even though I hadn't.

"I'll have to stay with Catherine when she prepares her recipe," Frannie said.

Kyle gulped at her. "Impossible."

"She has asthma," Frannie countered with a shrug. "I have to be there with her inhaler and her tablets. I'm the only one who can judge the severity of an attack and give her the proper dosage. In fact, she had an attack last night and I told her to stay in bed until the actual time of the contest."

Kyle tried to stare her down, but eventually conceded. "Yeah, as long as you don't help her prepare her entry. Nobody else has any medical problems, right?"

We all shook our heads, and I hoped I was the only one who heard Ruby Bee mutter, "Except for that man in the kitchen. I'd call being dead a downright serious medical problem."

Kyle glanced our way, but merely said, "Well, then, why don't you have more coffee while we wait for Geri. She said she'd be here at ten." He looked at his watch, and then at the window. "I'd better check on Brenda. I think it'll be better if we're all here when Geri comes. She's still a little upset after last night's reception."

I watched him as he walked across the lobby, futilely punched the elevator, and disappeared into the stairwell. He was uncomfortable in his role as drill sergeant, but he was doing fairly well. Sure, he'd ruined his tie, and his jacket was so sprinkled with crumbs that he might have been in the throes of terminal dandruff. To his credit, his voice was breaking no more than every third word and his eyes were slightly less panicky than those of an animal caught in a steel trap. It was only a silly contest, I told myself as I finished my coffee. He'd been tense the day before, but now he was so wired that he might detonate any minute.

"What's bugging that Kyle fellow?" Ruby Bee said, paraphrasing my thoughts. "It ain't like he has to run the contest by his lonesome. Geri's coming back, so all he has to do is toady around and pretend he's important."

Estelle nodded sagely. "He's acting like someone stuck a piece of dynamite up his rear and struck a match." She made sure Durmond and I were the only ones paying any attention, then lowered her voice. "Maybe he had something to do with that corpse in the kitchen . . . The first time I laid eyes on him, I knew he was a sneaky sort. After all, a ferret ain't nothing but a domesticated polecat."

"Neither he nor Geri is staying in the hotel," I pointed out. "Rick may have conceded the kitchen key, but I can't see him handing over the key to the hotel. They weren't even here at four in the morning."

Durmond, in a whisper almost as theatrical as Estelle's, said, "And there was no corpse in the kitchen. Arly and I checked very carefully."

"There most certainly was!" Ruby Bee protested.

I managed to control my temper, for the most part. "No, there wasn't, dammit! Not unless he waited for you to leave, and then hopped up, grabbed a mop and a dishrag, got everything cleaned up, and wandered out the door with four cases of Krazy KoKo-Nut in his pocket!" For the most part, as I said.

I might as well have been arguing with Particular Buchanon—after his funeral. Ruby Bee thought for a minute, and said, "I think you're on to it. Somebody came into the kitchen after I left, moved the body, and cleaned up that awful mess. Who'd do a thing like that?"

Optimist that I was, I tried again. "If there was as much blood as you claim there was, no one except a band of elves could have accomplished all that in the short amount of time."

"It wasn't all that short an amount of time." Ruby Bee gave Estelle a nervous look. "I'd say we discussed what to do for a little while before we decided we'd better tell you about what I saw in the kitchen."

"We didn't want to disturb you," said Estelle, trying to act as if that were one of their priorities.

I knew them too well. "How considerate of you. Exactly how long did you dangle on the horns of this particular dilemma before you came to my room?"

"It could have been most of an hour," Ruby Bee mumbled. "I believe I'd like another donut. How about you, Estelle? The ones with the lemon filling are nice and tart."

"An hour?" I said wonderingly. "You debated the delicate issue of disturbing me for an hour? I am impressed, ladies. Ruby Bee's been known to call during the first sneeze to tell me she's coming down with a cold. But a body covered with blood—hey, let's take plenty of time."

"Shhh!" Estelle said, gesturing at the others in the room, all of whom were hearing enough of our conversation to look worried, if not scared sick.

Or then again, they might have spotted Geri striding down the sidewalk and through the lobby door. Maybe they could hear her grinding her teeth. Those with telepathy might have been hearing some colorful language, if her fierce scowl was any indication of her thoughts.

She slammed the briefcase down on a table, took out her clipboard, and in a voice nearly primal in its hostility said, "Let's get this damn thing over with, shall we?"

CHAPTER
TEN

Geri remained rigidly angry as she repeated what Kyle had said concerning the schedule, nodded grimly when Frannie presented her case for inclusion, and ordered the contestants to follow her to the kitchen.

"Isn't this exciting?" Frannie said as she, Ruby Bee, Gaylene, and Durmond trooped out the door. No one answered.

I refilled my cup and sat down across from Estelle. "Okay, we're here all by ourselves. I'm not saying Ruby Bee found a body in the kitchen, but if she did— what was she doing down there in the middle of the night?"

"You'll have to ask her why she went there. I ain't her psychiatrist, for pete's sake, and I gave up a long time ago trying to second-guess her motives for most everything she does."

"Don't try to spoonfeed me that nonsense. Why'd she go to the kitchen at three in the morning?"

Estelle took a compact and a tube of lipstick from her purse. "Maybe she was looking for a glass of warm milk. I myself was asleep, so I didn't even know she was gone until she came back and pounded on the door." She deftly outlined her lower lip in a shade I would have dubbed "Virulent Cerise," clicked the compact shut, and dropped it and the lipstick back in her handbag. "I wonder how long they're gonna be in there? I was thinking we might try again to go to the Statue of Liberty and—"

"You didn't ask her why she'd been creeping around the hotel in the middle of the night? Get off it, Estelle. I don't know what you two are—"

"Has either of you seen Jerome this morning?" Kyle asked from the doorway. We shook our heads. "Brenda's locked herself in the bathroom of 211 and she won't come out. She's not making much sense, but she sounds really upset about Jerome. You don't think she'll ... do something, do you?"

"I have no idea," I said uneasily.

Kyle groaned as if someone had crunched on his toes. "Oh, God, this is the last thing we need. Has Geri come yet?"

"She took the contestants to the kitchen about five minutes ago," I said. "If Brenda's locked in the bathroom, how'd you get into her room?"

"I got a passkey from Rick." He stared down the hallway, his expression increasingly bleak as he no doubt visualized the likely scenario. "Maybe you two could go up to her room? She might be more willing to talk to women. I'd call Jerome's office to see if he's there, but I don't even know where it is. They live out on Long Island somewhere, so his office could be there or in the city or almost anyplace, and I have no idea what the name of the firm is." His knees buckled, and he grabbed the back of a chair to catch himself. His voice rose in pitch and volume as he gazed imploringly at us. "Please see if she'll talk to you. I don't know what else to do. If she harms herself, the police will investigate and I might as well go ahead and slit my own throat."

"We're going," I said before he wet his pants in front of us. "Take it easy, Kyle. Brenda and Jerome were bickering last night. I didn't hang around for the finale, but it's likely that he stormed away to his house, or to his office, or even to another hotel. Of course she's upset about it. That doesn't mean she's going to end it all by drinking an entire bottle of Pepto-Bismol."

"She sure was upset at the reception," Estelle contributed thoughtfully. "She might be depressed enough to slash her wrists like Fizzy Westend did when his third wife ran off with that janitor at the high school. I can still see him staggering down the road like a three-legged calf, and bleating like one, too, while the blood spurted out like ribbons."

I grabbed her elbow and hustled her to the stairwell before she could come up with any more bright ideas. I knew we were both thinking about the purported corpse and the missing man, and I was not ready to dismiss it as a whimsical coincidence—if there had been a body. Estelle was convinced Ruby Bee had seen one, but she was as gullible as the local girls who swore you couldn't get pregnant if you were drunk. We have a lot of youthful mothers in Maggody.

I opened the door of 211 and cautiously said, "Brenda? Are you okay?"

Opting for the less delicate approach, Estelle pushed past me and knocked briskly on the bathroom door. "Brenda, honey, it's Estelle and Arly. Kyle said you were upset, and we thought we'd better come up and see if there's anything we can do for you."

The only response was the flushing of the toilet. While Estelle continued to make soothing noises to the scarred door, I ascertained that the only clothes hanging in the closet were Brenda's. All the shoes were pastel pumps. There were no manly items on the top of the dresser, and only one bed had been disturbed.

"He's gone," I reported quietly. "It's obvious he packed his bags and left at some point last night. We're dealing with a straightforward marital problem, not some dark mystery. They fought, he left, and she's crying her eyes out in the bathroom."

Estelle nodded, then raised her voice. "Brenda, there's no point in staying in that little bitty room for the rest of your life, just because your husband walked out on you. Why doncha come out? You could call your daughters. Wouldn't it make you feel better to talk to them?" She waited for an answer that failed to arrive, and she tried a new approach. "If I have to, I'll stay out here beating on the door the rest of the day.

Unless you want to be responsible for some bruised knuckles, you wash your face and come out here on the double, you hear?"

The door opened, and Brenda emerged, her face blotched and puffy, her eyelids so swollen they were almost closed. Her hair was damp, as was her night-gown, and she was shivering despite the feebleness of the air conditioner.

Estelle took her arm and solicitously placed her on the bed. "That's being more sensible. You want me to dial the telephone for you?"

"I don't want to call them," Brenda said dully. "It's not going to make me feel better to tell Vernie and Deb that their father's a satyr and a sadist. They probably know it, but I'm not going to be the one to say it aloud."

"Oh, honey," Estelle said, sitting beside her to hold her hand, "you and Jerome just had a spat, that's all. All married couples do, even newlyweds on their honeymoons. He'll come back before long, his tail between his legs, and apologize for being such a brute. I'll bet he's already sitting at his desk, feeling guilty and fretting over what to say when he calls you. Why, I wouldn't be surprised if he showed up real soon with flowers and a box of candy."

"I would be," she said in the same listless voice. "For one thing, he and his girlfriend are on an airplane to some city in South America . . . Rio, I think. I can just see them with their champagne and caviar, chuckling about how poor, stupid Brenda never knew a thing until he was packed and halfway out the door. All I can say is she'd better keep an eye on him, or she'll find herself replaced by the next young thing that rumbas into the room and snuggles in his lap."

"That's awful, but maybe it's for the best. You've still got your girls, and your house, and your bridge game, and your volunteer work. You'll stay so busy you won't even miss him."

Brenda toyed with her wedding ring but sounded a bit brighter as she said, "Jerome insisted on watching ball games on television every night. I've always been fond of those exotic nature programs, myself."

"Like the mating rituals of insects?" Estelle suggested. "I saw the most amazing thing . . ."

I let myself out of the room, relieved we hadn't found Jerome wrapped in a shower curtain and Brenda attempting to drown herself in the commode. As I'd tried to tell Kyle, it was nothing more than a man with a midlife crisis and a sudden interest in the mating rituals of younger women. Not all of them flew to Rio to play out their pathetic fantasies; I personally knew of one who'd settled for a seedy residential hotel two blocks away from his paramour until she could dispose of her spouse and free up some closet space.

I went to my room and lay down on the bed to think—not of the maladies of marriage but of more current events. Jerome was not missing, in a manner of speaking, and therefore no longer qualified as our mischievous corpse. Perhaps Ruby Bee had been sleepwalking, I proposed to myself. She'd managed to get outside the room, gripped by her bloody vision, and awakened when she found herself in the corridor. It had taken her an hour to persuade Estelle to buy her story, and then they'd come knocking on my door.

As for the missing cases of Krazy KoKo-Nut, it was more likely that Geri or Rick had arranged for them to be moved to a less obtrusive location, such as the pantry. All the other odd little things that had happened didn't matter one damn bit. Durmond had been mugged by an overly conscientious sort who wanted to make him comfortable in Ruby Bee's bed. Mr. Cambria was a doorman in Miami, and this was a busman's holiday. Magazine reporters were earthy.

The telephone rang. Remaining supine (mentally as well as physically), I fumbled for the receiver and said, "Yes?"

"Oh, Arly, it's awful!" Eilene shrieked, nearly piercing my eardrums. "There was gunfire at the café last night! Nobody's real clear what happened, but the police haven't seen either of the kids this morning!" She began to hiccup so loudly that I could barely understand her. "The killer's not dead, though. The police know that much."

"How do they know that?"

"He ordered a pizza. A large supreme with anchovies and extra cheese. The delivery boy had to take it right up to the door, hand it over, and then run for his life. The deputy said the poor boy had the tip clutched in his hand so tightly they had to pry his fingers open."

I searched the ceiling for guidance, but all I saw were waterstains, one of which bore an eerie resemblance to a pizza. "Well," I said weakly, "it sounds as if everybody's okay. They're certainly not starving if they've got pizza."

"But, Arly," she wailed, "Kevin hates anchovies!"

It occurred to me that despite my earlier bout of self-congratulatory analysis, I didn't exactly have things under control.

Mrs. Jim Bob figured no one could possibly recognize her, not dressed as she was in a shapeless tan raincoat, drab scarf, and sunglasses. She'd driven all the way to Fort Smith just so she could do her business in private. In that she was the brightest beacon of the congregation, along with being the president of both the Missionary Society and Citizens Against Whiskey, she didn't want to risk letting any of the more impressionable members get the wrong idea.

She parked on the far side of the lot on the off chance someone might see her car and start speculating about why it was parked in front of a store called "Naughty Nights." Clutching her handbag with the tenacity of a quarterback, she darted across the lot and into the store, and only when she was well away from the window did she take a breath.

"Hi," said the teenaged girl seated behind the counter. She put down a magazine and idly tried to guess why the woman was dressed like a Russian spy. "Need some help, ma'am? All the teddies on that rack

are on sale this week, and we just got in a new shipment of peekaboo bras."

Mrs. Jim Bob recoiled, but managed to stammer,
"I—I don't believe—no, not anything like that." The
girl merely waited. "I'm looking for—a gift. It's for a
niece who's getting married. I don't approve of this
kind of thing, naturally, but her mother said it was exactly what she—the bride, not her mother—wanted."

"What exactly does she want?"

"Not a peekaboo bra," Mrs. Jim Bob said, getting
hold of herself. "Something to wear on her honeymoon
to make her look"—she struggled but couldn't bring
herself to say the pertinent word—"romantic. Cut kind
of low and with lace, made out of material you can almost see through."

"Would she prefer black, scarlet, or apricot cream?"

This was harder than Mrs. Jim Bob had anticipated.
Here she was in a store with shameless underwear, being forced to choose from colors that sounded filthy.
But she had vowed to herself to do it to save her marriage. She was on a Christian mission, even if it might
look otherwise to ignorant busybodies, and she wasn't
going to allow the snippety clerk to deter her. "Black
will do nicely," she said.

The girl went over to a rack laden with perverted
merchandise. "What size does your niece wear,
ma'am? Does she prefer long or short? These little
nighties are cute, and they come with bikini-cut panties."

"Long, I should think, and without any bikini-cut
anythings," Mrs. Jim Bob said, proud of her steady
voice. "She's about my size, so she ought to take a me-
dium."

Various gowns, all long and black, were pulled out
for consideration, and within a few minutes one had
been selected and whisked to the back room to be gift-
wrapped. Mrs. Jim Bob kept an eye on the door, but
she righteously avoided letting the other eye drift to
racks that might have items like peekaboo bras and
bikini-cut panties.

"Here we go," the girl said as she returned with a

box wrapped in silver paper and a white ribbon. "Will this be cash or charge?"

"Cash." Mrs. Jim Bob took out her wallet. "How much is it?"

"Thirty-seven fifty. With tax, it comes to forty dollars and twelve cents. There's no charge for gift wrapping."

She counted her cash, then sighed and took out a credit card. "Use this, I guess."

"Sure," the girl said as she accepted the card and read the name. "If you'd prefer, you can put it on your charge account, Mrs. Buchanon. That way you can settle it with one check at the end of the month."

"My charge account?"

"Your husband opened one more than three years ago; he's one of our best customers. Haven't you ever noticed the gold NAUGHTY NIGHTS stickers on our boxes?"

"Yes, of course I have," Mrs. Jim Bob said with a tight smile. "The gold stickers with the name of the store, right there on the boxes for the last three years. I forgot all about it, but indeed, let's put this on the charge account. In fact, before you ring it up, maybe I'll take another look. My cousin Sharon in Shawsville has a daughter who'll be marryin' soon, and this way I can save myself another trip. Why, now that I think about it, the McIlhaney girl's engaged and so is the oldest Riley girl."

Mindful of her commission, the clerk came out from behind the counter, and an hour later she was in the back room, gift-wrapping half a dozen lacy gowns of all lengths, a silk teddie with a little satin bow, and a single black peekaboo bra for some cousin or other with an approaching birthday.

Mrs. Jim Bob nodded when she was presented with a charge slip. "Four hundred twenty-seven dollars and eighty-two cents," she murmured as she wrote her name very carefully. "But worth it, don't you think? This will save me so much bother down the road."

"Yes, ma'am," the clerk said dutifully.

"Yoohoo," Estelle called as she knocked on my door. "Brenda's feeling chipper enough to go down to the kitchen. You want to come with us? Ruby Bee ought to be finishing up afore too long, and if she's not supposed to make her cake till later in the afternoon, I thought we might do some more sight-seeing."

"No," I called back, too appalled at the idea to lift my head, much less unlock my door. "I think I'll take a nap."

"Suit yourself. Come on, Brenda, Miss City Slicker is too high and mighty to visit the Statue of Liberty."

I listened to their voices until they faded, then rolled over on the bed and burrowed my face into the scratchy bedspread. Despite the temptation to call the airline and find out when I could catch the next flight south, I was reluctant to do so. Or perhaps too cheap, since I might get a call from Estelle the minute the plane landed in Maggody, and find myself in the identical position I'd been in two days earlier—but this time with a depleted bank balance.

A noise from beyond the adjoining door caught my attention. It had occurred to me that Geri might not react well if the cases of Krazy KoKo-Nut had disappeared without a flake. She was angry enough to turn on Kyle, who was dangerously tense. We very well might end up with more than one bloodied body in the kitchen, this time along with a handful of witnesses.

I went to the door and tapped. "Durmond? I was wondering how it went in the kitchen."

There was no response. I told myself it was a helluva lot more sensible to go downstairs and see for myself, then eased open my door and gave his a tiny push. Marveling at my lack of judgment, I opened his door and said, "Durmond? Are you here?"

He was not, nor was anyone else. Guilt battled with curiosity, but it was a piss-poor war and two seconds later I was at the dresser, stealthily opening drawers and flipping through the neatly folded shirts, handkerchiefs, and socks. In the bottom drawer I found a faded red sweatshirt emblazoned (at one time, anyway) with the logo of a school called Drakestone College. That answered one question of noticeably minor significance.

One of greater significance came to mind when I saw the butt of a gun under said sweatshirt. It turned out to be a .38 Special just like one all the way back in Maggody, although mine was rustier from not having been used since the year before Eve ate the apple. He'd mentioned having a gun, but he hadn't elaborated on his reason. It was obvious he hadn't been kidding, though.

I replaced the sweatshirt, closed the drawer, and did a quick search of the rest of the room, the closet, and the bathroom. He'd not left his wallet for my perusal, nor had he written any letters and forgotten to mail them. I would have settled for a postcard. The wastebasket held only a crumpled potato chip bag, the copies of the insurance paperwork from the hospital, an empty bourbon bottle, and the stub of a train ticket. His toothbrush was in sorry shape, as was his encrusted razor. Wet towels had been kicked in a corner.

I went back to my room and stood in front of the window. A creature lacking opposable thumbs could do a better job of putting the puzzle pieces together than I was doing, I thought as I watched the traffic inch along. I was trying to come up with something clever when Gaylene Feather appeared below, crossed the street, and took off at a brisk clip, a large leather purse bouncing off her hip with the beat. A moment later, Ruby Bee and Estelle stopped at the curb, exchanged remarks inaudible to me but likely to be heard on Staten Island, and headed in the direction Gaylene had gone.

I would not have described myself as suspicious by nature, but the nurturing of the last thirty years had left its mark. Ruby Bee and Estelle were not taking a nice walk; they were following Gaylene. It did not give me a rosy glow of contentment to see they'd found a new hobby.

As they disappeared around the corner, I looked down to spot yet another intrepid traveler. It was Durmond's turn to hesitate for a moment, cross the street, and walk past the coffee shop to the corner. He stopped, however, as the door of the coffee shop opened and a man in a khaki jacket came out to the sidewalk. The grime on the hotel window prevented me from seeing with perfect clarity, but I got a fairly decent view of the man's long, stringy hair and unkempt beard. After a furtive glance toward the hotel, Durmond slapped the man on the back, and the two began to talk as they went around the corner.

I didn't know what to make of it, but I was certain something ought to be made of it. Morose professors from Drakestone College in Connecticut did not seem the type to relish the company of disreputable street bums. To add to the problem, the encounter lacked spontaneity. I may have been a bumpkin cop, but I could spot a prearranged meeting a block away, and just because I hadn't seen any lip-licking didn't deter me from leaping to a conclusion, maybe two.

It seemed like a good time to go downstairs and persuade Geri to part with information about various contestants. How I was going to do this was not clear, but I figured inspiration would come to me before I arrived in the lobby. I made sure my bun was firmly pinned, grimaced at my image in the cracked mirror above the dresser, and went down the stairs.

The front desk was deserted, as usual. Brenda sat alone in the dining room, a cup of coffee and an untouched danish on the table in front of her. She was studying a recipe card rather than a dagger, so I continued to the kitchen.

"He called me at home," I heard Geri say, and not in a pleasant voice. "I cannot believe you went tattling to your father like a little snot-nosed crybaby!"

Kyle sounded no more convivial. "Just run the damn contest like a big girl, okay? Stop with the princess on the pedestal routine, unless you'd like to end up without a nose or anything else. All you have to do is let them make their entries, and then we'll taste them, decide, and present the prize. If you can't stomach it, we don't have to taste them. We'll draw straws. This nightmare could be over in ten hours, if you'll keep your eyes dry and your act together. We're not messing with a bunch of clowns from Ringling Brothers."

I went into the kitchen in time to see Geri start toward him, her fingers curled into a fist and a less than regal expression on her face. "How's it going?" I asked.

Geri reluctantly lowered her fist. "Peachy. We've worked out the time frame and everyone's checked to see he or she has the necessary items. We begin at one with Catherine."

The four cases of Krazy KoKo-Nut were stacked ever so innocently next to the wall. On the island were the five boxes, now crisscrossed with silver tape. If Geri and Kyle were standing in a puddle of blood, with a mutilated corpse at their feet, they were handling it with admirable aplomb.

"Well, good," I said with what aplomb I could muster, which wasn't worthy of anyone's admiration. "Where are all the contestants now?"

Geri stiffened. "How should I know? I'm not a babysitter; I'm a marketing professional—to my regret. I'd imagine they went out sight-seeing or to grab a bite of lunch. Now that we've confirmed times, no one is obliged to hang around this dismal dump except for me."

"I'm here," Kyle said sulkily.

I hadn't yet been blessed with inspiration, but I forged ahead. "I was wondering how the contestants were selected for the finals of the contest. Did a panel of judges make all the submitted entries and select the five best ones?"

"In your dreams," Geri said with a harsh laugh. "Mr. Fleecum himself selected the winners, based on demographics. He then sent the list to the Krazy KoKo-Nut office for approval. Had his list not been trashed, we would have had a second man and better geographic representation to lure in regional press."

"So how did you end up with these five?" I asked.

Geri pointed her finger at Kyle. "You'll have to ask him. He's the one who blundered into my office with the updated list of finalists."

"I got the list from my father," Kyle said, squirming at her scarlet talon, "and he got it from Interspace Investments. They'd asked to see it, and he could hardly refuse, could he? Some of the finalists were unavailable, and they produced the replacements."

"Which makes this whole thing even more of a travesty," Geri said. She paused as a garbage truck rumbled and squealed to a halt in the alley, then added, "The integrity of Prodding, Polk and Fleecum is on the line. If word ever gets out on the street that the finalists are nothing but a bunch of ringers, we'll be the butt of cocktail party jokes for months."

"Not all the finalists," I said over the increasing din as the truck jockeyed with a dumpster, the men yelling and metal cans clattering as they bounced against the pavement. "Ruby Bee was on the original list, wasn't she? Who else was?"

Geri touched her temples. "This is giving me a migraine. Can't they do whatever they're doing out there and go away? Why must they make so damn much noise?"

"Maybe they're doing their job," Kyle began, then stopped as we were engulfed in silence.

"Oh, sweet Jesus," said a stunned male voice. "We got one."

"Why the fuck can't these deadbeats find a better place to sleep?" said another. "It's too late for the medics. You guys wait here and I'll call the cops from inside here. Damn it to hell, I was counting on getting off early so I could take my kid to the ball game."

Geri, Kyle, and I waited with all the animation of the teenaged finalist in one of her sulks. Even though we were anticipating the knock on the back door, we froze as if it were a spate of gunfire.

"I'll get it," I said at last.

I admitted an odoriferous man in a jumpsuit, who shrugged and said, "We got a sleeper in the dumpster. Would you call 911 and tell them we're waiting in the alley out back? And tell them we don't got all day."

"A sleeper?" Geri said carefully.

"You know—one of those homeless people who sleep wherever they can. This one chose your dumpster for his final resting place. Could you call the cops?"

Geri and Kyle crowded behind me in the doorway. The sanitation truck had opened its mouth to receive another meal, and the dumpster hovered above, having dislodged its contents. Resting on the mound of garbage within the truck was a body, one arm thrown back and the face turned toward us. Dried blood and rotting vegetable matter made a garish mask, but Jerome Appleton's features were identifiable. Behind the shattered lenses of his glasses, his eyes were wide and flat.

"The cops?" the man repeated. "We're already behind schedule for the rest of the run. You want I should make the call while you enjoy the view?"

Geri began to whimper. "This is too much. I was packed and ready to leave for the Cape when Mr. Fleecum called and ordered me back. I was willing to make the effort one last time, but this is it." Not surprisingly, tears began to dribble down her cheeks. "I don't care if Mr. Fleecum fires me or not!"

Kyle put his arms around her and allowed her to sob on his shoulder. I beckoned to the bemused sanitation worker and took him to the office midway along the hall, pointed out the telephone, and left him there while I went to break the news to Brenda.

The dining room was dark, and all that remained of her earlier presence was the untouched danish and coffee cup. I started for the stairs, then spotted Mr. Cambria at his post and veered out the front door.

"Good morning, good morning," he said, beaming at me. "Are you off to shop or are you meeting your mother and her friend for lunch?"

I shook my head. "Did Brenda Appleton leave the hotel a few minutes ago?"

"The little woman with the dark hair?"

"Yes, and wearing"—I tried to remember something that had been of no interest—"a dark blue dress with white buttons."

"Then I must admit she left not five minutes ago, and in such a hurry that the litter has not yet settled back in the gutter. Is she the one you're meeting for lunch?"

Sirens shrilled at the end of the block as two police cars sped by, their blue lights flashing. I had a pretty good idea where they were going . . . and whom they would want to question about the body in the garbage truck. Simply because she'd been questioned two days earlier about an attempted homicide.

I gave Mr. Cambria a goofy smile. "I think I'll run along now. So many shops, so little time."

"I wish you much success."

"So do I," I muttered as I headed for the corner. Only when I was out of sight of the Chadwick Hotel did I slump against a concrete wall and permit myself the luxury of a howl. In Maggody, someone would have rushed over to inquire about my health. This was not Maggody, not by a long shot.

CHAPTER
ELEVEN

Once I'd finished feeling sorry for myself, I considered my dilemma. The fact that I'd fled the scene of the crime was hardly worth stewing over; New York's finest would be hard-pressed to assign me a motive, and I was prepared to plead temporary insanity. I doubted it would be difficult to persuade them—or anyone else, including myself.

No, the dilemma circled around how to find Ruby Bee and Estelle in a city that stretched from the top of the Bronx to the bottom of Battery Park, less than fifteen miles but all of them a tad more congested than, say, the cow pasture out behind the Flamingo Motel.

They, along with Gaylene, Durmond and his disreputable friend, and Brenda, might come home to the hotel, wagging their tails behind them, but I wanted to talk to any and all of them before the police took charge. Somewhere in the city was a veritable parade of Krazy KoKo-Nut finalists. All I had to do was find it—and be damn quick about it.

Gaylene was the head majorette, I thought as I began to trudge toward Broadway. She could have taken off for any of a million destinations. Then again, I told myself with weary optimism, she could have gone to her apartment to practice her kabobs. It wasn't an especially brilliant theory, but it was the best I could produce, and I went into a stationery store and asked to borrow a telephone directory. After a short discussion with a woman larger than Dahlia and twice as surly, I became a bona fide customer with the purchase of a large bottle of aspirin. The directory hit the counter with a thud.

If she had a number, it was unlisted. I thought about calling Geri to ask for Gaylene's address, but decided it would not be prudent to call attention to my absence, or anyone else's. I tried for a moment, and then came up with the name of the club where Gaylene worked. The Xanadu had a telephone, along with an address only a few blocks north of where I was.

I kept my eyes averted as I walked past porn shops, peep shows, and posters extolling the talents of both bosomy women and young men who aspired to be bosomy women and were dressed accordingly. Chains and leather seemed to be the fashion, as were whips and masks and a lot of things that I was unable to identify. It was sleazier than I remembered, but it may have been my fault. On sleepless nights in Maggody (and there'd been more than a few), I'd allowed myself to romanticize the city, to think of the theaters and galleries and museums, rather than of the deteriorating infrastructure, the growing population of homeless, the pervasive crime, the expressions of those who had been victimized and those who knew it was only a matter of time.

I instinctively tightened my grip on my purse as I went past a derelict sprawled in a doorway and kept my face averted as I passed a huddle of teenaged boys. The paranoia was coming back like a recurrent case of the flu, and I picked up my pace. When I arrived at the pertinent street, I looked both ways for any sign of the Xanadu, sighed, and headed to the right because it was easier than crossing Broadway to go to the left.

Halfway down the block I found a sunbleached poster that proclaimed the Xanadu Club to be the home of THE WORLD'S SEXIEST WOMEN. The neon sign was dark, however, and the door was locked. This was not earth-shattering, since the poster also proclaimed that the first show would start in roughly eight hours. No cover charge, but the tab on the two-drink minimum might startle good ol' Toledo Ted.

As I turned to retrace my path to the hotel, I noticed an alley beside the building. It was as inviting as the weedy path to Raz Buchanon's cabin, but I'd walked a long way to do nothing more than gaze at the exterior of the nocturnal habitat of the World's Sexiest Women. And I had to admit I was running low on brilliant ideas.

The alley was lined with metal garbage cans, most of them filled to overflowing. The walls on either side of me were decorated with unsavory suggestions in a rainbow of spray paint—New York's only indigenous folk art. Things rustled as I walked by, and I was unhappily aware of the sweat spreading across my back and slinking down the sides of my face. It was nearly as much fun as stalking a still on Cotter's Ridge, I thought with a grimace as I came around a corner.

The small parking area was defined by a chain-link fence and dominated by a white Cadillac. A few hardy weeds had cracked the asphalt and were flourishing as best they could in perpetual shade. Two steps led up to a blue door with a sign that discouraged trespassing, as did the descending line of locks and the bars on the window beside it.

I righteously told myself I had no desire to set foot inside the place, continued to the window, and stood on my tiptoes. Through a wire mesh and a veneer of accumulated grime, I could see a dark office crammed with standard furniture—and a three-quarter profile of Brenda Appleton, who was seated at the desk, her fingers tapping the arms of the chair and an impatient look on her face.

I sank back on my heels, but before I could get my jaw off my chest, the blue door opened. I ducked behind the front of the Cadillac, anticipating at least one bullet between my eyes, and asked myself how I could be so incredibly stupid. Nothing came to mind.

"You're such a sweetie, Mr. Lisbon," Gaylene said. "I know it's awful of me to miss even more work, but when a girl's got a free trip to Vegas, she's gotta take it." I heard a murmur; then she giggled and said, "Who knows? Maybe I'll win the ten-thousand-dollar prize, too. Wouldn't that be something!"

The door closed, and her high heels echoed down the alley. I peeked over the hood of the car, but ducked as a light came on in the office and a darkly tanned man with a crewcut appeared. His mouth was moving as he reached for a cord and closed the curtains on whatever the hell was going on in there.

I stood up slowly, ascertained my forehead was as last I'd seen it in the cracked mirror (with the exception of a heavy glaze of sweat), and eased around the Cadillac to the edge of the building. Gaylene was gone.

I arrived at the sidewalk in time to see her turn at the corner and head down Broadway. Seconds later, two figures emerged from a deli and took off after her at what I'm sure they felt was a prudent distance for amateur sleuths hot on the trail of Manhattan's version of Mata Hari.

Half a block later said sleuths yelped loudly as I clamped down on their shoulders. Ignoring the pedestrian traffic that flowed around us as if we were submerged rocks in Boone Creek, I said, "What the hell do you think you're doing?"

"You'd like to give me a heart attack!" Ruby Bee said, clutching her chest and blinking at me.

Estelle looked no more thrilled to see me. "I can't believe you don't know better than to sneak up on folks like that! Why, the very first thing that flashed across my mind was that that psychotic man had finally caught up with us and was aiming to murder us right here in broad daylight."

"In broad daylight on Broadway," I said agreeably. "It has a certain poetic ring to it, doesn't it? At the moment I'm the only one thinking about murdering you two, but I'm willing to hold off for a few more minutes. We can discuss your behavior here, or we can do it in this bar. God knows I could use a beer."

Ruby Bee glanced down the sidewalk, but her prey had vanished. "I could do with one myself, come to think of it. But I don't have all the time in the world to sit and chat. I'm supposed to be in the lobby at two o'clock sharp so Geri can fetch me to fix my cake for the contest."

I followed them into the bar, and we found a table near the window.

"This is right nice," Estelle commented, nodding at the wide mahogany bar and row of padded stools. "Of course it ain't at all as homey as yours, Ruby Bee, but I must say those ferns add a summery feeling."

"Ferns shed," Ruby Bee said. "I'm not about to have to sweep the floor any more than I already do, and—"

I unclenched my teeth long enough to say, "Stop it!" then subsided as a waitress approached our table and took our orders. "We are not going to debate the decor. You are going to tell me what the hell's been going on, and why you were following Gaylene just now."

"Following Gaylene?" Estelle chuckled at the very idea. "We wanted to see Times Square, so we figured we had enough time to walk over and look around. It's kinda odd how the famous theaters are stuck between those nasty shops, isn't it? It seems to me the police ought to—"

"We're not going to debate the zoning, either," I said coldly. "I came to find you because Jerome Appleton's body was discovered in a dumpster behind the hotel less than an hour ago."

Estelle gasped. "But that can't be! He's on an airplane going to South America."

"Not anymore," I said. "I recognized him."

"Then that's who was in the kitchen last night," Ruby Bee said. "I thought that might be who it was, but Brenda's such a dithery thing that I didn't want to worry her. I took a real fast look and almost fainted on account of the blood being as awful as it was . . ."

The waitress banged down two beers and a glass of sherry, regarded us with a frown until I'd paid the tab, and returned to the stool at the end of the bar to resume her conversation with the bartender. I suppose she'd overheard worse.

"Why did you go to the kitchen?" I demanded.

She looked at Estelle, who took a sip of sherry and said, "I already told Arly that you might have been in the mood for a glass of warm milk."

"And I already said I didn't believe one word of it." I realized I was strangling an innocent beer glass and forced myself to uncurl my fingers.

"I reckon you don't have much choice," Ruby Bee said with a mulish frown.

"May I point out that the police do have choices? The most obvious one is to drag you back to that cold, dirty cell and leave you to regale the rats with your silly lies. Then again, they might choose to interrogate you night and day until you come up with a better explanation."

Her lower lip may have quivered just a tad, but she shook her head, finished her beer, and put down the glass. "I need to get back to the hotel and study my recipe. Come on, Estelle, you can coach me on the order of the ingredients."

"There is no contest!" I said so loudly that the waitress and bartender stared. "There has been a murder, dammit! The police will be there to conduct an investigation, not to sample the entries and pick the winner! They may even want to ask you some questions—none of which will have anything to do with teaspoons and measuring cups and pinches of salt and Krazy KoKo-Nut!" I could hear myself getting more strident with each sentence, but I was unable to stop myself. "You found the goddamn body, Ruby Bee! Don't you remember?"

"How could I forget a thing like that? Do you really think they'll stop the contest? Jerome wasn't a contestant, you know." She shrank under my glare, then took a tissue from her handbag and dabbed at her nose. "Maybe you're right about the contest being canceled. It'd be hard on Brenda to fix her entry not ten feet from where they found her husband's body."

"She'd be fumblin' like a pup," Estelle added. "Of course he was supposed to have left her for a younger woman, so it's not like she planned on seeing him anytime soon."

I gestured at the waitress for another round. "I can see you're both too distressed by Jerome's murder to discuss last night. Let's talk about the night Durmond was mugged and tucked into bed in your room. Where were you before you came back to the room?"

"Shopping," they said in unison, although not with the melodious effect of the Methodist choir.

"At nine o'clock?" I took my sweet time raising my eyebrows. "I would have thought you'd be worn out from the trip, if not a tiny bit intimidated about prowling after dark in a big, bad city. Where did you go?"

"Just here and there," Ruby Bee mumbled. She stared at Estelle, who nodded nervously in agreement.

"What did you buy?" I persisted.

Estelle hesitated until the waitress had replaced our glasses with full ones, then cleared her throat and said, "I picked up some souvenirs at a shop at the end of the block. Nothing really interesting."

"A shop at the end of the block?" I said. "Do you mean the porn shop at the end of the block? What exactly did you buy—a leather bikini? Handcuffs? Edible underwear?"

She turned bright pink. "It's none of your business, missy. I just browsed for the most part."

"You didn't tell me it was that kind of place," Ruby Bee said, then realized her error and got real busy with her beer.

"And where did you go?" I growled at her.

"I decided to visit a few grocery stores, just to compare what they carry with what's at the SuperSaver back home. I went into one place that was run by these Asian people. You'd think one of them could speak American, but they were all gobbling in some language that I couldn't make heads or tails of. They sounded like a flock of turkeys the way they were carrying on."

She was turning pinker than Estelle, and her hand shook as she picked up her glass. Despite her years of intensive practice, she was not a particularly glib liar.

"I get it," I said slowly. "Did you?"

"Did I what?"

"Did you get a package of coconut so you could use

it in your cake instead of the soybean flakes? You've done some lowdown things before, but I'm amazed that you would stoop to cheating in a cooking contest, Ruby Bee." I tried not to grin, but I couldn't help it. "I'm disappointed in you, to say the least. What would Lottie and Elsie think if they heard about this?"

Ruby Bee hung her head in a fine display of penitence. "It seemed like a good idea at the time. It's not my fault that Krazy KoKo-Nut tastes so dadburned awful that it'll ruin the best recipes. I just couldn't bring myself to make my chocolate chip bundt cake and use that stuff. I have my reputation to think of." She gave me a look meant to be remorseful, but it reeked of slyness. "You won't tell anybody, will you? I don't know what Geri would do if she heard about it, but I'd as soon lick the sidewalk in front of the hotel as be thrown out of the contest and sent home in disgrace."

"I may, or I may not," I said archly. "Is that why you snuck down to the kitchen last night—to put the real coconut in your box?" She nodded warily. "Well, did you make the substitution or not?"

There was a pause that didn't just reek of slyness; it literally stank of it. "No," she said, "because of the shock of finding the body like I did. I was so discombobulated that it was all I could do to get myself out of there before I was murdered."

"Speaking of which," Estelle murmured, "maybe we ought to go back to the hotel? Geri's likely to be in a real tizzy this time, what with the police and all. She'll be sobbing louder than a passel of preachers outside the Pearly Gates."

"Yeah?" Jim Bob said into the receiver, not sounding real friendly. He held a towel around his waist, but he could feel the water dribbling onto the floor, which meant he'd catch hell unless he mopped it up hisself and that was a goddamn pain in the ass. He was on the verge of saying as much when he realized who was calling. As he listened, his hand turned numb and the towel slid down his body to form a beige puddle around his feet. Even though it was a nice, warm day, he started shivering worse than a wet hound, and it was all he could do to keep from howling like one, too.

"So I'll just stick it in the mail," the female voice concluded, wished him a nice day, and hung up.

Jim Bob was well past worrying about some water on the hallway floor, but he made a swipe at it with the towel before returning to the bathroom and sinking down on the seat of the commode. It seemed like an appropriate place to sit, considering the deep shit he was in.

According to the cute lil' clerk, Mrs. Jim Bob had inadvertently left her credit card on the counter—when she'd decided to use the charge account. He'd gone to the trouble of drivin' all the way to Fort Smith to do his shopping, and damned if she hadn't waltzed into the exact same store. And learned all about the charge account.

She was a lot of things, but the one thing she wasn't was stupid. Naughty Nights wasn't easy to mistake for a bookstore or a drugstore (except, maybe, for the display of fruit-flavored condoms). To add to his bewilderment, the clerk had said Mrs. Jim Bob'd bought a damn armload of merchandise. Just what was she planning to do with a black peekaboo bra, fer chrissake? Wear it to Wednesday evening prayer meeting? Prance down the road to the SuperSaver and show it to the stock boys? Dance half-naked in the moonlight?

Something real peculiar must have come over her, he thought as he tossed the towel in the corner and walked to his bedroom, his pudgy white flesh glistening with a mixture of bath water and sweat. It wasn't like she would be caught dead in some sexy little nightie—not the saintly Barbara Anne Buchanon Buchanon. She was a sight too fond of reminding him of the sins of lust and fornication. She could reel off the thou-shalt-not's without pausing for breath, even though she'd added about a dozen more of her own making, most of them involving booze, muddy boots, and bodily functions.

He tried to picture his wife in almost anything from Naughty Nights, but it was harder than picturing her snugglin' up with Raz or belching after a cold beer. Sweet Covita over in Emmet had looked right dandy in the little gift he'd given her the week before, and she'd expressed her gratitude with imagination and skill. Even Winona had been a knockout in her nightie, despite her buckteeth and fat ass and tendency to forget to shave under her arms, and she'd been generous to a fault. The padded dashboard had been the only thing saving 'em from a concussion.

He realized he was letting his mind wander from what was likely to be a fuckin' nightmare starting the minute Mrs. Jim Bob walked through the door. If he was there, that is. If he was long gone, she'd have some time to simmer down, and when he came back, she might not skin him alive.

It wasn't like he was afraid of her, he told himself as he began to stuff shirts and jeans into a suitcase. Hell, he was three inches taller and outweighed her by a good fifty pounds. Socks and jockey shorts went into the suitcase. He was the man of the house, the breadwinner, the provider and protector. A magazine from under his mattress followed the underwear. He sure as hell wasn't scared of any damn woman, and never would be. A handful of T-shirts and he was done.

He grabbed the suitcase and went out to the telephone in the hall. After a couple of fumbles that resulted in nasal admonishments that the call could not be placed, he managed to dial Larry Joe Lambertino's number.

"Listen up," he said, seeing no reason to waste time, "we're gonna spend a couple of days at that fishin' camp on the county line just past Chowen. While you're throwing your crap in a bag, I'll call to get us a cabin and make sure we can use one of their boats if we're a mind to." He flinched as he heard a faint noise downstairs, then assured himself it was only the furnace kicking on. "And fer chrissake, don't go blabbing all over town about it. I got some reasons why I don't want one single person to know where we'll be. Once we get there and get started on the bourbon, I'll explain. Put your scrawny butt in gear, and be ready for me to pick you up in ten minutes."

He hung up and called the assistant manager to tell him to run the store and just this once to keep his greedy fingers out of the cash register and out of Winona's panties. The assistant manager choked out a promise (although he was lying through his teeth about one or both). The ol' boy at the fishing camp said he'd reserve the best cabin.

Jim Bob picked up his suitcase and went downstairs to the kitchen. He loaded a grocery sack with cans and what he could find in the refrigerator, including a good-sized hunk of meatloaf and half a strawberry pie, and took all of it to his car. After he'd fetched his fishing gear from the garage and stowed it in the trunk, he was feeling a sight more cheerful.

Only one last chore remained. He went to the kitchen and hunted up a pad of paper and a stumpy pencil. He laboriously wrote a note telling her he'd gone away on business for a few days and would see her when he got back. He signed it with his initials and, whistling, went out the door.

All the way across town, which wasn't even a fraction of the distance from the Bronx to the Battery, Joyce Lambertino was still frowning at the telephone. She didn't so much as look up when something crashed in the kitchen and Saralee began to screech bloody murder.

There were no police cars in front of the Chadwick, nor was there a doorman. Just inside the door, however, was a uniformed cop with a grim look. "Who're you?" he asked us.

I told him, and was told to go to the dining room and wait. Ruby Bee and Estelle were told to wait in their room, and they hurried toward the elevator without so much as a word of compassion for yours truly. I did as ordered and was sipping coffee as a middle-aged man in a brown suit came to the doorway. He had the jaw of a pitbull and the manners to match.

"You Arly Hanks?" he demanded.

I wiggled my fingers and said, "I am."

"Where the hell have you been for the last hour and a half? Sight-seeing? Shopping? Did it occur to you that you might have stayed around the hotel until we arrived? You may be some toad-suckin' hick from Arkansas, but surely you've seen enough cop shows on television to know you're supposed to wait for the police?"

This was not a good beginning for a deep and abiding friendship. I looked at him for a minute, then took a breath and in my twangiest voice, said, "Shit, Mr. Policeman, I dun reckon I was out there, just a-gawking and a-gaping 'cause I ain't never seen buildings higher than three stories. My eyeballs dun near popped out like a bullfrog's, and I was nigh onto swallowing my tongue, lemme tell you."

He harrumphed as he turned around to converse with a younger man in an equally drab suit. After papers were exchanged, he turned back and said, "I'm Lieutenant Henbit of the homicide division. If we could cut the crap, I'd like to know what you heard last night when you were skulking in the hall upstairs."

"Skulking, Lieutenant Henbit?"

"According to"—he consulted a paper—"Kyle Simmons, you told him that you overheard a conversation between the deceased and his wife, during which harsh words were exchanged."

"I reckon I might have told him that," I said, the hayseed still firmly between my teeth. " 'Course Bubba and Elmer are always saying I'm tetched in the head. Bubba's my uncle, and my brother, too, on account of our family tree bein' a mite short on branches. Elmer ain't related to nobody what we can figure, but he lollygags out back a-tryin' to court the prettier heifers."

"I apologize, Ms. Hanks," he said, his voice as strained as his smile. "I'm sure whatever errand you went on was justified, and I had no business making any wisecracks about your state. We are investigating a murder, and I would appreciate your full cooperation."

I related what I'd heard through the Appletons' door and described the scene earlier in the morning when Brenda had been bullied out of the bathroom. "She really did seem to think he was on his way to South America," I concluded.

"He's on his way to the morgue," Henbit said as he fixed himself coffee and sat down across from me. "She, on the other hand, seems to have disappeared." He was trying to be affable, but his jaw trembled and his eyes were intent. "The doorman said she left before the body was discovered. Do you have any idea where she is?"

"Try the Xanadu Club," I said, giving him the address. "She was in the back room not too long ago, talking to a man with short blond hair."

He gave up on the affability business. "How do you know that, Ms. Hanks?"

"I saw them through the window. I don't know why she was there or what was being said, and I didn't actually hang around outside very long. The garbage cans seemed an ideal home for rats." I paused as Durmond came into the dining room. "Have you heard about Jerome?"

"Yes, indeed." He glanced at Henbit. "May I join you, or would you prefer that I wait in my room?"

Henbit shrugged. "Sit, Mr. Pilverman, and join in the fun. I was just about to ask Ms. Hanks why she was in the alley behind the Xanadu. She's quite witty. You might enjoy her response as much as I know I will."

"In the alley behind the Xanadu?" Durmond echoed. "Is this true, Arly?"

I was chewing on my tongue and trying to concoct a mildly plausible story to explain my presence without indicting my mother. "It's true," I said. "I was looking for Gaylene. I couldn't go to her apartment because her telephone's unlisted. She'd mentioned that she worked there. The front door was locked, so I went around to see about the back door." There may have been a little hole in the story, about the size of a tank, but it was the best I could do on such short notice.

"Stay here," Henbit said. He went to the door and sent his minion away to fetch Brenda Appleton.

"Why were you looking for Gaylene?" Durmond asked in a low voice.

Henbit returned to loom over me like a tombstone with an epitaph mentioning my name. "A very good question."

I wished I had a very good answer. "There's something fishy about her. She's hardly the sort to enter a cooking contest. If she owns an apron, it's liable to be made of leather." I glanced at Durmond. "I happened to see her leave the hotel late this morning. I wondered where she was going and decided to try the Xanadu."

"This is after the body was found in the dumpster?" Henbit said. "You didn't have anything else to do, so you decided to stroll over to some nightclub to see if one of the fishier contestants happened to be there? You have fertile imaginations in the backwoods, don't you?" Sighing, he stood up and straightened his tie. "If you think of anything else, please don't hesitate to share it with me, Ms. Hanks. I would be most grateful."

I could think of a couple of little things I'd omitted, but I smiled sweetly and watched him stomp away. Once he was gone, I said, "Gaylene's not the only one I saw leave the hotel this morning, by the way. At one point, I characterized it as a damn parade."

"Did you, now?" he murmured, then gave me a look that bordered on reproachful. "Did you happen to tell the lieutenant about what Ruby Bee claimed to discover in the kitchen very early this morning?"

"Don't change the subject," I snapped.

"It's really much better if I do, Arly. The situation's a bit more complex than what you're accustomed to in Maggody. More complex, and more dangerous. It's unfortunate that you went to the Xanadu and saw Brenda, but it can't be helped now. Tell yourself she put on a nice blue dress and went to apply for a job. You'd better downplay your involvement for your mother's sake, if for no other reason, and let the lieutenant investigate in his own way."

I opened my mouth to offer a polite rebuttal when Henbit came to the door. His jaw was out as far as it could go, and his expression was noticeably less than genial. "I've had a call from the Xanadu. We don't have a positive I.D., but we're fairly certain that Craig Lisbon, who appears to be the manager, was shot and killed within the last hour. If you're not willing to be candid with us, Ms. Hanks, we'll book you as a material witness and let you cool your heels for a day or two. I'm sorry we can't offer more luxurious accommodations, but we're jammed and you'll have to share a cell with hookers, derelicts, perverts, and whatever psychotics we've invited to join us."

"Is Brenda there?" I asked, struggling not to envision his scenario.

"No, but when we pick her up, she'll be held pending charges for first-degree murder. It may take a little longer, but we'll probably get enough to book her for her husband's death, too. This is in no way going to alleviate your responsibility to tell me the whole goddamn story. Understand, Ms. Hanks?"

"Not at all," I admitted.

CHAPTER
TWELVE

Refusing to be bullied, I stuck to my story that I had followed Gaylene to the Xanadu because I suspected her motives in entering the contest. I explained how I'd happened to meet Ruby Bee and Estelle while they were exploring the neighborhood, glossing over a few details and stressing that I'd left Mr. Lisbon in good health inside his club. Due in small part to Durmond's bland gaze, and in large part to my real aversion to jail cells, I finally got around to the events of four o'clock in the morning.

Lieutenant Henbit seemed gratified by my candor, but mystified by my disclosure that the murder had most likely occurred in the kitchen and someone had gone to the trouble of removing the body to a dumpster and tidying up. I added that the cases of Krazy KoKo-Nut had also taken a trip, although they'd been returned some time between four and ten o'clock.

"Just what is this KoKo crap?" Henbit asked, scribbling a note.

"That pretty well describes it," said Durmond. "A perverse sign of progress, I suppose. No doubt there's a scientist out there who's devising a scheme in which someday everything that passes our lips will be synthetic."

"Yeah, maybe." Henbit read through his notes for a

moment. "What's puzzling me is why your mother went to the kitchen."

"You'll have to ask her."

"She have any kind of relationship with Appleton?" he continued ever so craftily. "They ever go off by themselves for a time, or have cozy conversations in the corner?"

I finished my coffee and stood up. "I really couldn't say, but I'd be surprised if they've so much as exchanged nods since they arrived. He wasn't polite to any of us, including his wife." I thought about how he'd looked in the dumpster and shook my head. "Even so, it was a damn nasty trick to dispose of him like that. How was he killed?"

"Bullet in the neck," Henbit said. "It destroyed the carotid artery, which was why it was so messy."

"And the weapon?" Durmond asked quietly.

"We haven't come up with it yet, but there're some unhappy men out back sifting through garbage. We won't see the ballistics report for a couple of weeks, much less the results of the autopsy. We pulled a stiff out of the river more than a week ago, and we're still waiting to hear something on that, not that it's gonna be any big surprise. Not that this one will, either. As for Lisbon, he was shot in the back of the head with enough caliber to take off his face. Real nasty, according to the first officer on the scene."

I wished him luck with Ruby Bee and Estelle and went into the lobby. Mr. Cambria was back on duty, but I didn't feel overly safe and secure in the hotel, even with cops in the kitchen and cops in the dining room and cops in the alley out back. Hell's bells, I was a cop, and I sure wouldn't have depended on me for anything more than a neatly written parking ticket.

I was under orders not to leave the hotel, which was fine with me. I lingered in the lobby, trying to overhear the conversation between Henbit and Durmond in the dining room, but one or the other had closed the doors. Thinking about my room upstairs was enough to give me claustrophobia, and I was reduced to sitting on a sofa in the lobby when Kyle and Geri came out of the office.

Her blotchy face and swollen eyes reminded me of Brenda's grand exit from her bathroom. "This entire debacle is your fault, you know," she said to him. "Right this minute I could be in the chaise lounge on the deck, but instead I'm going to have to deal with negative press. I hate negative press!"

"Speaking of the press," I inserted politely, "did you confirm the credentials of those people at the reception?"

"Why would *they* lie?" she countered, making it clear they were likely to be the only unimpeachable souls in the entire city, if not the state.

"Ruby Bee and Estelle were interrupted in the middle of a conversation about how someone in the room resembled a plumber."

"And I should know what a plumber looks like?" Geri said, then turned on Kyle. "I find it reprehensible that one of your contestants not only killed her husband, but also went to some seedy nightclub and killed the manager. If I'd had the slightest inkling that you were including homicidal maniacs on your list of finalists, I never would have set foot in this place."

"I told you the names came from Interspace Investments," he said sulkily.

"Which ones?" I asked.

"What difference does it make?" Geri said, but put her clipboard on the counter and flipped through the pages. "The two contestants from the original list are Ruby Bee and Catherine. We were supposed to have a cab driver from Brooklyn, a taxidermist from Boise, Idaho, and some hack mystery writer from Hansville, Washington. Instead, we get a hooker, a professor, and a homicidal maniac. It's rather obvious that this sort of decision process should be left to professionals, isn't it?"

She had a point. I thought for a minute (an increasingly alien activity), and said, "Why did the original three decline?"

"Ask him," Geri said as she let the pages flutter down.

Kyle stared at the floor. "They all called the same morning. The cab driver fell and broke his leg, and the taxidermist accidentally severed a finger. The writer said he'd decided to take a three-month cruise to Alaska. Someone from Interspace called that afternoon and said they'd found alternates."

"Lucky us. We got a hooker, a professor, and a homicidal maniac," Geri added with a sneer.

"They didn't phrase it quite that way," he said. "I'd better call my father with the news that the contest is off. He'll be pissed, but there's nothing we can do about it—except pray they find Brenda and arrest her without giving the media all the details about the purpose of her stay here."

He started for the office. Geri stared for a minute, slammed down the clipboard, and took off after him. "Just a minute, buddy boy. If your father calls my boss again and tries to blame this mess on me, I'll personally swim to the Cayman Islands and bury him up to his neck in the sand so the crabs can chew off his face!"

They continued their discussion in the office. Beyond the closed doors of the dining room, Lieutenant Henbit and Durmond sat with their backs toward me, intent on their conversation. On the counter not ten feet away, the clipboard lay abandoned on the counter, just begging to be given some attention and a few kind words.

Soft-hearted kid that I was, I sauntered over to the alcove, ducked beneath the counter, and removed the clipboard and myself to a shadowy corner. There were a lot of lists, some scratched into illegibility and others fresh with ill-fated optimism. I finally found the list of contestants and jotted down the addresses of the three replacements.

As I returned the clipboard, I glanced up. Mr. Cambria was regarding me from the sidewalk, not with his usual twinkly smile but with a cold impassivity that caused the hairs to rise on my arms and a lump to settle in my stomach. I felt like an animal on a stainless steel table in a laboratory.

The smile reappeared as he turned to speak to someone, and seconds later Gaylene came into view, laden with shopping bags, her purse, and yet another suitcase. I ducked back under the counter and hurried toward the stairs, not sure I'd interpreted his expression correctly but no longer in the mood to linger in the lobby. Nobody ever died of claustrophobia, for pete's sake.

Once I was in my room with the door locked, I sat down on the bed and looked over what I had scribbled. Unsurprisingly, Gaylene had a local address. Brenda lived in Peabody, New York, which I seemed to remember was on Long Island. I called information and got her number, then took a deep breath and dialed it. A male voice answered.

"Is Brenda home?" I asked.

"Who's calling?"

"Just one of the girls. I wanted to know if she wants to play bridge tomorrow at her house or at the club."

"Who is this?"

"I'll call back later," I said and hung up, aware I'd been chatting with a cop. Brenda hadn't gone home, apparently. If she'd murdered her husband and/or the nightclub owner, she might well have chosen a less obvious haven. But it was equally possible that she had no idea that either murder had taken place and was shopping at Saks or having a three-martini lunch in honor of Jerome's departure (albeit for a destination noticeably farther than Rio).

I looked back at the list. Durmond Pilverman resided in Beaker Lake, Connecticut, and taught at Drakestone College. He taught something "very obscure," he'd said. The college might not be in the same town, but it was apt to be in the same area.

It turned out to be in the same area code. I first called his home number and was not amazed when no one answered, in that he'd told me his wife was deceased and implied he lived alone.

"How obscure is it?" I muttered as I dialed the

number of the college. The switchboard operator refused to put me through to his office on the grounds that he didn't have one and was not a member of the faculty. I insisted that he was. After a few rounds of "is too," "is not," I asked for the administration office.

"May I help you?" asked a bored young woman who did not sound dedicated to the proposition.

"I'm trying to get some information about Durmond Pilverman. I was under the impression he's a professor there, but the switchboard operator seemed to disagree."

"Yeah, hang on," she said, then punched a button that allowed me to be entertained by a saccharinized Beatles' medley. We were well into "Yesterday" when she returned. "He used to be here, but now he's not anymore. That's all I can tell you on account of our policy."

"Can you at least tell me what department he was in?" I asked before she could cut me off.

"I dunno. It's like we've got this really strict policy about not giving out information about faculty and students. I think there's a law or something."

I put on my smiliest voice. "There's no law against naming his department. It's in the old catalogues, which means it's already in the public domain."

"Yeah?" she said dubiously.

"You can tell me."

We discussed the issue at length. After I'd defined "public domain" and assured her several times that I was merely tracking down a dear old friend, she told me he'd been in the sociology department. I went back through the switchboard and found myself speaking to the department secretary, a bored older woman. Her vocabulary was better, as was her attitude (when I explained that Durmond had inherited property in Idaho), and she suggested I speak to Dr. Ripley. I professed willingness to do so immediately and was told Dr. Ripley was conducting a graduate seminar and could not be reached the rest of the day.

All this had taken most of an hour. I now knew Durmond was no longer on the faculty of Drakestone

College. I also knew he had a gun in the dresser and a peculiar affinity for disreputable friendships. Then again, I didn't know how his mugging related to the murder, but I was convinced it did. He'd been shot in the stairwell by someone thoughtful enough to put him in a bed. Jerome had been shot in the kitchen by someone who'd felt the need to clean up afterward. Thoughtfulness and cleanliness were not traits I associated with the local criminal element.

I lay down on the bed and began at the beginning.

"I've just about had it with you," Dahlia growled, not at her captor but at her husband, who was in a corner, tied up like a bale of cotton. Marvel had done a competent job of it, although he'd been careful not to cause any pain and had inquired solicitously throughout the process. Kevin had been real grateful, sort of.

"Now, honey bunny," he said, his Adam's apple rippling against the clothesline, "there's no cause to get all upset again. We'll get out of this somehow—I promise. And when we do, why, we'll just go right to Niagara Falls like we planned. You're really gonna like it."

"I ought to drop you in the water while you're still tied up so's I could watch you bobble around like a cork." Dahlia was going to elaborate, but Marvel came out of the kitchen and gave her a mean look. "What's your problem?" she said to him, figuring she could get back to Kevin whenever she had a mind to. He sure wasn't going any place farther than he could roll.

Marvel peeked out the front window. "My problem is two cops out back and about ten of them out front. Jesus, you'd think they had Al Pacino holed up in here." He took another look, then glumly shook his head and sat down near the window. "You doing okay, man?"

"Yeah, I'm just fine," Kevin said eagerly.

"Some honeymoon," Dahlia sniffled. "I've been

dreaming of our honeymoon since the day we got engaged. All this year I've been lying in my bed thinking of how romantic it sounded, and how I'd be Mrs. Kevin Buchanon and we could ..." She snatched a napkin from the holder and blew her nose. "Aw, Kevvie, 'member when I was working at the Kwik-Screw, and we'd go back into the storeroom and it'd be like there was violin music playing and we were in heaven in each other's arms?"

Kevvie gurgled in agreement, although he wasn't thinking about her arms or fool violins.

Marvel was getting pretty damn bummed out by the situation—and with Big Mama and his main man. He hadn't had more than a few minutes of sleep for several days, and although he'd washed up as best he could in the restroom, he was feeling dirty and sweaty and real tired of his hostages.

And there didn't seem to be a solution, not with the battalion of trigger-happy cops outside. He knew damn well they'd turn him to Swiss cheese if he so much as came to the door and tried to give himself up. They sure as hell weren't going to let him hustle the hostages out to the station wagon so they could all go to Niagara Falls. No, somewhere along the line they were likely to get tired of sitting on their asses and blow up the diner like it was nothing but a target on the practice range.

He went back to the kitchen to make sure they weren't pulling any tricks.

As Mrs. Jim Bob arrived at the rusty sign proclaiming the limits of Maggody, she slowed down, not out of respect for a sign telling her to do so, but out of a growing sense of dismay for what she'd done at Naughty Nights. Well, maybe not exactly dismay, since Jim Bob deserved to pay through the nose for the sin of having a charge account at a store that specialized in lasciviousness.

"One of our best customers," the girl had said, just as if Mrs. Jim Bob looked like the sort of woman who'd be caught dead in a peekaboo bra and bikini-cut panties. He was buying presents for someone else, most likely a slut with brassy hair and makeup slathered on with a trowel.

The elegantly wrapped packages piled high in the backseat had a redolence of sinfulness that was beginning to suffocate her. She'd bought them in a rage, but what could she do with them now? Distribute them at the Missionary Society's next meeting? Donate them as door prizes at Jim Bob's SuperSaver Buy 4 Less? Hide them in a closet where her cleaning woman, Perkins's eldest, might come across them and see those gold stickers? Perkins's eldest was taciturn, but she might take a wicked pleasure in spreading the word around town.

Mrs. Jim Bob turned off the air conditioner and rolled down the window, but the sinfulness emanating from the back seat was worse than swamp gas. It was . . . Satan's flatulence. Ruby Bee's Bar & Grill was closed, which saved her from having to keep her chin up while she drove past a bunch of rednecks who could tell just from looking what was in the backseat. The police department was closed, too. If that smart-mouthed Arly Hanks ever found out, she'd laugh herself silly before settling down to needling Mrs. Jim Bob till the morning of Judgment Day. Roy Stiver was sitting in a rocking chair outside his antique store. Although he failed to do anything except keep whittling on a chunk of wood, she was sure there'd been a funny look on his face as she went by. The willowy hippie woman who owned the Emporium Hardware was on the porch, talking to disgusting Raz Buchanon. They both looked at her, as did Marjorie from the back of Raz's pickup truck, and the hippie even smiled and waved—just like she could see right through the car door.

There was only one thing to do, she concluded grimly as she pulled into the grass beside the rectory of the Voice of the Almighty Lord Assembly Hall. She had to seek spiritual guidance. She had to get down on her knees and beg for forgiveness for whichever sin applied, after which she could tell Brother Verber to dispose of the packages in a discreet manner. The episode would be over with. Jim Bob would never dare to mention the charge slip (not if he valued his skin, anyway), and she would simply get back to the Christian business of cleansing the community of illicit whiskey.

After a quick look to make sure no one was watching, she took the packages out of the backseat, careful not to inhale the miasma, and knocked on the metal door.

"Brother Verber, open this door immediately!" she called. "I have no intention of standing here like a salesman with a case of brushes. Open this door!"

Brother Verber did as ordered. "Why, if it isn't Sister Barbara behind that stack of pretty boxes. Are they gifts for the little heathen orphans in Africa?"

She went past him, checked to make sure he wasn't in the midst of counseling any errant members of the flock, and dumped the packages on the dinette table. "They are not for little heathen orphans in Africa," she said with a pinched smile. "They are proof of Jim Bob's perfidy. I brought them to you so you could get rid of them in a manner befitting your position as spiritual leader of the flock. We have to pray over them until Satan flees, and then burn them until they're nothing more than ashes." She'd been planning to suggest he run them out to the Farberville landfill, but this new idea was better, more symbolic, more likely to keep her secret. In fact, she thought with a slightly wider smile, she could scoop up the ashes and put them in a bag to present to Jim Bob. Wouldn't his expression be amusing when she explained they represented over four hundred dollars of lasciviousness?

"What's in 'em?" Brother Verber asked uneasily.

"It doesn't matter. What's important is that they reek of depravity, and we have a duty to make sure they never fall into the hands of some innocent child or good Christian. Go ahead and sprinkle them with holy water, Brother Verber, and we'll commence to pray over them until we see the fierce red devils go swarming off to find another home."

He approached the table, dearly hoping the fierce red devils weren't residing amongst sticks of dynamite. "If that's what we have to do, we'll do it, Sister Barbara. I'm fresh out of holy water, but I do have some sacramental wine in the ice box. If that's not sufficient, I 'spose I could drive over to the Church of Christ in Emmet and ask ol' Cornell about borrowing a cup of holy water."

"Fetch the wine," Mrs. Jim Bob said as she settled down on her knees on the kitchen floor. "The fewer folks that know about this, the better. I cannot in good conscience risk the mortal souls of members of another congregation." She closed her eyes and assumed an appropriately pious expression. The Almighty, in appreciation of her effort, sent down another idea, this one even better than the first one. She looked up at Brother Verber, who was hovering in a way not dissimilar to a blimp. "What's more," she told him, "as soon as we finish this business, we'll take these packages and drive to Cotter's Ridge to destroy Raz Buchanon's still. We can pour his wicked moonshine on them, and they'll blaze all the way to heaven so the Almighty can see we're doing our Christian duty. He'll approve of the way we're killing two birds with one stone."

The earlier conversation had put Brother Verber off balance, but this was enough to slam him into the nearest wall, metaphorically speaking. He snatched his handkerchief out of his pocket and tried to stanch the rivulets of sweat on his face and neck. "Why, I don't think we should waste any time destroying these ... proofs of perfidy, Sister Barbara. We can just use my barbecue grill out back. I think I have most of a can of lighter fluid, but I can always get more at the Emporium. We can be done in no time flat."

Mrs. Jim Bob was not about to risk being seen at the grill, doing something odd enough to rouse speculation and provoke pointed questions. "No, the Almighty won't mind waiting while we drive to the still. You told me that you knew exactly where it was, Brother Verber, and I would never doubt so much as a single word from your lips, what with you being a man of the cloth."

"Thank you, Sister Barbara," he said, although he was a ways from being overcome with gratitude. He thudded to his knees and started praying that the Almighty, who seemed real generous with His suggestions, might feel inclined to share some with him. The location of the still, for starters.

Ruby Bee and Estelle were waiting for the policeman to come knocking on the door of 219. They were doing it with about as much enthusiasm as a couple of coons treed by a pack of hounds.

"I think you're better off with the warm milk story," Estelle said from within the bathroom, where she was trying to stabilize her hair without bruising her elbows every time she moved her arms.

"You've said that about a million times already," Ruby Bee said, sighing. "I jest don't know what all Arly and Durmond told the policeman. If you hadn't gone and said something about visiting a porn shop, then Arly wouldn't have figured out what I was doing in the first place. She'll be smirking the rest of her born days, at you for shopping at such a place and at me for doing what needed to be done to win ten thousand dollars. It won't matter one bit to her that I planned to use part of my winnings to buy her some decent clothes." She wiggled around on the bed, trying to find a comfortable spot. She might as well have been lying on a corncob mattress. "Now that I think about it, what all did you buy at that place?"

There was a moment of silence in the bathroom, followed by a muttered response.

"You'll have to speak up. I didn't hear you," Ruby Bee said real nicely.

"I said there's not enough room in here to turn

around. My poor knees are gonna be black and blue, and I still can't get the bobby pins in at the right angle."

Ruby Bee got to her feet and crept over to Estelle's suitcase. "I'll bet that outhouse behind Robin Buchanon's cabin is a sight bigger," she called as she squatted down and began to rummage through the dirty laundry that had accumulated over the last few days. "I can't imagine how Dahlia and Kevin managed to spend all those hours locked in there the night they thought a killer was after 'em. They must have felt like the stuffing in a Thanksgiving turkey, don't you think?"

"I'll thank you not to go pawing through my personal belongings," Estelle said from the doorway. She waited until an abashed Ruby Bee scuttled back to the bed, then added, "I was thinking about something more important than a couple of silly souvenirs, Miss Snoopy Britches. I was recollecting about how Durmond came to be buck-naked in your bed and you had to go and shoot at the police."

"All I did was pick up the gun," the accused said sullenly. "I came into the room, and there he was, all bloody and indecent. Then out of the blue there's footsteps and pounding on the door and yelling like a bunch of drunks in my parking lot. The gun was right there on the floor. I picked it up and was going to answer the door when it liked to explode in my hand. Things took a downward turn after that."

"I'll say they did," Estelle muttered as she sat down on her bed and took out an emery board. "The thing is, I myself heard the shot as I stepped off the elevator. I was right there in the hall when the policemen took to butting the door until they broke the lock, which is why I was there to see them tackle you like they did. You ought to get yourself a lawyer and sue 'em for it, if you ask me."

"What's your point?"

"Didn't you hear what I just said? I swear, Adele Wockerman listens better than you do, when she ain't got her hearing aid tuned to her favorite Martian station." With an aura of smugness she knew would irk Ruby Bee, Estelle began to file her nails.

"You were yammering worse than a schoolmarm who's found a frog in her drawer. I heard everything you said. I just didn't find it all that earth-shattering." Ruby Bee picked up the travel guide and made a production of flipping through it. "This says there are some real quaint stores in Greenwich Village. If the contest is canceled like Arly says it'll be, maybe we ought to shop there tomorrow."

"I said I was coming out of the elevator when I heard the shot. Not one day later, Durmond's telling everybody he had to take the stairs on account of the elevator was broken. If it was so all-fired broken, how come I could sail right up to the second floor in it?"

"Maybe it was temporarily broken," Ruby Bee offered.

"And that snooty manager grabbed his tool kit at ten o'clock at night and climbed the cables like a darn monkey to fix it?" Estelle put down the emery board and frowned something fierce. "There's something real fishy about Durmond's story, if you ask me."

As reluctant as she was to do so, Ruby Bee said, "You may be right. If the elevator was working, he must have gone up the stairs for another reason. He doesn't strike me as one of those fitness freaks who think it's fun to dress up in pastel underwear and run alongside the road, or ride a bicycle in the living room. It wasn't like he had to wait more than a few seconds for the elevator to come; there's no one else staying here but us, and we're all on the second floor."

"Are we?" Estelle said, rolling her eyes toward the ceiling.

All Ruby Bee could see were cobwebs and some patches of bare plaster, but like Estelle, her eyes were aimed at a higher target.

CHAPTER
THIRTEEN

Staring at the ceiling produced nothing more illuminating than an awareness that it needed new sheetrock. Oh, I'd posed some fascinating questions to myself, but unlike "Jeopardy!" contestants, I was shy on answers. I decided to forego this beginning business and focus on the corpse.

Jerome had been killed in the kitchen. In theory, the kitchen was locked and Kyle Simmons had the only key. It had been in his possession from the moment the four cases of Krazy KoKo-Nut arrived until, I assumed, the police took it away from him in order to secure the scene.

I forced myself to replay the hour or so we'd spent preparing for the contest. The key had been in the lock when I entered the kitchen, and when we left . . . it had been left as well. Kyle had returned several hours later, at which time Geri had berated him for not having left the key at the hotel. But he had—and in a rather obvious place for it.

Clutching my pillow, I muddled for a while and came up with a tenuous idea. Someone had chanced upon the key in the lock, removed it for a period of time, and then replaced it before Kyle arrived with the bags of utensils. And unless Kyle had unlocked the door for Jerome in the middle of the night, there was now another key floating around in someone's pocket.

Who had borrowed the key long enough to have a duplicate made? Ruby Bee, Estelle, Durmond, and I had been busy making total asses of ourselves in various locales along Fifth Avenue. Catherine and Frannie had departed for a beauty salon; later in the afternoon, however, Frannie had returned laden with shopping bags and mentioned that Catherine was napping. Implying she'd been in her room, Brenda had come looking for Jerome—implying he hadn't.

He was a candidate, although no stronger a one than a boyish Democrat confronting a rich Republican incumbent. Geri had been in the hotel, but she needn't have bothered to go through convolutions to get a duplicate key; all she had to do was keep the original. Excluding the workmen, the only other people within spittin' distance were Rick and the enigmatic doorman, Mr. Cambria.

I was approaching a full-scale migraine, but I squeezed my eyes closed and continued my mental meanderings. Rick had been seriously perturbed when Geri demanded the key. In fact, he'd been on the verge of combat when twinkly ol' Mr. Cambria had suggested that he cooperate. And what had provoked this sudden interest in the not especially interesting kitchen? The arrival of four cases of Krazy KoKo-Nut.

No one had admitted a fondness for soybean flakes, tinted or otherwise, and it was more than challenging to come up with a reason why anyone but a full-fledged wacko would kill for them. Yet an awful lot of people were behaving oddly over something Ruby Bee'd sworn was unfit for a sow (okay, a pedigreed sow, but still . . .). Interspace Investments, Inc. had bought the company and were enthusiastic enough to move up the date of the contest and host it in their own hotel. They'd rounded up replacements when the three original contestants had dropped out . . . with a broken leg, a severed finger, and a sudden desire to explore the Alaskan coastline for several months.

Gawd, I hated coincidences almost as much as I hated the island on which I was currently prone. I dealt with the latter by standing up, gazing sullenly at my re-

flection, and heading out the door to find Lieutenant
Henbit and impress him with my insightful logic.

This proved to be a veritable piece of cake as the elevator doors slithered open and he and Durmond came
out. "Ah, Ms. Hanks," he said, politely ignoring my
gasp, "I was on my way to your mother's room to have
a word with her. Several words, to be more accurate.
Mr. Pilverman has convinced me that her discovery of
the body in the kitchen was . . . well, not fortuitous, but
perhaps serendipitous. However, neither of you has an
explanation for her untimely presence. Let's hope she
does."

Durmond looked in need of a dry cleaner's establish-
ment, and not just for his clothes. He was watching me
with such gloominess that I had to restrain myself from
tweaking his cheek and assuring him everything was
just dandy. "I'm going to lie down for a few minutes,"
he said to both of us, and then to me, "but you're welcome to join me for a drink later."

"I don't know," I murmured, not at all pleased with
the emotional turmoil he'd managed to stir up with his
morose eyes and smile. "I'll have to see how I feel, but
now I'd like to have a word with Lieutenant Henbit."
I waited until Durmond went into his room, grabbed
Henbit's arm, and dragged him down the hall toward
the higher numbered rooms.

"Ms. Hanks," he said as he removed my hand, "I really have more important things to do than to play secret agent with you. I'm aware that you're the chief of
police of your little town in Arkansas. I have no doubt
you're skilled in the art of running speed traps and
tracking down foxes in the chicken coops. This, however, is not Arkansas, and I must insist you—"

"Wait just a goddamn minute, Lieutenant Henbit!
I'm getting sick and tired of being dismissed as a two-
bit cop from a one-bit town. I'm coming to you with
valuable information, possibly what you need to deter-
mine who killed Jerome Appleton and why." I held up
my palms and moved backward. "But if you're too
busy to listen, I'll run along and have myself a high ol'

time with a bug zapper and a six-pack of beer. Golly, I may jest go git myself another tattoo."

His jaw was out and trembling just a tad, but he took a breath and said, "What information do you have?"

"I think it's likely that the cases of Krazy KoKo-Nut contain contraband of some sort. Based on several oblique references to Florida and the Caribbean, I'd suggest you test the contents for drugs."

He gave me an indulgent smile. "We have. The lab tests aren't completed yet, but the preliminary word is that the four cases contain nothing more than foultasting, rubbery soybean flakes with artificial flavor and artificial color, all packaged in unsullied plastic bags. It ought to be illegal, but it's not."

"Are you sure?"

"I just told you this was preliminary, so in that sense we're not sure. Why don't you go take a nice nap like Mr. Pilverman, or even with him, if that appeals? I need to ask your mother some questions, and then go back to my office to see what kind of progress we're making on the current whereabouts of Mrs. Jerome Appleton." With a nod, he went down the hall toward Ruby Bee's room, leaving me to stand there gawking like a damnfool tourist in the mean streets of the city.

And to think I'd skipped lunch to concoct my brilliant theory that had explained a helluva lot of things—perhaps not every itsy-bitsy bugaboo, but some of them, anyway. I was leaning against the wall, watching Henbit knock on Ruby Bee's door, when I heard voices and footsteps in the stairwell. I eased open the door in time to hear a male voice assessing the chances (not good) the Mets would win the pennant. A second male voice concurred.

They continued down and presumably out into the lobby. I went to the landing and confirmed as much, then twisted my neck and looked up at the seemingly endless stairs leading into the darkness. With all the confidence of someone walking into a subway tunnel, I went to the third floor, where the remodeling supposedly continued.

The door was not locked. I opened it far enough to stick my head out and ascertain the existence of a table saw, a pile of mismatched lumber, a rusted air conditioner surely on its way to its burial, and other debris appropriate to a remodeling job. It was pretty much what I expected, and I was about to duck back into the stairwell (and go find some lunch) when I heard the unexpected from around a corner.

"Then you think lead pipes are the answer?" said Rubella Belinda Hanks of Maggody, Arkansas. "I always thought copper was the way to go."

"Well, the rust factor's what you got to worry over," said a genial man, identity and hometown unknown.

"Ain't rust just a royal pain in the butt!" chirped Estelle Oppers of Maggody, Arkansas.

They were heading in my direction. I let the door click shut, hesitated long enough to scratch my chin and frown, then scurried up to the next landing and waited. I was gratified when the door below me opened and the two adventuresses began to descend.

"All I can say is that it's a good thing he works for that magazine at night!" Ruby Bee said with a sniff. "Imagine not knowing your copper pipes from your lead pipes."

Estelle sounded equally disdainful as she said, "I doubt he knows his spigots from a hole in the ground! I'm glad we don't have to count on him when pipes start bursting in the winter."

"I should say so. Do you remember back in 'eighty-six when we had that hard freeze right before Christmas and—"

"It was 'eighty-seven, the same year my cousin Carmel was electrocuted in the bathtub. His wife said he always played the radio, but she was seen at a bar less than a week later and dressed in jeans so tight—"

The door banged closed on yet another diverting incident in the Chadwick Hotel.

"I told you to make sure you had the maps," Dahlia said, her tone as deflated as her chins. "Right before we got in the car at that horrible motel, I asked point-blank if you had the maps, and you said you did, even though the maps were in the room and your head was up your behind. I was gonna make sure, but then you had to go and drop my suitcase so everyone in the parking lot could see my underwear just a-flutterin' in the breeze. Right then and there I should have told you to take me home so I could call a lawyer and git myself a divorce."

Kevin tried not to whimper from under the chair where he'd gotten himself wedged more 'n an hour ago. Sweat was gathering in his eyes and leaking into his ears something awful, but there wasn't anything he could do on account of being tied up. "I guess I deserve it," he said, trying to be brave like a frontiersman surrounded by hostile Indians and down to his last bullet. "It's all my fault, my darling. I dun everything wrong from the minute we hit the highway leading out of Maggody."

"You're darn right it's all your fault," Dahlia said. "If someone like Ira was here, he'd know what to do about it. I keep asking myself why I had to be kidnapped with you instead of a real man who ain't afraid to protect his woman from danger."

Marvel, who was once again in the kitchen making sure the cops weren't getting ready to do something stupid, eased away from the window, and took the last piece of bread from the wrapper. Shit, he thought, they were running out of food. Big Mama wasn't much fun, but there'd be hell to pay if she found out they might have to make do on water and crackers. He could order another pizza, he supposed, but just remembering her reaction to the anchovies was enough to make his stomach go sour.

"Beloved," Kevin whined from the front room, "if I was a policeman or an FBI agent, I'd just gnaw my way out of these ropes and shoot that fellow until there weren't nothing left of him."

She responded to that, but Marvel wasn't listening. He was thinking, and after a minute, he hurried to the front room and picked up the telephone on the counter.

He punched for the operator and said, "I want to talk to someone at the police station in whatever this hell-hole is called. If you don't put me through, I'll kill one of the hostages and kick the body out the back door."

"Kevin," said Dahlia, although in a tone that suggested he engage in volunteerism rather than heroics, "do something."

Marvel pointed the gun at her until she subsided. "Okay, listen up real good," he said into the receiver. "I'm fed up with this and ready to negotiate. Thing is, I don't trust you honky rednecks. I want you to get a dude from the FBI and send him in here to work out the details. What's more, my man, I don't want some local asshole putting on a three-piece suit and claiming to be a fed. The only man I'll deal with is gonna be a brother." He listened for a moment. "Yeah, a black man, and I don't care how you're going to get one. All I can say is that if he doesn't come up on the porch at precisely nine o'clock, his arms in the air and his credentials between his teeth so I can read 'em, I'll shove my gun up one of the hostages' noses and splatter brains and blood on the wall."

"Kevvie . . ." Dahlia wailed, covering her face (and nose) with her hands and slumping across the table. He couldn't see any of this, wedged as he was, but he could hear the distress in his beloved's voice and it was worse than being poked in the eye with a sharp stick.

"And while we wait," Marvel said, "why don't you send over a big bucket of fried chicken and some biscuits and gravy?"

To Kevin's relief, Dahlia's wails dribbled off with a hiccup or two.

As I came out of the stairwell, the door of 215 opened and Frannie, after a hushed word over her shoulder, came into the hallway. "Catherine's resting," she said. "I thought I'd find out what we're supposed to do about food, since the kitchen's off-limits and we're not allowed to leave the hotel. I really don't know what to think about this whole thing. Brenda seemed like such a pleasant woman. Jerome was beastly, but I can't imagine her actually going so far as to . . ."

For some reason I couldn't define, I shot a quick frown at her door before I said, "He was brutal during the press reception, wasn't he?"

"But Geri certainly upstaged everyone," she said with a dry smile.

"She's worse than some of the teenaged girls back home. She doesn't have half the poise your daughter's shown these last few days, although Catherine did seem . . . excited last night. Whatever did she mean about the little piggies?"

Frannie eased me away from the door. "She's not accustomed to alcohol, and she was unable to handle it. This is our first visit to Manhattan, and what with the pressure of the contest and meeting the media, she was simply not herself. She told me afterward that she was trying to lighten everyone's mood with a silly joke."

"Oh," I said wisely. "Have you and she given statements to the police yet?"

"That lieutenant came to the room earlier. Catherine was sleeping, but I went to the lobby and talked with him for a few minutes. There was very little I could tell him about poor Brenda and Jerome, and Catherine's had almost no contact with them at all, beyond the few times Geri gathered all the contestants to discuss the schedule."

She headed for the elevator, forcing me to follow her. I still couldn't figure out what was bugging me about her room, which was apt to be as dingy and cramped as everyone else's. Not even in my wildest flights of whimsy could I hypothesize a majestic suite behind the peeling door.

"Catherine seems to spend a lot of time in the room," I said as Frannie pushed the elevator button.

"It's her allergies. There's something in the air that's giving her dreadful headaches, and she's hardly been able to sleep at night because of the noise outside the hotel. The horns never stop, do they? It doesn't do one bit of good, but they seem to enjoy leaning on their horns and shouting obscenities at each other."

"You're from Kansas, right?" I said, wily professional interrogator that I was. She nodded and, when the elevator door slid open, stepped inside. At the last second, I joined her with a witless chuckle, and continued. "I assume Catherine's in school. What do you do, Frannie?"

She gave me a narrow look, as if I'd asked her for the name of the madam who ran the whorehouse. "I work part-time in a little store. I think it's important that I be there when Catherine comes home from school. I drive her to all her lessons, and sometimes we go out to the mall to shop and have supper in the food pavilion. She's in the honors program, so she's always loaded with homework in the evenings. I sew or occasionally read a magazine. I've tried to watch television, but Catherine cannot concentrate unless the house is very quiet."

"I guess you have to be careful when you turn the pages," I said. It didn't exactly enhance the atmosphere between us, but I was getting tired of hearing about mama's little monster. Definitely a sour pickle, and sour enough to turn one's mouth inside out.

We arrived at the first floor without further discussion of delicate Catherine's needs and desires. Frannie headed in the direction of the office, no doubt willing to vent her maternal instincts despite Geri's propensity for hysterics. I opted for a sofa in the lobby rather than a ringside seat and was getting settled in when Lieutenant Henbit stomped out of the dining room.

"Where're your mother and this other woman who's with her?" he barked at me.

"I am not my mother's—" I stopped as I remembered the last time I'd tossed out the phrase.

"Your mother's what?"

"Keeper. However, if I were you, I'd try her room."

"She wasn't there," he said, still all red in the face

and tacitly accusing me of some nefarious scheme to deprive him of his opportunity to speak to her.

"She's probably there now. She and Estelle felt some imperative to discuss their pipes with a plumber on the third floor. By now they're back in their room, arguing the wisdom of lead over copper and analyzing the mysterious death of Cousin Carmel back in 'eighty-six. Or was it 'eighty-seven?"

" 'Eighty-seven," Rick said from behind the counter. "It was a very good year for mysterious deaths and chablis with an impudent personality."

Lieutenant Henbit did not look amused as he continued across the lobby and took the stairs. Once the door banged closed, I looked at Rick and said, "What's the matter? Can't take the heat in the office?"

"That Gebhearn dame is driving me friggin' crazy. If she's not jabbering on the telephone, she's sobbing like someone ran over her poodle. She was not doing well on account of her boss calling, but then the queen mother barged in and started carrying on, too. Jesus! Was there ever a time when this hotel was calm and everybody was just going about his business?"

"I wouldn't know," I said truthfully. "I came only after my mother was arrested for attempted homicide, if you recall. I've been thinking about the so-called mugging in the stairwell, and I can't figure out why Durmond was placed in 217—or who called the police."

He sneered, albeit faintly. "The police seem more concerned about murder these days. They might be willing to assign a special task force to alleviate your curiosity, however. You should ask the lieutenant when he comes down."

"He does seem preoccupied with this other business, doesn't he?" I said, refusing to allow him to irritate me. "But I think there's a parallel between the two crimes that he's ignoring."

"Do you now?" Rick twisted his ring, but his eyes were on me. For the record, they weren't the friendliest I'd seen and didn't begin to compete with Mr. Cambria's twinkle.

"In both cases, the bodies were relocated before they were discovered. Durmond was taken to 217, and Jerome to the dumpster in the alley. This means that someone went to a lot of trouble when it would have been so much easier and safer to depart the scene with all due haste."

"How do you know Jerome was taken to the dumpster? Maybe he went outside to play with the rats or something and was shot out there by some punk. The cops are not making an effort to keep me informed of their investigation, but I would not be surprised to learn Appleton's wallet and watch are missing."

"As is his luggage," I said with a frown.

Rick stooped under the counter and came to the sofa. "But why is it that you say he was killed someplace else and moved to the alley?" he persisted.

"Because my mother went to the kitchen for a glass of warm milk and saw the body," I said. "She didn't mention seeing his luggage, though. What happened to it?"

I'd been talking to myself for the most part, barely aware of Rick's presence, and therefore was startled half out of my skin when Mr. Cambria said, "What else did Ruby Bee see while on this quest for warm milk?"

I held back a giggle that would have been on the manic side. "Nothing else that I know of, but the lieutenant may be able to worm something more out of her—if he's as clever as he thinks he is. I wouldn't bet on it."

Rick looked at Cambria. "I swear this is the first I've heard of this. The cops didn't say a word about the guy being shot in the kitchen, or about his luggage disappearing. From what I've picked up, they were perfectly happy with him going out to the alley on his own two feet and then either his wife or some punk shooting him there. Only now am I hearing how that screwy broad was in the kitchen while the body was still warm."

"I was there, too," I said, "but after the body had

been moved and before the four cases of Krazy KoKo-
Nut had been returned."

Rick was twisting his ring hard enough to rip off his
finger, and his face was turning paler by the second.
"It sounds like there's a history of sleepwalking in this
family. First the mother and now this chick go roaming
around in the middle of the night, and both spouting
off nonsense about what they saw and what they didn't
see. I think maybe their brains are packed less carefully than Appleton's suitcases."

I was on the verge of verbalizing my displeasure
when a truck squealed to a stop in front of the hotel.
All three of us watched a man grab half a dozen flat
white boxes and come charging across the sidewalk.

"I told you to make some calls," Cambria said
softly.

"I did, just like you said," Rick said, gulping. "I got
hold of everybody I could think of. The word's out. I
dunno what this guy is doing . . ."

The door opened. "Pizza man!" said the newcomer.

Brother Verber was puffing as he scrambled over a
patch of loose rocks in what would be a bubbly, gushy
creek in the springtime. He was having a hard time
keeping his balance, in that he could barely see over
the boxes he was carrying. Every now and then the
white ribbon tickled his nose enough to provoke hearty
sneezes that sprinkled the slick silver paper like tiny
drops of dew.

"I presume we're almost there," said Mrs. Jim Bob.
She wasn't as worn out as he was, but the humidity
was getting worse by the minute. Heavy gray clouds
had massed over the ridge, with occasional flickers of
lightning and rumbles that threatened a downpour at
any minute. "We haven't got all day," she continued,
her beady eyes boring into his back, "and we can't
have much of a fire in the rain. What's more, it's getting chilly."

He almost apologized for the weather, but decided he'd better save his breath and concentrate on picking up any stray cosmic suggestions as to the location of Raz's still. It had to be around there somewhere, he told himself as he stumbled and fumbled through the brush.

"How much farther is it?" demanded Mrs. Jim Bob.

"Why, not all that much farther," he said with what confidence he could muster. "The problem is with the directions Raz gave to me after he finished repenting. I'm almost certain he said to take the second logging road and keep to the right all the way, but he was such a pathetic wretch that he might have been addled at the time and meant to have said to keep to the left."

"Then we may be on the wrong side of the ridge? Is that what you're saying?"

"Of course not! We're here to do our Christian duty, and the Almighty wouldn't let us stray down the wrong path, much less the wrong side of the ridge. Any time now we'll come around a clump of trees and feast our eyes on that soul-pollutin' moonshine still."

Mrs. Jim Bob glanced up, but there was no Divine Finger pointing the way to go. "We'd better find it right soon and get this nasty business over with before we find ourselves soaked to the skin." She wrapped her sweater more tightly around her shoulders, wishing she'd thought to bring a coat, not to mention an umbrella. Then again, maybe a shower from heaven would cleanse her soul of the gritty residue of guilt lingering from the night she'd lain in her bed and allowed herself to think about things that violated everything she'd learned from rigorous Bible study and services three times a week.

Brother Verber was shivering, too, although the dipping temperature was not the sole cause. What a tangled web he'd woven, he thought with a wheezy sigh, all because he allowed Satan to hand him a glass and force the wicked whiskey down his throat and into his belly, where it'd festered and boiled and done its best to seep into his loins and turn him into nuthin' more than a sinner driven by mindless lust. Luckily, he'd

seen fit to fight for his immortal soul and had won fair
and square, and now was again pure of heart and free
of lust.

He looked benignly over his shoulder. "Sister Barbara, you are such an inspiration to me and to all the
members of the congregation." He was planning to add
more, but his foot came down on a loose rock. The
boxes went flying every which way as he fell to the
ground heavily enough to compete with the thunder
and startle the birds into silence.

"Are you all right?" said the inspiration.

He kept his eyes closed while he pondered her question. His head was spinning, to be sure, and his backside was screaming so loudly he was a little amazed
she couldn't hear it. He continued his assessment. His
back didn't feel broken, which isn't to say it felt good
or even so-so, but he made sure he could wiggle his
toes just the same. He was getting ready to announce
his findings when the Almighty, who'd been real quiet
up till now, finally decided to put forth a proposal.

Sister Barbara was slapping his cheeks and making
agitated noises, but Brother Verber waited for a moment before letting his eyelids flutter open and his
mouth curl into a grimace.

"It's my ankle," he said, making it obvious that the
only thing stopping him from whimpering was his res-
olution to be brave. "It feels like it's on fire."

Mrs. Jim Bob pulled up his trouser leg. "This one?
It looks fine to me. If it were broken, wouldn't the
bones be sticking out?"

"It's the other one, and I don't think it's exactly broken. It's more like sprained real badly and afore too
long will commence to swell up and turn purple." He
sat up and squinted at it. "Yes, I can see some bruises
right below the surface of the skin. I'm afraid this puts
a damper on our plans, Sister Barbara, and I'm as disappointed as you are that we can't continue forth to do
our Christian duty. I just hope I can hobble all the way
back to the car."

Mrs. Jim Bob wasn't overly impressed with his
speech, but she wasn't ready to accuse him of lying,

not just yet. Instead, she left him to rub his head while she gathered up the boxes, which weren't nearly as festive after having been flung hither and yon. She couldn't leave them on the ridge, she told herself as she made a neat stack. Some fool hunter might come across them, and with her luck, there'd be a receipt in one of them with her name written in big, bold letters that might as well spell S-E-X.

Taking them back to Maggody meant driving down the road while folks out and out smirked at her. Brother Verber's barbecue grill was not an option.

"What we'll do," she said, ignoring his moans and facial contortions, "is sit for a spell and see how much your ankle swells up. If it's not too bad, we can continue on our mission and be back at the car before it starts raining. You do want to destroy the still and these perfidious packages, don't you?"

The fact that she was standing over him with her hands on her hips and a real tight look on her face prompted him to say, "Of course I do, Sister Barbara." He realized he was staring at her trim ankles only inches away. "Of course I do," he repeated numbly.

CHAPTER FOURTEEN

I stayed in my room the rest of the afternoon, eating pizza (no anchovies) and trying to sort through everything I knew. Or what I thought I knew, anyway, which was a whole 'nother ball game. The Chadwick Hotel had not seen fit to provide its guests with embossed stationery, but I scrambled through drawers until I found a scratch pad, took a pencil from my purse, and sat cross-legged on the bed while I made numerous lists and drew little arrows all over them. The arrows had points; the lists did not.

I was having such a fine time that I was seriously annoyed when the telephone rang. Furthermore, I hadn't had much luck with calls lately. I let it jangle for a long time, but finally I got tired of listening to it and picked up the receiver.

"Oh, Arly!" Eilene shrieked (her standard approach these days). "There's been a breakthrough! They're still being held hostage in Lebanon, but it looks like they'll be released if negotiations are successful. A man's on his way from Washington, D.C., to act as the go-between. Their nightmare may be over after all this time, and they can come home to their families and loved ones."

"That's great news," I said, feeling as though I was linked to CNN. "Why is the guy having to come from Washington?"

"The terrorist demanded to speak to a black FBI agent, if you can imagine. I didn't know there were any, but the policeman said they tracked one down and sent for him. He's more of an office worker than one of those agents who goes around with a gun chasing drug smugglers and folks who want to shoot the president. He has to fly into Frankfort, and they'll fetch him in a car and take him straight to the café."

"Great news," I repeated weakly.

"I'm just beside myself! I've been pulling out my hair and pacing up and down like a caged animal in a zoo. Earl's just as distraught as I am, although I must say he ain't missed any meals—or any ball games on the television."

"Well, it sounds as if it'll be resolved soon and the bride and groom can resume their trip to Niagara Falls." I tried to think of something else to say, but I'd worn myself out with all the lists and arrows. "Thanks for calling, Eilene. I'll be sure to tell Ruby Bee and Estelle the good news."

"You don't have to tell them about it, Arly. I talked to 'em a while back. Just tell them that Earl says even a plumber's apprentice knows that copper is better than lead. It costs more, but you come out ahead in the long run. Earl couldn't believe a real plumber'd say something that stupid. He says it sounds more like Kevin."

I asked her to call back when the hostages had been released, then replaced the receiver and pretended I was studying my lists. So Ruby Bee and Estelle were still on the case, were they? Lieutenant Henbit might not be pleased to hear they were dabbling in his water. I sure as hell wasn't. Whatever was going on under the guise of a cooking contest was a damn sight more dangerous than the chemicals enhancing the soybean flakes.

Rehearsing a few acidic phrases under my breath, I was halfway across the room when there was a knock on the adjoining door, presumably from the hand of a man who was no longer a professor but was professing to be one just the same. And had a .38 Special in his dresser drawer. Yeah, that man.

I opened my door. "I was just on my way to have a word with some meddlesome broads from Maggody."

Durmond stood there, his shoulders slumped and his face as gray and limp as an old washrag. I'd seen better color on a cadaver. Beneath his eyes were half-crescents darker than bruises. He had on a different shirt, but it was as wrinkled as if he'd changed before he took a nap. I was about to repeat myself when he sighed and said, "May I come in, Arly? I've just had a call from Alex Ripley, and I think we'd better talk before you jump to a lot of erroneous conclusions about me."

"I already have," I said crossly, then gestured for him to enter the room. "Although I doubt they're all that erroneous, unless the entirety of Drakestone College is conspiring to play a practical joke of some kind. I didn't speak to anyone who sounded as though she had that lively a sense of humor."

"I was on the faculty until it was determined that my wife's cancer was inoperable. I stayed home to take care of her, and I just ... never returned to the classroom." He gave me a quick look as he sat down, and although his voice remained soft, it took on an edge—the kind with which you can slice a ripe tomato—as he added, "I find it odd that you called Drakestone to check on me, but what's even odder is that you knew the name of the college."

"You must have mentioned it. Maybe Geri said something, or Kyle heard it from this investment corporation and passed it along."

"I wasn't added by the corporation, Arly. Kyle Simmons's father arranged to have me included as a contestant. I suggested that he put my name in with the other two replacements, and he did it right before he left for a vacation." The edge became sharper than anything advertised on late-night cable. "But I didn't mention Drakestone to anyone because I didn't want any snoopy sorts to attempt to verify my credentials. There's only one way you could have come up with the name of the college."

"Okay," I said, leaning against the wall.

"Which means you must have noticed the weapon in the drawer. I wish you hadn't searched my room, Arly. I guess your cop instincts got the better of you, but it's unfortunate and will cause complications I'd hoped to avoid."

I regarded him, uncertain what I ought to admit and how much mendacity he might buy. "I'm sorry if it was inconvenient," I said at last, opting to be obtuse, "but possessing a concealed weapon has that risk. So you're not a professor, and the president of Krazy KoKo-Nut was so enamored of your recipe that he arranged for you to participate in the contest. What was his approach—physical violence or cruise tickets?"

Durmond winced. "The tickets, please. Mr. Simmons is not the sort of CEO to resort to severing fingers or breaking bones."

"That's good to know. But why did he do you such an inestimable favor?"

He picked up my scratch pad and shook his head as he looked at it. "Why do you think?"

I was almost positive that Rick and Cambria were members of an organization that preferred the physical violence approach, and over several generations had perfected it. But I couldn't quite envision Durmond in the role—maybe because I didn't want it to be true. "Beats the hell out of me," I said as I went into his room, fixed myself a drink, and came back to the doorway with a glass and a guess. "Unless you're a cop?"

"A cop of sorts," he said wryly. "More of a federal agent, to be precise. I retired from the DEA fifteen years ago, but a couple of the guys dropped by while I was spending my days out in the boat, and their invitation had more appeal than returning to my classroom at Drakestone. My wife taught there, too. We used to eat lunch in her office every day and complain about campus politics, the escalating ineptness of the students, disappointing movies, and the weather."

I watched the ice cubes melt while I considered him in this new role. It eventually began to make sense, along with dealing with some of the bugaboos mentioned earlier. "How about the overly friendly psychotic in the khaki jacket? Is he a fed, too?"

"Sonny's been trying to keep track of the contestants when they leave the hotel. He thought his cover would make him invisible, but he didn't count on the Arkansas contingency. They scared the shit out of him in the subway."

"And you're here because this whole thing is a sham to cover drug distribution," I said as I sank down on the end of the bed and took the pad from him. "Interspace Investments, Inc. is a mob organization. They bought the Krazy KoKo-Nut company in order to launder money and insisted the contest be held in this"—I gazed at the room—"dump in order to divert attention from the dealers going in and out with their tool kits and boxes. No wonder the plumber didn't know his spigots from a hole in the ground."

"Plumber?" he said, justifiably puzzled.

"Ruby Bee and Estelle recognized him at the reception, although initially they assumed a family resemblance was responsible. Being the meddlesome broads that they are, they trotted up to the third floor this afternoon and chatted about plumberly subjects. He failed the test, although who knows what the two concluded about his lack of expertise." I paused to scan my notes. "The lobby was used before the contest. They then moved to the third floor and continued the remodeling ruse to cover the comings and goings."

"That's our theory," Durmond said, although it seemed to me he ought to show a little more appreciation for my display of deductive prowess. "The big shipment came in the Krazy KoKo-Nut cartons, of course. Geri screwed up the plans when she insisted the cartons be secured in the kitchen, as did whoever shot Jerome Appleton at the same site. The last thing Rick and Cambria wanted was to draw attention to the shipment and provoke undue interest in it."

"So they moved the body out to the dumpster!" I said, getting into the rhythm of it. "They cleaned up the blood and borrowed the cartons long enough to exchange the drugs for innocent packages. But why would they kill Jerome there to begin with? It would make a helluva lot more sense to escort him out to New Jersey or sink him in the river or whatever is the current vogue these days."

"Drive-by shootings outside of restaurants are gaining in popularity," Durmond murmured, clearly impressed with my enthusiasm if not my logic.

I stood up and began to pace as best I could, rubbing my hands together and gnawing on my knuckles as I careened around the tiny room. Pacing in Maggody's a lot easier; I've been known to resolve sticky problems out in the pasture behind the Flamingo Motel, despite the prevalence of cow patties. "The corpse in the kitchen was a problem for them, to put it mildly. And why kill Jerome in the first place? That's what destroyed their scheme. They must have been alarmed when Geri snagged some of the dealers and insisted they were magazine reporters, but they managed to get things under control again." I reeled around, tripping over my carry-on bag. "After Geri's boss called her and ordered her to continue, that is. Kyle had called his father and was shaking in his boots after the conversation. All these executives know darn well what's going on in the hotel this week. Why didn't someone call the police?"

Durmond tapped his chest. "The department approached the senior Mr. Simmons, after which he agreed to put my name down as a contestant in exchange for immunity. He then felt the need for a long vacation, as did Geri's boss. Sure, they both know who owns Interspace Investments, but coupled with fear was a significant amount of greed. They're also keenly aware of the wisdom of distancing themselves from anything that might lead to indictments."

"So they threw a couple of kids into the pit to save their hides? That's not exactly sporting." I resumed my flight pattern, although I did keep an eye on the carry-on bag. "Rick's a kid, too, which is why Cambria rushed here from Florida after the incident in the stairwell and agreed to take the role of doorman. Neither of them wanted an outside security man to monitor the arrivals."

"You're not bad at this business," he said (and high time). "But we don't have any proof that the Krazy KoKo-Nut cartons contained cocaine, and you've produced a very good reason why Rick and Cambria *didn't* shoot Jerome. Then, of course, we still have a problem with the murder at the Xanadu and the subsequent disappearance of the recently bereaved widow."

"I can't handle every last detail," I said gracelessly. "After all, it's what you get paid for, isn't it? I'm just a hick from Arkansas. You're the big-time fed. You can have a long talk with Lieutenant Henbit about this—while I pack my bags, gather up the overgrown girl detectives, and find out about the next flight out of this absurd city. I didn't want to come in the first place, and I don't want to hang around a hotel owned by mobsters." I snatched up the carry-on bag and opened it with enough vigor to rip the teeth out of the zipper. It was merely a gesture, in that none of us would be allowed out the hotel door, but as gestures go, it had a certain style.

"Well, then," he said, moving his hands aimlessly as if he were a confused conductor, "I suppose I'll call Henbit from my room. He already knows who I am and why I'm here, naturally, but he might have further information that Sonny and I can use. I'll . . . talk to you later, if you're in the mood."

I jerked open the door and stood there until he was in his room. I didn't exactly slam it, but I may have failed to ease it closed. Why was I in this snit? Because I was sick and tired of people not being who they claimed to be, from the professor who was a fed to the plumber who dealt drugs to the ex-husband who was a philandering son of a bitch whose concept of morality rose and fell with his prick (inversely, that is).

Flopping onto the bed and bursting into tears appealed enormously, but I resolutely clenched my teeth, jammed my fists in my pockets, and stared blindly out the window until I was cooled off enough to think.

Another bugaboo bit the dust. I reopened my adjoining door, confronting his, and loudly said, "And you weren't mugged between the first and second floors, either! You were on your way to the third floor when—"

The door opened. Durmond had removed his shirt, and the sight of the vivid red scar and heavy bruising around it took the wind right out of my sails, so to speak. It was a damn good thing I wasn't vying for the America's Cup.

In a much calmer voice, I continued the sentence. "When you were shot, not by some punk but by one of the dealers—or even by Rick. They had the same problem as they did in the kitchen. In order to draw attention away from that part of the hotel, they moved you into one of the rooms and stripped you to add to the muddle. Rick must have called the police and been pleasantly surprised when Ruby Bee returned in time to take a wild shot through the door. I wonder what he thought when you came up with your story?"

"That I was confused, I suppose." He flushed as he realized I was staring at his seminude torso. "Ah, let me grab a shirt and we can . . . Would you like another drink, Arly? I'm out of canapes, but . . ."

It was obvious he was still confused, but he didn't deserve to be in any better mental shape than I was. We regarded each other with varying levels of bemusement, neither of us quite sure what to do next. We finally figured it out and tacitly decided to do it in his room. And did it damn well, too.

Once again, Brother Verber was staggering up the hillside, panting like a Lamaze student, sneezing every now and then, sweating copiously, and praying with impressive sincerity that the moonshine still would pop up from behind a rock any minute. The major differences were that he was obliged to limp and that the storm was squarely overhead and making it clear it was gonna get down to business real soon.

"Around these rocks?" Mrs. Jim Bob said, trudging behind him. "Are you sure it's there, or are you still addled from your fall? We have been up here and down there and over this and behind that to the point I couldn't find the car if you paid me. I'd like to think you would have known if Raz was lying to you, you being trained in that sort of thing, but I'll admit I'm beginning to wonder, Brother Verber."

"We have to keep the faith, Sister Barbara. That's the only way to tell the saints from the sinners, and we both know which side of the bed we get up on, don't we?" He wished he could wipe the sweat out of his eyes, but there wasn't any way to juggle the boxes and get to his handkerchief. A raindrop bounced off his balding head, adding to the ambience of impending doom. "It sure does look like rain. Maybe we ought to think about putting off this Christian mission until we have a nice, sunny day?"

"We are not putting this off for anything," she said firmly, although she was equally dismayed by the growls from the sky and the occasional raindrop. "You're the one who said it wasn't all that far, if I recollect, and you're the one who's going to lead us to the still and light the fire. If you ask me, you'd better save your breath for the climb."

The two differences have already been mentioned. Now two things were about to happen, neither expected and neither to be savored in the manner of a glass of iced tea on a hot afternoon. The first happened right off. Just as Brother Verber was finding the courage to admit he was confused (if not as lost as a flea on a sheepdog), he saw the still in a clearing.

"Oh my gawd," he said, blinking in disbelief. "I mean to say, praise the Lord. Sister Barbara, we have reached our goal. Let us fall to our knees and offer thanks for the success of our mission to rid the community of moonshine and perfidy."

"It's about time. We've been wandering in circles for more than three hours."

Brother Verber was too amazed with his luck to insist on an impromptu prayer meeting in the woods. He would have patted himself on the back, had it been possible, but had to settle for a smug chuckle and the knowledge that he had been guided by the Lord on account of the undeniable purity of his soul. He put down the packages and studied the still, a real artistic arrangement of copper coils, a big ol' vat, some gallon jugs, and a goodly collection of mason jars in wooden crates. The remains of a fire, nothing more than some charred wood and feathery white ashes, were visible below the vat.

Something twitched from underneath. He was curious enough to squat down and poke the shadow with a stick. "Something's under here," he said. "One of the Lord's little critters needs to be on its way afore we commence our mission."

"What is it?" she said, joining him. Destroying the still and burning up unspeakable lingerie was one thing—two, actually—but she didn't want any roasted groundhogs on her conscience.

This led almost immediately to the second unexpected thing. The *Mephitis mephitis* (also called polecat, zorrino, and, by the less couth, wood pussy) was frightened by the jabs to its hindquarters. Instinct took over and it backed out from its haven, lifted its tail, and spewed out a message that had stopped many a predator ten times its size. Having succeeded, it stalked indignantly into the brush to hunt up some tasty grubs for supper.

Mrs. Jim Bob and Brother Verber were grappling with each other as they tried to escape the yellow mist that stung their eyes, clogged their throats, and seized their lungs. Both of them were screeching something awful; the words weren't intelligible but the messages were pretty much identical. By the time they reached the far edge of the clearing, Mrs. Jim Bob was sobbing uncontrollably and Brother Verber was on his hands and knees and in the process of tossing his lunch.

"You idiot!" Mrs. Jim Bob howled between sobs. "I can't believe what an idiot you are!" She staggered to her feet and tried to wipe the miasma off her face. She might as well have tried to wipe off her nose or her chin. "You stupid idiot!"

He caught hold of a sapling and pulled himself up, in some corner of his mind obliged to agree with her. "I didn't know! I thought it was a—a—I dunno! I didn't think it was a skunk, for pity's sake!"

"You idiot," she repeated for good measure, "look what you've done. I can barely see. What if I'm blind forever after? How are we gonna find our way out of here?"

She remained hysterical for another ten minutes or so. Brother Verber missed some of it because of recurrent nausea, but it finally eased up and he offered her his handkerchief. She was still making disparaging remarks when lightning crackled. Not more than a few seconds later, thunder exploded with such fury that the whole ridge trembled.

"Now what?" she shrieked, immediately lapsing back into hysteria. "Now what? What do we do?"

A fine question, worthy of the beacon of the flock, he heard himself thinking as he spun around and gazed at nothing more useful than scrubby brush and the creek bed they'd come up. He couldn't recall which way the car was, but he was certain it was a long, long way. And they had a short, short time to find shelter.

"Stay here a minute," he said, then hustled himself past the still to the other side of the clearing. There wasn't much of anything there, either, and he plunged into the brush, his feet moving of their own accord and his mind nigh onto blank. He thrashed this way and that, feeling as if he were covering miles but actually making a loppy circle, and therefore was a little surprised at how quickly he returned to his companion.

"Well?" she snapped.

"There's a cave not too far from here," he gasped. "It ain't a Holiday Inn, but it's deep enough that we can get out of the rain. I think Raz uses it to store his whiskey."

"What about this disgusting stench?"

Thunder reverberated, this time clearly a warning that the preliminaries were over and the rain was coming any minute. Brother Verber snatched up the packages and said, "I didn't see a shower in the cave, if that's what you mean. We'd better hurry, Sister Barbara. Time's a-wasting."

The heavens proved him right. They hurried to the cave, but by the time they arrived, they were soaked to the skin, shivering so hard neither could speak, and their clothes, rather than being rinsed off, smelled all the worse for being clammy. Mrs. Jim Bob sat down on a crate and blotted her face, then took a look at the decor, which consisted of a dozen crates of moonshine, a few stubby candles, crumpled candy wrappers, and a vast quantity of crushed acorn shells on the muddy floor.

She wrapped her arms around her shoulders and began to sniffle. It was retribution, she thought despondently. She'd sinned, and now she was being made to suffer for it. She'd entertained notions of lust, and to make it worse, had envisioned herself in the arms of another man. "Thou shalt not commit adultery," she mumbled under her breath, "and thou better not even thinketh about it." She'd said those very words to Jim Bob, time and again, once going so far as to write them down on a paper and leave it pinned to his pillow the night he hadn't come home until the roosters were crowing and the first yellow school bus was sucking in a child at the edge of the county.

"Beg pardon?" Brother Verber said as he fumbled with the buttons of his shirt. He took in her startled gaze and said, "Don't you mind, Sister Barbara. I have on an undershirt. I'm hoping it won't smell quite so bad and I can put my shirt way off in the corner behind those crates."

"I'm not about to take off my dress," she said primly, or at least as primly as anyone could who was shivering, shaking, stinking, and dripping onto the floor of the cave. "I shall not sink to indecency, no matter how trying the situation. Now you fetch some wood and build a fire."

They both looked at the rain coming down like Niagara Falls. "I don't reckon we'll have much luck with a fire," he said as he threw his shirt down and determined sadly that his undershirt was just as wet and just as smelly. Lordy, it was cold. Poor Sister Barbara was twitching from her head to her ankles, and it was all he could do to stop himself from rushing to her side and wrapping his arms around her to share his warmth and to comfort her in this time of trouble and despair. "I wish we could get out of these wet clothes," he said as he put that idea right out of his mind and sat down at a decorous distance. "They might dry if we spread 'em out for a time, but of course I know we can't do that on account of being good Christians."

Mrs. Jim Bob plucked at her sodden skirt. "You're probably right about getting out of these clothes. However, I am a married woman, and under no circumstances would I behave immodestly in front of another man. Or in front of Jim Bob, for that matter." Her teeth began to chatter so hard she had to stop talking. Her knees were knocking against each other as if they were applauding, although there sure wasn't anything worthy of ovation. There they were, stuck in a cave with whiskey. They were wet, cold, stinking to high heaven, with no good idea of how to find the car should the rain ease up, and it was all her fault. She clenched her hands together and hung her head.

"I don't think you ever said what's in these boxes," Brother Verber said, picking up one and peering at the splattered paper and listless white ribbon.

Ruby Bee was still irritated from the interview with Lieutenant Henbit and had been making it known going on several hours now. At the moment, she was flipping through the guidebook, but for not the first time. Then she slammed it on the bed and said, "I don't know when I've met a less mannersome man. He acted ruder worse than Leadbelly Buchanon did when those kids tipped his outhouse. I swear, I thought ol' Leadbelly would never quit griping about that."

Estelle decided not to mention an uncanny parallel that happened to be lying on the bed. "At least you didn't tell him about the purpose of your mission last night. Gawd only knows what he would have said if he'd been told. He might have arrested you for tampering with the contest rules or something, and you'd be back in the slammer before you knew what hit you."

"If we could get this mess straightened out, maybe Geri could go ahead and have the cookoff," Ruby Bee said, again not for the first time. "Ten thousand dollars ain't chicken feed, not by a long shot, and I sure could use it. I might just buy some ferns for the barroom, after all. Dahlia doesn't do much more than mope around as it is, so she could be in charge of sweeping up the leaves."

They discussed the tragedy in Lebanon for a while, but they didn't know much. After they'd agreed how awful it was and how they couldn't imagine such a thing happening on a honeymoon and maybe this hotshot black FBI man might help, the conversation dribbled off. It did get them back to the problem with the plumber, however, in that Eilene was supposedly looking into the lead vs. copper situation.

Estelle snorted and said, "I'm having some doubts about this fellow, even if he really is just a bad plumber. Why would he be moonlighting for a snooty magazine? It seems to me he'd make a lot more money making emergency calls at night, when people are obliged to pay an arm and a leg to keep the house from flooding."

"That old boy in Emmet charged me forty-five dollars when the commodes backed up on a Saturday night," Ruby Bee muttered, getting steamed up just thinking about it. "He had the audacity to tell me that if I didn't want to pay the extra charge, he'd see if he could come by Monday or maybe Tuesday. Now how am I supposed to make do without commodes for two or three days?"

"Why would he say he was a plumber if he wasn't?"

"And what is he?" Ruby Bee mused aloud. There was a truckload of other questions, but she decided to chew on this one for the moment. "If he's not a plumber, then maybe some of these other so-called workmen aren't what they say, either. I'll tell you one thing: Gaylene Feather is no cook. I asked her a few questions about her recipe, kind of assessing the competition, and she was as addled as a snake with feathers. I don't know how she ever got to be a finalist."

"It's odd, her going to the Xanadu yesterday," Estelle said. "If Arly hadn't turned up like a bad penny, we might have figured out what she was up to. But you had to start asking that clerk about the lottery and how it worked, and that's why Arly snuck up on us like she did."

"I seem to recollect you were slobbering over my shoulder at the chance to win all those millions of dollars."

"That ain't the point. If those television detectives were as sloppy when they tailed someone, they'd end up dead before the second commercial."

Blame was cast back and forth, but in a perfunctory way, and again the conversation dribbled off and both of them took to eyeing a spider on its way across the ceiling.

"It's too bad we didn't go up the alley alongside the Xanadu," Ruby Bee said. "We might have seen Brenda Appleton inside, shooting that fellow—or someone else shooting him. I suppose the police looked around for clues, but they sure seem to think Brenda's their culprit."

Estelle assumed Ruby Bee had done her homework well. "Does she know how to cook?"

"Yeah, but she mentioned funny things like matzoh balls and chopped chicken liver."

"Instead of fried? Does she cook it first, or is it raw?"

Ruby Bee held up her hand. "We didn't swap recipes, Mrs. Pillsbury Doughgirl, and that's not important, anyway. What matters is why those men keep going to the third floor and pretending they're regular workmen. I'd be willing to say there's something going on up there that doesn't involve Krazy KoKo-Nut or lead pipes."

"Something illegal," Estelle said, nodding. "Something so awful that they shot Jerome Appleton because of it and most likely the manager at the Xanadu. Maybe we ought to warn Rick about them. He could tell the lieutenant, and then the next time they come prancing in with their toolboxes, the police could arrest 'em on the spot."

"I don't know about that. After all, they've been remodeling this hotel for a time, and you'd think Rick would know if they weren't who they said. Remember that man at the table saw? He was sure acting like he knew what he was doing, and doing it real loud, to boot. It's not all of them, but just some, like our ignorant plumber." She glanced at the bedside alarm clock she'd had the foresight to bring, since the Chadwick Hotel had failed to supply one. "It's well past quittin' time, so they've probably cleared out by now. What do you say we have a look around and see if we can figure out what's going on besides remodeling? Then that rude lieutenant can arrest the murderers and we can have the contest."

"And the ten thousand dollars?" Estelle said, wiggling her well-drawn eyebrows.

Ruby Bee allowed herself a smug smile. "And the ten thousand dollars. I got this contest tied up tighter than bark on a tree—if we ever get to fix our recipes."

They made sure they had the room key, went out into the empty hallway, and headed for the elevator, doing all this real quietly so's not to attract the attention of anyone in the rooms (Arly, for example). Once they were safely in the elevator, however, Estelle rolled her eyes and said, "These Yankees are the strangest folks I've ever met. They put the Buchanon clan to shame. Can you imagine eating raw chicken liver?"

The topic was more than adequate to entertain them as they rode toward the third floor.

CHAPTER
FIFTEEN

The knock on Durmond's door was more than mildly inopportune. I grabbed my clothes and hightailed it to my room, then leaned against the adjoining door while I caught my breath and reminded myself I was well past the age of consent—and had done more than my share of any consenting. Hell, I'd initiated it. There was no reason to feel like a kid caught necking on the porch. We were both single, sober, and attracted, and we'd been heading in this direction since we first laid eyes on each other. For all I could tell, I'd been heading in this direction since the stewardess had offered me a complimentary beverage of my choice and a foil packet with six lightly salted peanuts. As far as directions go, it wasn't a bad one.

I regarded my flushed face in the mirror while I dressed and repaired my hair. There was no scarlet message written on my forehead, but it was obvious I hadn't been flipping through a magazine during the last half hour, not with a complacent smile like mine. I peered more closely at my eyes, which were simmering with the frustration born of being interrupted during a more leisurely expedition. It then occurred to me that I'd fled so quickly that I didn't know the identity of the intruder in the next room. I gave up analyzing my recent behavior—not repenting, mind you, analyzing—and went to the adjoining door to knock.

My hand froze as I heard Lieutenant Henbit's dulcet voice.

"Yeah, we picked her up at Grand Central," he said. "She had a hundred thousand in her bag, but refused to explain it or anything else. One little phone call, and this sleazy lawyer comes barging in, bitching about a lack of evidence, and advising her not to say a word."

"A hundred thousand," Durmond said with a whistle.

"This particular sleazy lawyer has been on retainer for certain unsavory families for the last decade. Why would a nice suburban housewife call him?"

"Because her husband worked for them," I said as I came into the room. Henbit made a burbulous noise, but I ignored it. "I heard him and Rick in the office the day I arrived. Jerome Appleton was their accountant. That explains why Brenda was invited to be a contestant, and why she knew the name of a sleazy lawyer." I resisted the temptation to make a more generic remark about the profession and waited for Henbit and Durmond to congratulate me on the significance of my comments.

"We know that," Henbit said. "What I was about to point out when you barged through the door"—he paused to smirk at the rumpled sheets from which we could all see steam rising—"or back through the door, was that we now know that Mrs. Appleton was aware of her husband's association with the Gabardi organization. Our theory is that he decided to walk out on her, packed his bags, and tried to split. She didn't go for it, so she followed him through the kitchen to the alley, where she shot him."

"Ruby Bee saw the body in the kitchen," I protested.

"So she says. The lab boys are testing the floor and walls for blood, and we'll have the results before too long. Thing is, she could have shot him there just as easily and dragged him out to the dumpster, set his luggage where it could be stolen by the first bum that staggered by, and then, being a finicky homemaker, felt obliged to clean up the mess she'd made. I'm aware Pilverman here is convinced there were drugs involved, but we haven't turned up so much as a gram and I don't have the manpower to crawl over every inch of this place in search of one."

"Where'd she get a hundred thousand dollars?" I asked.

"From his suitcase. Maybe he's the sort who prefers to pay cash instead of putting it on plastic."

Durmond gave me a warning look. "I talked to Sonny earlier about this. Let me share our thoughts with you. Appleton went to the kitchen to avail himself of a package or two of Colombia's finest on his way south. Rick and Cambria were there, getting ready to replace the contents of the cartons with what was supposed to be in them, and they were unhappy about Appleton's plans. One or the other shot him, and they took away the cartons to complete the substitution. Ruby Bee saw the body before they'd had time to move it to the dumpster, clean up the blood, and replace the cartons."

It wasn't quite what he and I had come up with, but I merely frowned and said, "The cocaine's liable to be on the third floor, Lieutenant Henbit."

"Ms. Hanks," he said, his frown a great deal less winsome than mine and his drawl more pronounced, "we have searched the third floor. There is a great deal of evidence that the remodeling continues. We're talking tools and lumber and sawdust and sheetrock and all those subtle hints even we could hardly miss. If there ever was cocaine, it's long gone from this hotel. I don't give a shit what you, Agent Pilverman, and his undercover cohort think, and to be blunt, the last thing I need is a one-bullet cop and a pair of feds messing up my investigation."

I was going to tell him I had three bullets, but I sensed it was not the moment to quibble about such details. Nor did I offer the information that he had a couple of amateurs on the prowl, partly because I had no idea what they were up to and partly because I was pissed at his attitude. He'd find out in good time. "What are you doing with Rick and Cambria?" I asked meekly (I do great meek).

Henbit bristled like a sow. "I can't do anything. Despite Agent Pilverman's invitation to avail ourselves of his department's thick files on the suspects, we can't do a goddamn thing without proof. So what if they shot Appleton and moved the body? Do you know how long we could detain them on the evidence we've got? They wouldn't have time to finish a cup of coffee before the lawyer was there to escort them out the door, and I'd be explaining to my superior why I'd booked them in the first place. I can hear him mentioning the night shift in Flatbush."

"The department's been after these guys for four years," Durmond said, sighing. "Two good men were executed last year in Florida when their covers were blown. We've got three of the lower echelon in the witness relocation program, whooping it up on tax dollars, but nevertheless ready to testify if we can get indictments. Gabardi's organization is responsible for maybe a third of the drugs in this city, and we can't nail the son of a bitch. I'd settle for Cambria, the second in command, but I'll be damned if we bust him for some misdemeanor."

He stopped as we heard the elevator arrive at the floor. There was yet another knock on the door; I had to bite my lip not to join in the game and shout, "Who's there?" Durmond admitted Geri and Kyle, both of whom looked frightened out of their yuppified wits.

"Lieutenant Henbit," Geri said, ruffling her hair with a pale hand and then beginning to toy with the buttons of her silk blouse, "what's the status of your investigation? For reasons beyond my comprehension, my boss insists we continue with the contest. I mentioned the murder, but he dismissed it as random violence and ordered me—ordered me, mind you, to pay no attention to it and . . ." Not surprisingly, tears flooded her eyes and she sank down on the bed. "I know how to deal with caterers and florists, but Mother never taught me how to work around a murder. I mean, a mugging is one thing. Mr. Fleecum is behaving like an absolute dictator and I simply cannot"—she sniffled but withstood a torrent—"handle this, no matter what he says."

Kyle cleared his throat. "My father was as adamant. He seems to think this murder in the alley is nothing more than a minor nuisance."

"The metropolitan force apologizes for any inconvenience," Henbit said coldly, "but we're going to continue the investigation, and the contest is canceled until this is cleared up."

"Maybe the contest would clear it up," I said under my breath. I noticed I had everyone's attention and raised my voice. "All the contestants are available. Durmond's here. Ruby Bee, Catherine, and Gaylene are in their rooms. Brenda's at your precinct and could be brought to the hotel, should you be amenable."

Geri had recovered from her watery decline and was regarding me with bright approval. "Yes, and then this ghastly contest could be done with and I could head for the Cape. This has played hell with my nerves, ever since it was dumped on me as if I didn't have luncheon engagements or aerobics classes or anything better to do with my time."

"Or with my kneecaps," Kyle contributed.

"How 'bout a drive?" Raz suggested to Marjorie, who was looking dejected on account of the latest twist on her favorite soap. "That ol' boy what lives over at Grazin says he can take a couple of cases tonight, iff'n I kin get 'em to him afore he heads out."

Marjorie blinked in confusion.

"You know the skinny peckerwood I'm talking about. He drives one of them monster trucks in contests clear across the country. He's willin' to pay right good cash for high-quality hooch, and ever'body knows I make the best damn hooch in the county."

Marjorie's eyes drifted to the window.

"Sure, it's nippy and rainin' something awful,

but"—Raz spat into a coffee can whilst he tried to think of a way to sweet-talk her into it—"you won't git wet iff'n you stay in the truck. It cain't take more 'n an hour to fetch the hooch out of the cave and run it over to Grazin, and afterward, we'll celebrate at the Dairee Dee-Lishus. Don't a chili dog sound right tasty?"

Marjorie drooled obligingly.

"We can't turn on the lights," Estelle whispered as they crept along the hallway of the third floor. "What if Mr. Cambria looks up and realizes someone's on the prowl? You think he'll just smile and go on opening the door for folks?"

"I couldn't say," Ruby Bee retorted, doing her best not to stumble over all the darn clutter on the floor. There was enough light from the windows at either end of the hallway for them to avoid the big stuff, but she'd already stubbed her toe on some fool thing and it throbbed like a boil. "Just what do you think we're gonna find up here, anyway? Another body, this time with a typed confession from the murderer safety-pinned to its chest?"

"So this is all my idea? Is that what you're saying, Mrs. Let's-Have-a-Look-for-Ourselves? I suppose it'll be all my fault if we get ourselves killed, right?"

Ruby Bee clutched Estelle's arm. "Hush up! I heard a voice."

"You heard my voice. As for this other voice, why—" She broke off with an intake of breath. "I hear it, too."

They continued around a corner, clinging to each other as they negotiated a particularly perilous roll of old carpeting, and stopped when they saw a ribbon of light beneath a door. A low voice was interspersed with a giggly one, and it took them a few minutes to identify both, take in a few sentences, and ease back around the corner.

"That Catherine sounds drunker 'n a skunk," Estelle said, disgusted.

"There's no doubt in my mind what she and that Rick fellow are doing," muttered Ruby Bee. "I ain't heard that kind of talk since they locked away ol' Harly Brad after they found out he was making those obscene telephone calls. To this day I don't understand why Elsie took notes every time he called her, but she sure seemed to enjoy telling me what he said down to the last dirty word, and doing the heavy breathing parts, too."

"His vocabulary was enough to curl my hair."

"So's Catherine's. Rick's ain't shabby, but he's a sight older and lives in Noow Yark City, so he probably learned all that on the playground. They ought to be ashamed of themselves, him for doing that sort of thing with a snippet of a girl, and her for going along with it. I declare, I don't know what the world's coming to!"

"Frannie sure would be unhappy if she knew about this," Estelle said, moving on since she didn't know what the world was coming to, either. "Her little princess behaving like a common slut, and doing it out loud, which is even more awful. We should have known when we saw her at the reception, drunk and crawling all over—"

"Jerome!" Ruby Bee said excitedly, then clapped her hand on her mouth as she remembered they were supposed to be whispering. "Do you recollect on the first night how he said he was going to his room to work and all of a sudden Catherine pipes up and says she's got a headache and leaves in the elevator with him?"

"And the next day, when she claims to need a nap all by her lonesome and Brenda can't find Jerome?" Estelle's mouth went drier than a wad of cotton as she tried to think. The blinking neon lights didn't help, nor did the misshapen shadows on the walls and the murky piles of sheetrock and lumber. "I don't know what it means, but maybe we ought to trot down to our room and call that lieutenant."

"To tell him what?" said a voice from behind them. A female one, but on the unfriendly side.

They spun around and gasped at the gun in Frannie's hand. "Nothing! We don't have anything to tell him. I didn't mean what I said," Estelle gabbled, her fingernails digging into Ruby Bee's arm so harshly they were close to drawing blood.

"We—we were just looking around," Ruby Bee said, "and there's nothing here but a big mess. You can see for yourself, Frannie. Why doncha put down that gun before you hurt someone?"

"I heard everything you said," Frannie continued, not putting down the gun and not getting any friendlier. "You said my daughter was engaging in tawdry behavior with that slimeball manager—and did the same thing with Jerome Appleton. Do you want to know what really happened?"

Estelle shook her head, while Ruby Bee bobbled hers. Frannie managed to overlook this display of mixed messages and said, "That man seduced my daughter, a girl of sixteen. She should have known better, but she allowed him to take advantage of her and use her as if she were a prostitute. I found out about it and made it clear to her that I would not tolerate that kind of thing. She's won several beauty pageants, you know. She's in the honors program and will be offered scholarships when she graduates. I've already begun to sew her college wardrobe. I have plans for her. I cannot allow her to destroy her future by . . . by . . ."

Estelle and Ruby Bee were as unnerved by Frannie's increasingly shrill voice as they were by the wobbly barrel aimed in their general direction. To make matters worse, Frannie slumped against the wall and began to cry, the gun bouncing as she shook with sobs. They waited for a minute to find out if they were gonna get shot, but Frannie seemed to have forgotten about them and was lost in her misery.

At last, Ruby Bee stepped forward and took the gun. She used her free hand to grab one of Frannie's arms, Estelle took the other, and they led the docile woman to the elevator. As they waited, a giggle drifted down the dark hallway.

Agent Clark Rhodes approached the porch of the café with his badge in his teeth and his heart in his throat, or thereabouts. His jacket was neatly draped over his arm so the terrorist could see he was unarmed, and his hands were in the air in the classical submissive pose and shaking like autumn leaves in a breeze.

He took his badge from his mouth. "Rhodes, FBI," he shouted, as worried by the heavy weapons aimed at his back as by what he assumed was leveled on him from behind the blinds. Rhodes did not relish melodramatic confrontations, which is why he had opted to be a statistician rather than a field operative. On the flight from Washington, it had occurred to him that he'd been chosen because of his expendability—not a cozy thought.

"I'm doing exactly what you ordered," he added. "I'm unarmed and alone, and by the way, my wife's expecting a baby in two months. It's our fourth." Actually, it was their first, but it couldn't hurt to paint a more touching portrait of the grieving widow and children at the graveside.

The door was opened by the largest, most sullen woman he'd ever seen. Her dark eyes were burning into him, and her mouth was harshly puckered above a bevy of chins. She wore a tent-sized dress that was badly wrinkled and stained. Her hair, a mass of greasy strings, brushed her mammoth shoulders like a wet mop. "Whacha staring at?" she demanded.

"I thought you were ... a brother," Rhodes said weakly.

"Then you ain't no Ira Pickerel. Do I look like someone who takes hostages and threatens to kill 'em?"

"You're not Marvel, then?"

"Lord Almighty! I wouldn't have bet a plug nickel

there was anyone on the planet stupider than Kevin Fitzgerald Buchanon, but now I ain't so sure! Are you gonna stand there all night like your feet are planted, or are you gonna do like Marvel said?"

Rhodes stepped inside and the door slammed behind him. He was so bewildered that he felt relieved when he saw the slender black man on a stool, a gun in his hand and a broad grin on his face. "Rhodes, FBI," he said, "and you're Marvin Madison Evinrood Calhoun, a.k.a. Marvel, right?"

Marvel nodded, since he didn't think it would be appropriate to high-five the dude. "I am delighted to see you, my man Rhodes. Big Mama and my main man over there in the corner are delighted, too. Make yourself at home, and how about a piece of chicken?"

"Let's have ourselves a daddurn picnic," Dahlia said as she trudged back to the booth and jammed herself in. "We can roll Kevin out in the middle of the floor and use him for a centerpiece. We can stick plastic flowers in his ear."

Marvel frowned at her until she subsided, then gestured for Rhodes to sit down on the last stool. "Good of you to come, brother. I seem to have gotten myself in a bad situation here, and you're just the man to help me out. By this time tomorrow, you can be flying back home and these fine folks can continue their honeymoon."

Rhodes looked around. "When I was briefed, I was told you have two hostages. I only see one. I hope you haven't . . ."

Marvel laughed. "Oh, he's over there somewhere. I guess he forgot his manners. Kevin, say yo to the brother."

"Yo," came a voice from the shadowy region beneath the corner booth.

"Now, let's move along," Marvel continued. "Big Mama, you sit real still and keep an eye on the door. My man Rhodes and I are going into the kitchen where we've got ourselves some talking to do. If I happen to come out and find you or my main man up to some nonsense, I'll put a bullet in your ear. Are we clear?"

Dahlia growled something, but Rhodes was too close to fainting to pay any attention, and when Marvel gestured with the gun, he barely managed to stand up and head in the indicated direction.

"My wife's name is Carol," he said as he went into the kitchen, exceedingly conscious of the barrel in his back.

"Let's just get this over with as quickly as possible," Geri said with the perky determination of a kindergarten teacher. "Originally, I'd arranged for each of you to have a two-hour block in the kitchen for security reasons. However, it's really much too late for that, so we'll have two in the first slot and three in the second."

We had a good-sized group in the dining room. Gaylene sat alone at one table, painting her fingernails a subtle shade of screaming scarlet. At the next table, I sat with Ruby Bee, Estelle, Frannie, and Durmond. Frannie had announced that Catherine was ill, and Ruby Bee and Estelle had backed her up with such gushy agreement that I had no idea what was going on, although I doubted it was anything I'd appreciate. Brenda sat dejectedly between Lieutenant Henbit and one of his detectives. Kyle hovered behind Geri, no less relaxed than he'd been when mentioning his kneecaps. I realized he'd known for some time that Interspace was owned by the mob; his father had been less reticent than Geri's boss.

Henbit had been reluctant to permit the contest, of course, and I'd had to take him to my room and present my arguments with enough skill to outshine the Broadway stars several blocks away. He'd finally admitted that it couldn't hurt to test some of my theories, called Geri in the hotel office and told her to round up the contestants, and then called his precinct to arrange for Brenda to be delivered in a fashion not unlike a pizza.

Durmond touched my knee beneath the table. "Are you sure this is the thing to do?"

Geri put down the clipboard in order to clap her hands, alleviating me from the need to answer that I had no idea whatsoever. "Please, let's all pay attention, shall we? If we insist on personal conversations, we'll be here all night, and I for one have plans for tomorrow that preclude this fleabag hotel." She glanced back as Rick came across the lobby. "Good, I'll use you as a judge, along with Kyle and that doorman person. I do hope that's acceptable to all of you, because I'm in charge and you really have no choice. The first two contestants will be Gaylene and Durmond. Come along and please don't dawdle."

The two obediently rose. Durmond looked unexcited at his big chance, but Gaylene giggled and waved, and she swept out of the dining room as if heading for the Miss America runway. The head count remained steady, however, as Rick and Cambria entered and sat down as far away from us as they could. Their conversation would have been diverting, had I been able to hear it. Rick was already damp, but drops of sweat were forming like pimples and he tugged at his ring so furiously that I had visions of the poor taxidermist in Wyoming or wherever. Cambria wasn't twinkling.

"I guess I'll check on Catherine," Frannie said, pushing back her chair.

"No one leaves the room." Henbit motioned to a figure beyond the French doors. "And that officer will encourage your compliance."

Frannie put her elbows on the table and cradled her face in her hands. Estelle patted her on the shoulder and said, "Don't worry. She'll be all right and will come on down as soon as she . . . freshens up."

"Sure she will," Ruby Bee said.

The lieutenant's presence did not encourage conversation, and we sat in uncomfortable silence for a long while. After what might have been half an hour, Catherine came out of the elevator, crossed the lobby, and sat down next to her mother. I'd hauled in enough teenagers to realize that, despite her purposeful motion and bland expression, she was under the influence of alcohol. On her face was a thick layer of pancake makeup that almost disguised a black eye.

Others could see it, too. Ruby Bee and Estelle began to whisper, and Brenda gaped as if Catherine were an alien. Henbit nodded at his minion.

Earlier I'd remembered why my flippant remark to the lieutenant had stirred up a sense of déjà vu. "I'm not my mother's keeper," I'd told him in the exact same tone I used on Jerome Appleton when he'd emerged from Catherine and Frannie's room. Frannie had been out shopping, however. Jerome had tried his bully routine on me because he'd been up to no good (in several senses of the phrase). I decided to risk the wrath of Henbit and see what I could learn about Catherine's most recent activities—and I knew just where to begin.

I tapped Ruby Bee's shoulder. "I called your room earlier and no one answered. I wanted to pass along a message from Eilene, all the way back in Maggody, Arkansas. It has to do with copper pipes."

"I guess I was showering," she said.

I looked at Estelle, who swallowed and said, "And I must have dozed off for a spell."

"The telephone didn't wake you up?" I gave them the full benefit of my incredulous gaze. "You've both been lying like a rug going on four days now, and it's beginning to get on my nerves. You couldn't have left the hotel. That gentleman in blue would have shot you in cold blood. Where were you?"

"Frannie's room," Ruby Bee said nervously. "We went down to have a nice chat about Kansas, and the town where she and Catherine live. It sounds like a mighty fine place."

I was going to see if Frannie would back up this latest lie, but she was whispering fiercely to her daughter, who was listening with a smile that . . . that I'd seen in my mirror a few hours earlier. Minus the frustration.

The suspects were present, and it wasn't difficult to settle on Rick. He now looked as if he were hearing the details of his upcoming live cremation, which he might well be, considering Cambria's moist tirade in his ear.

"Rick has a room on the third floor, doesn't he?" I said to Ruby Bee. Her twitchy shrug confirmed my hypothesis.

Geri came to the door. "Good, Catherine's here. I think we can speed things up, if we all work together." She consulted her clipboard. "Durmond's KoKo-Nut Kream Pie is almost ready to chill, and Gaylene has made enough KoKo-Nut Kabobs to allow all of you a sample. Isn't that lovely?" She was obviously much happier now that the contest was underway and she could see the light at the bow of the ferry. "Now we need Ruby Bee, Brenda, and Catherine in the kitchen. You may come if you wish, Frannie. If you please, ladies?"

Brenda glanced at Lieutenant Henbit, who nodded. As she passed our table, Ruby Bee joined her and murmured her condolences as they left (or one would think; she was more than capable of pedestrian interrogation). Catherine followed them, but at the last moment veered toward Kyle, wrapped her arms around his neck, and began to nuzzle his mouth and chin.

"Aren't you a little piggy?" she cooed.

Frannie yanked her back before Kyle could find a suitable response. As we stared, she slapped Catherine's face so sharply that the girl stumbled backward and fell across the sofa.

"Are you all right?" Geri gasped as she hurried across the lobby, knelt, and pushed Catherine's hair out of her face. This could have been motivated by compassion, but those of us with a cynical bent wondered if Geri was driven by terror that this somehow might delay the cookoff.

"Huh?" Catherine said, blinking, then put her hand on her cheek and began to moan. The sound did not ring true, however; there was an eerie undertone of satisfaction.

Geri stood up. "This child is drunk. Her breath absolutely reeks of it, and she's clearly out of control." To Frannie, she added accusingly, "As are others of us. I must insist that you take her upstairs and allow her to sleep it off. As for the contest, the rules specify that the contestant must be prepared to produce the entry at whatever time I specify. I'm not about to wait until she's sober. Therefore, she's disqualified. The Krazy KoKo-Nut company will still pick up your expenses, but under no circumstances is her participation to be included in any future résumés."

I was impressed. The others seemed appalled by the scene or stunned by Geri's announcement . . . with the exception of Ruby Bee, who was tallying up the contestants on her stubby, white, grandmotherly fingers. I could read her thoughts: and then there were four.

"She has to stay in here," Henbit said from the doorway of the dining room. "Both of them."

Frannie dashed past him and huddled in a corner, her face hidden. Catherine rose rather majestically, threw a kiss to Kyle, sauntered through the doorway, and resumed her seat as if nothing had taken place. Then again, she might have missed it all.

Geri herded Ruby Bee and Brenda down the corridor, and the rest of us sat back and tried not to stare at either Vervain. After a while, I asked Durmond if his cream pie would prove to be a work of art, a veritable tribute to artificial flavors and colors. He admitted he had reservations. This prompted Gaylene to wax poetic about her kabobs, and this served to keep us diverted for most of an hour. At some point Frannie sat down at a vacant table and picked at the crumbs on the tablecloth. Catherine's chin dropped as she nodded off, her snores faint and ladylike, her cheek still striped with four red marks.

Considering the proximity of the climactic moment of the Krazy KoKo-Nut Kontest, it was pretty dull stuff.

I was engaging in a lewd fantasy featuring the man sitting beside me and a boat in the middle of Beaker Lake (no doors) when Geri strode briskly into the room, a platter dotted with peculiar-looking lumps in her hands. Ruby Bee came next, her bundt cake on a plate, followed by Brenda with her Kut-ups, already cut up into oblongs, and Kyle with a pie masked by whipped cream. It was the official KoKo-Nut parade, this time with Geri as the prancing majorette.

"Perhaps you'd like to be a judge, too?" she asked Henbit as she put down her platter and gestured for the others to do the same.

"I think not," he said hastily. "How about you, Detective McRowan?" The invitee slithered down in his chair and shook his head, as any of us would do. "Well, then," Henbit continued, "why don't the four of you get this over with as soon as possible? It's getting late."

Geri produced a knife, but paused to say, "I can tell time, Lieutenant Henbit. I went to a very good preschool before I entered kindergarten. Rick, would you and your employee please take your plates and be seated at the table by the far window? Kyle, we'll need water to cleanse our palates and paper on which to make notes. I have nice, sharp pencils for everyone. Any questions?"

She was really rolling by now, the knife darting here and there, her smile vivid, her eyes glittering with visions of escape. She kept up the chatter until she'd gotten everyone where she wanted them, warned us not to approach the judges' table, and nodded approvingly at the scene.

Ruby Bee was beside herself with repressed anxiety, watching the table where forks rose to lips, bites disappeared, jaws moved slowly and thoughtfully, eyes drifted, throats rippled, faces reflected varying degrees of distaste.

"I just can't stand it," she whispered to Estelle, who was equally entranced by the solemnity of the moment. "Who'd ever think I'd be in Manhattan being awarded ten thousand dollars! I'm getting tuckered out thinking about it!"

Of the remaining three contestants, only Gaylene was watching the judges with any expectancy. Durmond was slumped in his seat, perhaps mentally writing a report—or engaging in the same fantasy I'd concocted. Brenda was wan, but she'd had a helluva day.

Ignoring Henbit's glower, I sat down next to her, produced a sympathetic smile, and quietly said, "You've been through a lot today, haven't you? First thinking Jerome had walked out on you, and then learning he'd been murdered." I tut-tutted for a moment. "Not to mention being arrested at Grand Central with all that money. Were you hoping to take a train to California?"

"I suppose so," she said so softly I had to lean forward. That was okay with me, in that I wasn't yet ready to share my ideas. "I wanted to get away from . . ."

"From your memories?" I said encouragingly. When she failed to be encouraged to share further confidences, I said, "I'm dreadfully sorry I had to tell the police that I saw you at the Xanadu, but it is a double-homicide investigation."

She played with her lip for a moment, then glanced at Henbit and said, "I truly didn't know Jerome was dead until the police told me. I was at the Xanadu, but Mr. Lisbon was alive when I left. We conducted some business, a private matter, and then I took a cab to the station."

If she'd shot Jerome in the kitchen, she might have gotten hold of some cocaine to sell to Lisbon. Then again, if Lisbon was the sort to buy it, he was also the sort to be unhappy with cocaine that rightfully belonged to someone as powerful as Gabardi. The only thing she could have sold, I thought slowly, was information. The most interesting (although erroneous) information she had centered on her errant husband's whereabouts.

I made sure Henbit was occupied in conversation with his minion, then gave Brenda a penetrating look as I said, "You told Lisbon that Jerome and his girlfriend were on the plane to Rio, didn't you? Did you also mention he'd stolen cocaine from the cartons in the kitchen? Is that what made your story so expensive?"

"Do you know . . . ?"

"I know about the cocaine, and I know he was working for the mob," I said softly but sternly.

"He'd squirreled away more than a million dollars in pre-laundered money," she admitted. "He was juggling the books for the remodeling so Rick could pay cash. Most of it comes in air conditioners from a Florida firm that coincidentally is owned by Mr. Gabardi and his associates." She took a deep breath. "Mr. Lisbon was willing to pay for me to get out of town before they caught up with Jerome and his hussy. Otherwise, I warned him, I might be so overcome with grief at Jerome's death that I'd blurt out everything to the police."

"You were blackmailing the mob?" I said, awed by this housewife in a nice blue dress, with a pleasant face that concealed the raw courage of an Apache warrior. "Weren't you afraid this Lisbon man wouldn't just . . . ?"

"Oh, no, they're not at all like that anymore. Craig and Charlotte Lisbon have been out to dinner several times, and he's my younger daughter's godfather. The religious kind, not that other kind. Only last summer Jerome and I had a wonderful time at Mr. Gabardi's condo in the Grand Cayman Islands. He even sent over his yacht so Jerome could go deep-sea fishing all week, and every December we get a lovely fruitcake and bottle of champagne from him. I had lunch with his wife on another occasion when we were down for a business meeting. She's a marvelous girl, so pretty and clever. You've been watching too many of those movies. They're really a nice group of people."

"Right," I said as I battled with myself not to allow one teensy giggle to escape. Silly ol' me was all wrong about Cambria, Rick, the manager of the Xanadu, and even the faceless Mr. Gabardi, who shared his condo and his yacht and was a reformed Scrooge. They were businessmen, and if their business was not yet socially acceptable, who was I to go around accusing them of dumping bodies in New Jersey like so much toxic waste?

"May I have your attention?" Geri said, tapping her fork on a glass. "We've arrived at our decision."

CHAPTER
SIXTEEN

"The grand winner of the Krazy KoKo-Nut Kontest is . . ." Geri patted down her hair and smiled at us, her shoulders squared with power and padding. "Before I make the announcement, I want to thank all of you for coming, and I'm sure Kyle Simmons, as the company's representative, will want to apologize at length for all this dreadful business with shootings and bodies and policemen disrupting my schedule. I think it's obvious to all of us that the contest should have been held as originally planned, in which case I could have arranged adequate publicity before and after. As it is, I'll have to write up the press releases and fax them from the Cape, and I doubt we'll get half the coverage I could have provided."

Ruby Bee rumbled like a truck changing gears. "I'm sure it'll be just fine. The winner?"

"It should have been Catherine!" Frannie said, slamming her fist on the table hard enough to send the crumbs bouncing into the air like frightened fleas. "I need the money to finance the pageants and take trips to broaden her experiences. The best colleges require that these days. If that awful Jerome hadn't encouraged her to start drinking again, none of this would have happened! He deserved to die for what he did to my daughter."

"He ain't the only one," Estelle added, pointedly

staring at Rick. "And it's a darn shame, her being sixteen and from a little town. I think the police ought to arrest that fellow sitting right there, instead of letting him be a judge."

Rick shot a paralytic look at Cambria. "Hey, I don't know what she's talking about. I didn't do anything to that girl."

"We shall discuss it later," Cambria said, his lips barely moving.

Gaylene stood up unsteadily. "I think we'd better discuss it right now, if you don't mind. What's this about Rick and this girl? Are you saying that before the contest he got her drunk and screwed her?"

"In what I would guess is 319, on account of it being above mine," Estelle said.

"It could have been 317, on account of—" Ruby Bee stopped when she realized we were not intrigued by details.

Gaylene marched across the room to tower over Rick. "Is this true, you son of a bitch? How could you do such a thing? Here we've been seeing each other for two years, and you go and screw the first girl that walks by? Do you realize I could have gone on a Caribbean cruise last summer and ended up with a really good tan? But no, I tell Mr. Gabardi that I have a steady boyfriend and I'm not the sort of girl to party behind his back with other men. And I had to miss three nights of work to be a contestant—as a special favor to you! When I get back from delivering that suitcase to Vegas, I won't even have a job because the club's closed! Unless my dancing career takes off, I'll have to go back on the street again."

Rick and Cambria sat like lawn statuary, neither reacting to Gaylene's sputtery outburst. One had a white face, and the other's was growing darker by the minute.

Lieutenant Henbit, in contrast, was blinking at her as if she'd accused Rick of murder and put the weapon on the table. "So you know Gabardi, do you?"

"Of course I do, and he's a swell guy. I wish I'd taken him up on his offer. One of the girls at the club went, and she came back with a diamond bracelet that almost blinded me." She curled her fingers as if to rip into Rick, then lost her resolve and returned to her table, saying to Frannie as she went, "I'm real sorry about what he did to your daughter, honey. It's sickening, and if you want to have his face rearranged or something like that, you let me know and I'll pass it along to some friends of mine."

"I think you ought to do just that," said Ruby Bee, possibly unaware of the implications of her remark—but I wasn't sure.

"She asked for it," Rick muttered, jabbing his thumb at the sleeping girl. "She came up to my room, her blouse unbuttoned to her waist, and grabbed my crotch before I knew what the hell was happening. She had my zipper open and was on her knees before I could get out a word. I've met her kind before, and lemme tell you, she's not a little virgin with ribbons in her hair. I tried to get rid of her, Gaylene honey, but she was all over me like hot tar."

"Hot tar," Cambria echoed with an approving nod. "I can't remember when we last used it." From Rick's expression, it seemed likely that he did.

During this, Geri had picked up her clipboard and was frantically scanning the top page, all the while mewing like a stray kitten. "I don't think we need to discuss this further," she said in a high voice. "Catherine's propensities do not concern the results of the contest. It's unfortunate that we had to listen to what should have been a private conversation, but it's really none of our business ..." She looked at Gaylene. "Please don't mention the product if you do go back to your former profession, and forget you were ever in this totally ridiculous contest. Forget the name of my firm, and forget me completely. Pretend I never existed."

Gaylene put a piece of gum in her mouth. "Suit yourself."

"We're down to three," Ruby Bee whispered to Estelle.

"Be quiet!" Geri snapped at her. "We're going to put

this unpleasantness behind us and be done with this
mess. I am going to announce the winner and head
straight out the door. My car is parked in the lot across
the street, and my luggage is in the trunk. I'm going to
say one name, and then I am history. History! Do you
people understand?" No one had the nerve to so much
as nod. "All right, then," she continued grimly, "the
winner is . . . No, wait a minute, she's been arrested for
murder. Wouldn't the media have a goddamn field day
with that? Interviews from a jail cell! A press conference with handcuffs! I'll have to redo the figures. Give
me a minute and I'll have the result." She sat down
and began to scribble on her clipboard, talking to herself in a shrill and distracted voice.

"I can't believe it!" Ruby Bee said in a voice re-
markably similar. "Are you saying that those bars are
better-tastin' than my chocolate chip bundt cake?
That's flat-out impossible, missy."

"Someone has to win," Geri snarled without lifting
her head.

Ruby Bee stalked over to the table where the entries
were placed and, with the solemn sincerity of a funeral
home director, said, "I have been making this exact
recipe for twenty-five years, and you can just ask Arly
if it's not the best dadburned cake she's ever had."

I smiled benignly. "I guess it doesn't come out as
well with the fake coconut. What a shame."

"But it ain't got that nasty stuff in it," Ruby Bee
blurted out, then realized what she'd done and clutched
her chest as if experiencing the onset of a heart attack.

"Actually, I gave it low marks for its rubbery texture," Kyle contributed helpfully.

"Rubbery texture?" Ruby Bee snatched up a fork,
took a bite and chewed it vigorously. After she'd swallowed, she gave him a bewildered look. "It is on the
rubbery side, I have to admit. But how can that be? I
made it the same way, and even though some of the ingredients are from these parts, I sure know how to fix
this particular cake and it always comes out the exact
same."

I decided to butt in, now that the stage was set. "You

bought a bag of real coconut and one of the Krazy flakes the evening you arrived. Yesterday afternoon in your room you switched the contents. Last night you went down to the kitchen, discovered the door was unlocked, and went in to make the exchange. Despite the necessity of having to step over a corpse, you completed your mission and stole away like a common thief—which you are, by the way—with what you thought was a bag of Krazy KoKo-Nut. Am I right?"

"I still don't understand how come there wasn't real coconut in my box tonight," she said, not willing to acknowledge any guilt.

"Because whoever cleaned up the blood in the kitchen took all the bags out of the boxes and replaced them with real Krazy KoKo-Nut," I explained. "We're going to have one unhappy drug dealer somewhere down the road."

Lieutenant Henbit came across the room. "Mrs. Hanks, what did you do with the bag you took from your box? You didn't flush its contents down the toilet, did you?"

"I was afraid it would stop it up, and I'd hate to rely on that stupid plumber to fix it. I just tossed it in the trash can with what I bought the other night."

Henbit ordered McRowan to take Ruby Bee's key and examine the contents of the trash can in 219. He then approached Rick and Cambria, saying, "If we find cocaine in her room, I'm going to find a way to link it to at least one of you."

"What if their fingerprints are on the bags that were used tonight?" I said. "Neither of them had any business fooling with the ingredients for the contest. Kyle's the one who placed the bags in each contestant's box."

Cambria opened his mouth, then closed it and sighed. Rick gasped for air as if he were drowning in the aura of disapproval radiating from his companion . . . who happened to be second-in-command of the Gabardi family.

"Okay," Geri said abruptly, having ignored this idle chatter while she realigned her notes. "The winner is

Durmond Pilverman. It's been fun working with you, but I need to run along now."

"No, I cannot accept," Durmond said, who'd been oddly quiet during the fireworks. "I'm a federal agent, here under false pretenses. I arranged to be included among the contestants in order to monitor the drug deal we knew was about to take place. The recipe was provided by another agent, and I've only prepared it once before to make sure I could."

"Then you!" Geri pointed at Ruby Bee. "You're the damn winner! You get the grand prize—okay? Your entry had the product in it, and that's all that matters. No one could make anything remotely edible with it, anyway." She burst into tears halfway through the door, but Kyle hurried over to offer his handkerchief and murmur soothingly. At Henbit's bidding, the officer at the door allowed them to sit on the sofa in the lobby.

"I won!" Ruby Bee shrieked, hanging on to Estelle's shoulder. "I won ten thousand dollars! I can't believe it."

"Well, sit down before you make a fool of yourself," Estelle replied tartly. She was going to continue, but suddenly screamed like a banshee that'd been goosed. "There he is! Oh my gawd, do something!"

From behind the window, the whiskery psycho watched us, his tongue darting across his lips and saliva bubbling in the corners of his mouth. He gave us a jaunty little wave, then sauntered out of our sight, a suitcase rather than an axe in his hand.

"He takes his roles too seriously," Durmond said apologetically. "I hardly ever let him go undercover anymore."

McRowan came back into the dining room. "Yeah, there's cocaine in the trash can, mixed up with some flakes. I did a quick search of the room to make sure I'd found it all, and came across a dozen of these."

Henbit took a small pink plastic object from him, studied it for a moment, and said, "This is interesting, although we may not need to confiscate it for evidence." He twisted a button, then set it down on the table and smiled as it began to hop around with a clicky sound. "It's the infamous Popper Penis," he added for those of us ignorant of Manhattan porn shop novelties.

We all watched it with mindless fascination as it hopped its way to the edge of the table. At the last second, Estelle grabbed it and buried it in her lap, her face almost as red as her hair.

"Goodness gracious, Estelle," murmured the grand winner of the Krazy KoKo-Nut cookoff.

Henbit told McRowan to place Cambria and Rick under arrest for possession and homicide.

"One minute," Cambria said. "You may have evidence of drugs in this hotel, and it is possible that this young man and I came across a body in the kitchen and felt it would be more appropriate to place it elsewhere. You may discover fingerprints on the bags used tonight, and I may need to discuss this with my lawyer before I explain why I may have handled them at some point. What you do not have is any evidence that this young man and I shot the deceased. He was, in fact, a valued employee. Only today did we learn he planned to leave the country with certain items that did not belong to him."

"That's right!" Rick said. "He was the only one who could deal with the bookkeeping. I myself cannot make heads or tails of—" Cambria's glower was as effective as a garrote.

Neither spoke as McRowan escorted them out the door. Henbit ordered the rest of us back to our rooms, but like Manhattan in the middle of the night, the lobby remained lively. Geri was sobbing while Kyle tried to calm her down, Ruby Bee was raving about money, Estelle was doing her best to explain to anyone who would listen (no one would) that her purchase was nothing but a gag gift, and Frannie and Gaylene were unsuccessfully trying to rouse a comatose ex-contestant.

Therefore, only Durmond and I rode the elevator to the second floor, although it felt more like a decompression chamber than the wheezy product of Mr. Otis's imagination. He (Durmond, not Mr. Otis) invited me into his room, but I wasn't yet ready to see the steamy sheets and insisted we go in mine.

I went to the window and watched the cars crawling below. "I didn't think it made any sense for the two mobsters to have killed Jerome Appleton in the first place. I was surprised when you suggested it to the lieutenant."

"It's a good solution," he said, "and it's possible the weapons used on both Jerome Appleton and Craig Lisbon will turn up in Rick's room on the third floor. When the registration is checked, the police will discover it belongs to Rick, or Ricco, as his Floridian friends call him. He'll refuse to talk, of course, and deny it all the way to the pen. In the meantime, Cambria will be occupied with the drug problem. If I were in the mood for wild guesses, I'd say another bag of Krazy KoKo-Nut cocaine might show up in his penthouse on the very top of the hotel. I'd like to think the police will search the back shelf of the closet."

"How very wild, indeed." I turned away from the window and sat down. Durmond gave me a wry smile while I muddled over the remaining bugaboos that had been haunting me for several days. He looked as if he were encouraging me to come up with answers, which perhaps he was.

"How did you know I saw Brenda at the Xanadu?" I asked him levelly.

"I was at the table when you told Lieutenant Henbit."

"You already knew it, blue dress and all, and if you didn't hear it from me, you must have heard it from someone else—or saw her there yourself."

"Through the same window you did, maybe," he said.

I considered it, then shook my head. "Ruby Bee followed Gaylene, and you and your pal followed them, although they had a healthy headstart—and they didn't go all the way to the Xanadu. They staked out a spot in a stationery store around the corner. If you did go there, you did it of your own accord, not because you were following meddlesome broads."

"The problem with Craig Lisbon was that it always took him time to decide how to deal with situations that might disrupt his business dealings. He was the sort who might think for a day or two, then realize that Brenda Appleton posed a threat of enormous dimensions. She knew names and faces, dates and addresses, and she might decide to file for a divorce and name everyone, including Gabardi, as a co-respondent. Scorned women have been known to do such things."

"Wait a minute!" I said, aware I sounded as shrill as Geri. "Are you telling me that you went to the Xanadu and killed Lisbon? I really don't want to hear this." Especially, I added to myself, from a man with whom I'd had sex not six hours ago and no more than ten feet away (did I mention the size of the rooms?).

"I'm not telling you anything," he said with a sigh that we both knew meant he was telling me everything—and reading my mind along the way.

"I heard the elevator last night," I said, "and I thought it was Ruby Bee returning from the kitchen. But she had come up an hour before she and Estelle cooked up an alibi and came to my room. How high's the penthouse?"

"Very high, and I'm still feeling the effects of the bullet wound. Don't ever get shot, Arly. It hurts like hell, and the scar never goes away."

"Why Appleton?" I asked, refusing to allow his words to get to me. I already knew more than enough about scar tissue.

"I was in the kitchen when he and Catherine appeared."

"So he was the one who had a copy of the key?"

"I would be more inclined to search Rick's pockets. Appleton didn't need one. The door was not locked when they tried it." He took a pick from his pocket. "I was a bit curious who might come prowling."

"Such as everybody in the hotel?"

"There was a lot of traffic," he agreed, "beginning with Jerome and Catherine. Although I'm not a parent, I could certainly see that what he was about to do would totally destroy the child's life. Three months and he would have abandoned her in Rio, possibly addicted to cocaine. She has some problems, including a violent mother, but I could not, in good conscience, allow him to take her with him. I sent her upstairs, and Jerome and I had a talk. He refused to listen to reason, I'm afraid."

"Why did Rick and Cambria come?"

"That was not my doing. I was hoping our Miss Gebhearn might actually produce reporters for the contest, and they would be present at the opening ceremony in the kitchen. In some situations, the media can be useful."

"Brenda was distraught about Jerome leaving her and also terribly chummy with members of Gabardi's big, happy family. She might have called Cambria to stop him."

"You're apt to be right, Arly. They came so quickly that I was barely able to duck into the office. Once they'd taken the four cases upstairs to switch the contents, I came out of the office and nearly encountered Lady Macbeth of Maggody in a flannel gown. Back into the office I ducked until I heard her running down the corridor to the elevator. I hoped she would call the police immediately, but she did not, giving Rick and Cambria time to clean up the blood and move the body outside. I was surprised she didn't, but I underestimated her determination to win the contest." He made me a drink and sat down on the other bed, carefully positioning himself so that our knees did not touch. "All in all, a busy night for everyone concerned."

"Yeah, the elevators really hummed." I assessed the distance between us. It wasn't quite two thousand miles, but it was damn close. "Sonny had a suitcase tonight."

"Cambria and Rick weren't aware that Jerome brought down three suitcases from his room, two with personal effects and one with an impressive quantity of cash. I felt it expedient to relocate the third one before they arrived on the scene to move the body and remaining suitcases to the alley. We did not feel Cambria would donate the money to a worthwhile charity. Besides, we're always mindful of overhead."

"So let me get this straight. Sonny's playing the psycho, and you seem to have decided on the role of white knight. You shot Jerome to save Catherine, and Lisbon to save Brenda. I sure hope you don't decide Ruby Bee's about to drive me crazy."

"I never shoot women," he said with a small frown. "None of us do. We do occasionally find ourselves frustrated in our inability to indict people who've murdered our agents."

"What am I supposed to do with this, Durmond? Try to convince Henbit that you and Sonny are responsible for the two homicides? That you're framing Cambria and Rick? That a government agency pays its utility bills with drug money?"

"I don't know what to tell you, Arly. You've got an old-fashioned sense of morality, which is not a criticism, but we're engaged in an outright war. It would be lovely if everyone played by the rules and the system worked. However, the courts are more determined to protect the rights of drug barons than those of the kids in the schoolyards. Most of us have been forced to succumb to the philosophy that the end justifies the means."

"And all's fair in love and war?" I murmured.

"I didn't want you to get involved and I sure as hell didn't want to get involved with you. If you forget this conversation, twenty-four hours from now you can be home in that little town of yours. I'll stay around here to tidy up the loose ends, and then I have no idea where I'll be sent on my next assignment—which could well be my last." He lifted his hand as if to touch me, then thought better of it and shrugged. "Sometimes I need to reassure myself that I'm not still in the boat in the middle of the lake, surrounded by nothing but flat brown water."

I returned to the window. Lights were on in the apartments across the street, very few with curtains or shades drawn. In one apartment, children sat staring at a television set; in another, a woman slumped on the sofa with a beer in her hand. On the floor above, an elderly man and woman were engaged in a hostile exchange. It was, I thought sadly, the ultimate gesture of defiance required for survival in a city: No matter what we do and where we choose to do it, you can't see me and I can't see you.

I looked at Durmond with the blind stare of an urbanite. "But you took the gun from Rick's room the first night you were in the hotel, didn't you? The scene in the kitchen wasn't all that spontaneous, not if you'd gone to the trouble to steal the gun to frame Rick. You had to shoot someone."

"So many crooks, so little time."

"I feel ridiculous," Mrs. Jim Bob said from the farthest corner of the cave.

Brother Verber thought she looked mighty fine, but he knew she didn't want to hear it and would fail to appreciate how he was merely admiring God's handiwork, dressed as it was in a scarlet nightie and cute lil' panties. The outline of the peekaboo bra was visible under the flimsy fabric, and one black strap had strayed along her shoulder.

He made all these observations from a crate on which he was perched. He'd selected an apricot nightgown, but the panties had torn when he tried to wiggle into them, so he was feeling a chill in his privates. "Don't be embarrassed, Sister Barbara," he said sonorously. "The Good Lord doesn't mind us doing this so we won't freeze to death. This rain'll have to let up before too long, and we'll just change back into our regular clothes and look for the car."

"Keep your head turned, Brother Verber. I don't care how many times you keep trying to act like we're dressed for prayer meeting, we aren't. I cannot believe what's happened, and all because of you."

"Of me?"

She wasn't about to explain, so she sniffed irritably

and tugged at the lacy hem that kept easing over her knees.

"I hope I haven't done anything to cause you all this grief and uncomfortableness, Sister Barbara. You know how much I respect you from that halo I can see all the way down to your trim ankles."

"Don't talk about my ankles!"

"It was just a figure of speech. Being a preacher, I get in the habit of using them to emphasize my message. At least take heart in knowing that no one will ever know about this. No one in the entire world. If we have to say anything, we'll just explain we got caught in the rain and waited in a cave. We don't have to say one word about changing into dry clothes. Let us offer praise to the Almighty for allowing us to keep this secret—"

"I won't be more'n a minute, Marjorie," said a voice from the darkness outside the cave. "Change the radio station if ye be a mind to."

"Who's that?" Mrs. Jim Bob hissed, clutching the collar of her scarlet nightie.

Brother Verber's privates turned icy. "I reckon we're hearing things on account of being cold and hungry. Why, there's no way anybody would be wandering around this godforsaken place in weather like this."

He was going to add more, or at least repeat his words with increased assurance, when a flashlight beam hit him square in the face. The beam moved down slowly, illuminating the lace of the nightgown and his quivery knees, then darted across the cave to linger on Mrs. Jim Bob's stricken expression.

"Well, what does we got here?" The figure silhouetted in the mouth of the cave cackled and spat. "Marjorie, git over here and have yerself a look at the preacher man and his floozy. You ain't gonna believe your eyes!"

Marjorie was most amazed.

"Fishing?" Larry Joe Lambertino said, studying the note with a bewildered frown. "Joyce hates fishing. This doesn't make a lick of sense. Are you sure she didn't say anything before she left?"

Saralee had her head in the refrigerator, rooting for food, so her voice was a little muffled. "Not a word, Uncle Larry Joe. All she did was make us go out to the treehouse in the backyard and have a tea party. Now my stomach aches awful, Uncle Larry Joe. I think I'm gonna throw up."

She was right.

"You know," Simmons (senior) said, balancing his drink on his belly while he paddled the raft toward the edge of the pool, "this place has class. Costs a god-damn fortune, but at least you get your value for your money."

Fleecum sat in a deck chair, a cap on his head and a damp towel draped around his neck. The lights around the pool glittered gently, as did the moonlight on the beach and the stars reflected in the water. "Value's a big seller these days. We stress value in all the major projects, even when the product's like that crap you make. Consumers like to be told they're getting good value, just like you said a minute ago." He gestured at a waiter. "Want to see about an early tee time tomorrow?"

"Whatever," Simmons said, handing his empty glass to the waiter and paddling back out to the middle of the water, where he could admire the moon hiding behind the palm fronds.

"I knew you were stupid the minute I laid eyes on you," Dahlia said from under the stool where she'd been tied so tightly her fingers were numb.

Her remark was aimed at Clark Rhodes, who was

tied to the next stool and dressed only in his underwear. His sock had slipped down around his ankle like
snakeskin, but he'd tried once to catch it with his teeth
and bitten himself. "He had a gun, and I didn't have a
whole heck of a lot of options. How was I supposed to
know he was going to pull this kind of stunt? I'm a
statistician. I do numbers in a nice, clean office in
Quantico, and then I drive home to my suburban home
and have a martini on the deck and read the newspaper
with my wife. Did I mention that she's pregnant?"

"Stupider than dog doo-doo," Dahlia said, not
touched by this poignant scene of domestic bliss.
Kevin was still over in the corner somewheres, but it
was pitch-black with the blinds closed, and she didn't
care anyway. "Stupider than Kevin," she added for
good measure, "and that's as stupid as it gits."

"Beloved," Kevin called from wherever it was he'd
most recently gotten stuck. "I'm on my way to gnaw
clean through your ropes and set you free."

"Wire, Kevin, and unless you got tools in your
pocket like Ira Pickerel, all you'll do is chip a tooth."

Rhodes was beginning to realize how grim his situation was. Marvel had promised to tell the police that
he had persuaded the terrorist to come out at sunrise
and surrender, which meant they might get suspicious
by noon or so. Rhodes had hoped the police would notice the switched identity, but they hadn't. One brother
looked just like the next one, especially in the dark.
The real problem, he thought with a sigh, was that he
was going to spend up to twelve hours being told how
stupid he was, how stupid Kevin was, and how smart
Ira Pickerel was. Rhodes already hated Ira Pickerel.

Marvel didn't hate Ira Pickerel anymore, now that he
was tooling down the road in Kevin's car, having cited
agency policy when he confiscated it for evidence. He
was munching cookies out of the picnic basket, fid-
dling with the radio every now and then to get away

from the redneck wails, and on his way to Niagara Falls, via Cleveland. The jacket was spread out neatly in the backseat, along with the dark red tie. Special Agent Clark "Marvel" Rhodes didn't know when next he might need to flash his badge, but when he did, he wanted to look slick.

"I don't want to file a report," Geri howled, standing beside her Mercedes. "Whoever did this is welcome to my luggage and the spare tire. Just let us go!"

Kyle winced at the harsh marks on the trunk. "Come on, Officer, it's not as though you're going to catch the guy, so why don't you allow Miss Gebhearn to come by the precinct when we return to the city. In the meantime, she'll send you a copy of the insurance and registration papers, and you can start the report with them."

"No, sir, that's impossible," the police officer said. "You have to come down now and fill out the paperwork. Otherwise, your insurance company won't pay up and you'll be amazed at how much this kind of damage costs."

"I feel as though I'm being taken hostage," Geri said, glaring at the officer and wishing Mother had instilled some tips about this sort of degradation.

"Sorry, ma'am."

Kyle took her arm and eased her into the passenger's side. "We'll be out of the city in no time. How long can paperwork take, after all?"

"Would you like some more peanuts?" the stewardess asked so eagerly that I wondered if she were on commission.

I took a package, but Ruby Bee stonily stared at the back of the seat, her hands grasped tightly on the armrests and her mouth clamped shut. Estelle also accepted another package, but she wasn't any chattier than her cohort in crime.

"So it wasn't cash," I said for the millionth time.

"And what am I supposed to do with a lifetime supply of Krazy KoKo-Nut? I don't care what they say about its value, it's nasty and gawdawful and I wouldn't even use it for compost. Just thinking about it arriving year after year's enough to push me in an early grave."

Fresh out of suggestions, I looked down at the clouds, then smiled as I realized I was longing to get back to Maggody, where nothing ever happened.

CHAPTER ONE

"You're a detour on the highway to heaven," sang Ruby Bee Hanks as she ran the dust mop across the minute dance floor of Ruby Bee's Bar & Grill. Her voice wasn't bad for a woman of modest years, she thought with a smile that lit up her chubby, well-powdered face. It weren't nothing like Matt Montana's, not by a long shot, but she carried the tune faithfully. That wasn't surprising since the song came on the jukebox every five minutes from noon till midnight.

There wasn't any question Matt Montana could sing, but nobody'd ever claimed he made the best scalloped potatoes west of the Mississippi. She'd bet her last dollar he'd never won blue ribbons at the county fair for his canned tomatoes and watermelon pickles. This last thought reminded her that she needed to check the apple pies bubbling in the oven, so she took the dust mop and went into the kitchen to get ready for the noon rush. Presuming there was one for a change.

* * *

"I am lost on the backroads of sin," warbled the checkout girl at Jim Bob's SuperSaver Buy 4 Less. The proprietor, Jim Bob Buchanon, who also happened to be the mayor of Maggody among his other sins, gave her a dark look, then went out the door to the mostly empty parking lot. Beneath his noticeably simian forehead, his eyes were yellowish. Those were the two dominant physical traits that proclaimed his lineage in the Buchanon clan, although a geneticist would be quick to point out that they were both recessive. There were about as many Buchanons in Stump County as there were varmints up on Cotter's Ridge. Some Buchanons were more intelligent (and less ornery) than these same varmints, but they were few and far between—and living elsewhere. Most of the rest regarded family reunions in the same fashion young executives did singles' bars.

Jim Bob leaned against the concrete block wall and watched a lone pickup truck rumble out of view. Business was bad; there was no getting around it. The cash registers weren't pinging, and his bank balance was dwindling to a worrisome level. He shaded his eyes and looked across the highway at Ruby Bee's Bar & Grill, which didn't appear to be faring any better. Down the road, no one was filling up with gas at the self-service pumps, nor was anybody waddling into the Suds of Fun Launderette with a basket of dirty clothes. There weren't any cars or RVs parked in front of Roy Stiver's antique store, and he'd heard that Roy was threatening to close for the winter and go flop on a beach somewhere to write more of that high falutin poetry he was so proud of. Jim Bob had written some in his day, although his had been calculated to melt comely maidens' hearts and soften their protests. Roy's stuff didn't even rhyme, and gawd help you if you tried to sing it.

Jim Bob figured he might as well be writin' poetry as standing in the parking lot looking at nothing. Like the ancient oak tree out behind his house on Finger Lane, the whole damn town of Maggody was in danger of crashing down in the next gust of wind. The best he could recollect, there were still seven hundred fifty-five citizens living along the highway and on the unpaved back roads that led to other depressing towns or petered out up in the mountains. There were more citizens buried out behind the Methodist church, but nobody he knew of had been planted—lately, that is. More folks than usual seemed to have been murdered since Arly Hanks had skulked back home to become the chief of police (and the entirety of the department). But, Jim Bob added to himself, trying to be fair about it, it most likely wasn't her fault. She hadn't brought back a busload of muggers and rapists with her from her high-and-mighty life in Manhattan. No, she'd just brought her smart mouth and snippety way of putting her fists on her hips and staring like a goddamn water moccasin when she pretended to be listening to him. He couldn't think when he last made her blink.

"I have got to get back on the four-lane," the checker was singing as he stomped back inside.

He was about to fire her on the spot, when he realized she wasn't all that unattractive, if you were willing to ignore her stained teeth and rabbity eyes and lack of chin, and concentrate on her undeniably round breasts.

"Malva, isn't it?" he said in a right friendly voice. "Why don't you take yourself a little break in the lounge? I'll get us a couple of cans of soda and a box of cookies, and then you can sing me some more of that pretty song."

Malva wasn't fooled one bit, but she was dim-witted enough to think she might get a raise (along with the rise) out of him. "Whatever you say, Mr. Buchanon."

His fingers tingling, Jim Bob took off for the Oreos.

"So that I can see Mama again," sang Perkins's eldest as she maneuvered the vacuum cleaner down the hallway and deftly turned into the living room, the electrical cord whipping behind her like a skinny black sidewinder.

"I wish she'd hush up," said Mrs. Jim Bob (aka Barbara Ann Buchanon Buchanon) as she came back into the sunroom with a fresh pot of coffee. Her hair was brown and sensible, her face devoid of the devil's paint, her eyes mostly brown with only a few flecks of mustard. She wore a blue dress and freshly starched underwear in case there was some sort of untimely disaster and she found herself submitting her résumé to the Lord.

Elsie McMay gazed solemnly across the table. "Did you hear those hippies what own the hardware store are talking about closing up and moving away?"

"It'd be a blessing if they did. They're lewd and lascivious, probably all sleeping in one bed. There's a fancy French name for what they do, but I'm too good a Christian to even know what it is. I told Brother Verber to go over there and give them a word of warning about eternal damnation, and he said he would just as soon as he had the time." Her thin lips grew thinner as she thought this over. "I seem to recall that was more than two years ago."

The mention of the pastor of the Voice of the Almighty Lord Assembly Hall led to a discussion of the latest uproar in the Missionary Society (too many ballots in the box) and several cups of coffee.

After Elsie left, Mrs. Jim Bob pulled on a sweater and went out to the front porch. It was a mite crumpy for November—maybe a ominous sign of things to come. If business was as bad as Jim Bob had sworn, then they were in trouble. He'd used all their savings to open the supermarket, even getting his hands on the nice little sum she'd inherited from great-uncle Arbutus Buchanon, who, for the record, was a Buchanon from her side of the family rather than Jim Bob's.

As befitted the mayor's wife, she had the finest house in all of Maggody, a two-story red brick structure on the top of a hill where everybody in town could see it, and a driveway that wound down to a gate with the letters *J* and *B* formed out of bricks and spanned by a wrought-iron arch. But if the store went broke, they'd be lucky to have a rusty mobile home at the Pot O' Gold.

Mrs. Jim Bob was shivering as she went back inside

to rinse out the coffee pot and have a stern word with Perkins's eldest about the baseboards.

"When Mama lay a-dyin' on the flatbed," sang Estelle Oppers, although the words were muffled on account of the bobby pins wobbling between her lips. More were scattered across the counter among bottles of shampoo and conditioner, combs, hairnets, plastic and foam rollers, hair dryers, curling irons, and other accoutrements of the profession she ran out of her living room.

Eilene Buchanon frowned at her reflection in the mirror as Estelle caught a wisp of brown hair and pinned it back in place. "Can you make it less fluffier on top? My niece—the one on the drill team over in Farberville—she says it makes me look like a French poodle."

Estelle gave Eilene a hand mirror and swiveled the chair around. "I think this looks real sweet, Eilene. These teenage girls today all think they have to wear their hair so it looks like they were lined up to be the next bride of Frankenstein." She glanced in the mirror at her own fiery red beehive, today festooned with a row of spitcurls across her forehead. Yesterday she'd tried a two-tiered effect, but this was undeniably more becoming. "Amateurs don't know about the artistry of cosmetology. Just the other day I offered to fix Arly's hair—not that she's a teenager by a good fifteen years—but she ducked her head and said her schoolmarm bun was dictated by the police manual. If that wasn't a platter of barbecued Spam, I don't know what is!"

"She still moping around the police department?" Eilene asked as she handed back the mirror and stood up, wondering in the back of her mind if she didn't look just a tiny bit like a dog that answered to Gigi.

"Moping like a wet mop. I can't tell you how many times Ruby Bee and I have tried to talk some sense in her. We might as well be arguing with a box of rocks. Arly says she's perfectly happy to spend her days at the police department and her nights in that shabby one-room apartment, except when she's wolfing down biscuits and gravy at Ruby Bee's or slurping cherry limeades from the Dairee Dee-Lishus. The most exciting thing that's happened to her in the last month was stopping a silver Mercedes for speeding out by the remains of Purtle's Esso station and finding out the guy was a state senator."

"She give him a ticket?"

"In a Noow Yark minute, and still giggling about it."

Eilene paid Estelle and booked her next appointment. "Kind of sad, isn't it? Arly's ain't bad looking, but she isn't going to find herself a man in this town. At the rate things are going, this may be a ghost town afore too long. Earl keeps busy repairing burst pipes and unstopping toilets, but he hasn't had a subcontracting job in months. He heard Ira Pickerell down at the body shop had to fire his own first cousin Jimson on account of business being so poor. I guess folks can't afford to get their dents fixed when they have to worry about rent and groceries. Christmas is gonna be real bleak this year, if you ask me."

Estelle went out to the front walk and stood watching as Eilene backed her car onto County 102 and drove away. As if she didn't know business was poor these days. All she had scheduled for tomorrow was a trim for Joyce Lambertino's little niece after school let out. She'd heard about the hippies leaving, and she wasn't all that surprised about Ira having to get rid of Jimson. More times than not, Ruby Bee's Bar & Grill was half empty at noon, and happy hour was downright gloomy these days. The poultry plant in Starley City had cut back the night shift. The used car lot was nothing but a field of weeds. Everybody was hurting.

Out by the ditch, the sign that read ESTELLE'S HAIR FANTASIES creaked in the bone-chillin' wind. What paint that hadn't flaked off was nearly illegible, and one corner of the sign dropped where a screw had fallen out. With a sigh, Estelle went back inside, switched on the television to her favorite soap, and settled back for an hour of somebody else's misery.

* * *

"She warned me not to truck with girls like you," sang Dahlia (née O'Neil) Buchanon. She had a sweet voice, but at the moment she was so depressed that the words were oozing out like molasses on a winter morning. Her eyes kept overflowing with tears that ran down her chunky cheeks and leaked into the cracks among her numerous chins. She was slumped on the sofa of what her new husband kept describing as "our little love nest," but anyone with a pittance of a brain could see it was nothing but the same house where she'd always lived with her granny. Her granny'd put up quite a fight when Dahlia made her move to the county old folks' home; lordy, how she'd covered her ears and squawked like a chicken whenever Dahlia tried to reason with her about how nice it would be to sit with the other old ladies on the porch every day. She was still clamming up when Dahlia visited every Sunday afternoon, but she'd stop being a crybaby sooner or later.

Dahlia heaved all of her three hundred pounds to her feet, wiped her face, and trudged into the kitchen to make supper for Kevin. Marital bliss sure wasn't the way they showed it on television. The honeymoon had been one disaster after another; then they'd come back to find out that Kevin had lost his job at the supermarket and Ruby Bee couldn't afford the salary for one barmaid—not even part-time.

Spilling a can of beans into a saucepan, she wondered if she'd done the right thing getting married in the first place. Kevvie'd talked about a cozy cottage and going to the picture show every Friday night, but he took the first job he could find—selling fancy vacuum cleaners in Farberville—and hardly ever got home before ten o'clock at night. Just what was the new Mrs. Kevin Buchanon supposed to do all day?

She popped a couple of cookies in her mouth and imagined herself on the Grand Ole Opry stage next to Matt Montana, whose photograph she kept tacked to the wall in the living room and whose face had been known to invade their double bed on those rare nights Kevin didn't stagger through the door and fall asleep in the recliner. In her daydreams, she was always as thin as Ronna (but with Dolly's bust), with Barbara's exquisite seashell blue eyes, with Wynonna's cascading blond hair, with Katie's stark and mysterious cheekbones. She was dressed in a white sequined gown and cute little cowgirl hat, and her boots were dainty as ballet slippers.

"But I was caught in the glare of your headlights," she recommenced to singing, this time in perfect two-part harmony with Matt, "and went joy-riding just for the view."

"Your curves made me lose my direction," sang Brother Verber as he stood in the doorway of his trailer parked beside the Voice of the Almighty Lord Assembly Hall. He dearly hoped the highway he was gazing at wasn't the one in the song, because it wasn't clogged with cars and trucks heading for the Pearly Gates. A cadaverous hound was asleep on the dotted yellow line, threatened only by an empty beer can rattling across the road.

The collection plate was getting lighter every week, which meant that not only were the little heathen orphans in Africa missing out on the opportunity to be enlightened (as soon as he got their address) but also that he'd been obliged to quote a verse from the Good Book to that sassy young woman who'd called that very morning. "The Lord is my light and my salvation: whom shall I fear?" he'd demanded of her. She'd suggested the rural electric cooperative.

Religion ain't immune to recession, he thought bleakly as he went to the kitchenette to pour out another tumbler of wine, and then lay down on the sofa. Why, he couldn't find the energy to change out of his pajamas and bathrobe, and it was already early afternoon. Hanging over the end of the sofa, his bare feet looked like a pair of dead fish. All in all, at the moment even he would admit he wasn't the epitome of evangelical inspiration.

Brother Verber got up long enough to turn on his television to one of those talk shows where people seemed eager to tell the whole world about how they'd lusted after their household pets, or dressed up in leather underwear and performed degrading acts on the kitchen floor, or both. Brother Verber didn't approve of this kind of thing being shown on television, but figured it fell into the realm of better preparing himself should a sinner come a-knockin' on the rectory door.

It occurred to him that he might could charge a small fee for eternal salvation—maybe even run some kind of special at Christmastime.

"But you were just one more roadside attraction," sang Kevin Buchanon as he walked up the sidewalk of a house in Farberville, "and it's been ten thousand miles since I prayed." He wore a dark suit and a tie, and despite the fact his trouser cuffs failed to hide a good three inches of white socks, he was sure he looked like a bright young businessman. After all, his manager, Mr. Dentha, had slapped him on the back and told him that exact thing at the regular morning sales meeting at the Vacu-Pro office.

Kevin tightened his grip on his case containing the body of the vacuum cleaner and its thirty-five attachments. The proud owner of a Vacu-Pro could not only clean her carpet, she could shampoo upholstery, sand wood, spray-paint walls, dust venetian blinds, strip furniture, and do so many other useful things it had taken Kevin more than a week to memorize the list. Now he could rattle 'em off in under a minute. And who wouldn't want the finest vacuum cleaner on the market, a contraption on the cutting edge of the technological revolution? Sure, a Vacu-Pro was expensive, but so was a jet airplane—and try to scale a fish with one of them!

His shoulders squared and his chin held so high that anyone in the neighborhood could see his throat rippling, Kevin pushed the doorbell.

The door opened slowly, and all of a sudden he was gulping and fighting for air as he found himself staring at a woman wearing a scarlet nightie, lace panties that hung on her shapely hips, and not another stitch. He jerked his eyes up to her face, which was wearing a be-witching grin amidst a cloud of crimpy blond hair that looked soft as cotton candy.

"Well, hello," she purred, her tongue curling along her scarlet lips. "I've been waiting all day to have my carpet shampooed. Nobody told me they were sending a handsome young man to do ... it. I've been told there are all sorts of interesting things to do with the attachments. You did bring your attachments, didn't you, honey?"

Kevin knew he was supposed to launch into the joys of owning a Vacu-Pro, but not a single word made it out of his mouth. All he could do was gurgle as she took his arm and pulled him into the house.

"So he did it again," muttered Pierce Keswick as he grimaced at his younger brother. They shared a family resemblance strong enough to give Pierce ulcers. Ripley had the same hawkish nose and washed-out blue eyes and the same sharp chin, but his hair hung to his collar in an untidy mess that begged for a comb (or, in Pierce's opinion, a weed whacker). Pierce wore silk; Ripley preferred corduroy and one hundred per cent cotton. They rarely—just short of never—communicated outside of the office, which suited both of them just fine.

"I am not overwhelmed with amazement," Ripley said with only a faint smirk.

"This is the second time since Matt won the award that he's been arrested. He was scheduled for a couple of telephone interviews this morning, but I called the radio stations and made excuses. He missed two shows in Memphis last weekend, just flatout didn't show up. Harry says he and the Hellbellies are thinking about backing out on the tour and just riding out the winter here in Nashville. This latest crap gets out, no one's gonna risk opening for him, and we might as well cancel the tour and kiss off the quarter of a million we've put in the album."

"I said right after he won the award that Lillian wouldn't be able to control him. The annals of country music have proven that small-town rednecks are notoriously incapable of handling fame and fortune."

"That's it!" Pierce said, hitting his desk with his fist so hard his secretary glanced up from her computer and inadvertently added a zero to some lucky devil's contract. He got up and went to stand at the wide window, smiling at the mountains faintly visible through what the Nashville Chamber of Commerce elected to describe as *haze*. "The club agents, the deejays, the fans, even the Hellbellies—they all need to be reminded that despite his newly acquired reputation as a total fuck-up, Matt's nothing but a simple country boy with treasured memories of his hometown. Tie in this Christmas thing—'tis the season, deck the halls, away in the manger. Help me here, Ripley. We need some kind of publicity about where he grew up . . . and we need it before the tour starts falling apart. Let the media see him surrounded by his kinfolk, decorating the Christmas tree, singing carols in the high school gym, and reminiscing about his beloved granny. Get him on the line and ask him where he grew up."

"I should think at the moment the poor boy's sleeping off what must be a ferocious hangover. In interviews, he talks about Little Rock."

"Little Rock's too big for a hometown. Come up with someplace quaint and honest, with hardworking folks and a café where everybody has coffee on Saturday morning."

"There's something in the file. . . . I seem to think he spent at least part of his childhood in some little cesspool in the Arkansas Ozarks. Let me check his bio." He left the room, then returned with a folder containing a few grains of truth and a lot of whimsy. "I was right, of course. On his AFM application, he says he was born in a place called Maggody. There's a next-of-kin listed, too."

Pierce rubbed his hands together. "Perfect! Matt Montana's going home for the holidays."